The Hidden Room

Kate Kae Myers

Kate Kae Myers
7-2-2018

Hi Cheri,
Thanks for your support. ☺
I hope you enjoy this teen
adventure, as it was a lot
of fun to write.
I appreciate your great example
of faith, kindness, and charity.
    Hugs,
    Katherine

First published in the United States of America in June 2018
by Kate Kae Myers, LLC
www.katekaemyers.com

The Hidden Room / by Kate Kae Myers – 1st U.S. edition

Summary: When sixteen-year-old Kenley is left in Indiana by her
mother, she does the one thing she shouldn't: she explores an
abandoned castle called the Chateau. There she meets Zefram, who
eventually enlists her help in hunting for a lost family fortune.

ISBN 9781986388016

[1. Suspense—Fiction. 2. Teen romance—Fiction.
3. Adventure—Fiction. 4. Impressionist art—Fiction.] I. Title.

Books by Kate Kae Myers

The Vanishing Game
Inherit Midnight

Praise for: *Inherit Midnight*

—**Entertainment Weekly:** "Myers has created a mash-up of *The Amazing Race* and *The Westing Game*—a madcap romp full of twists and turns that you hope will never end."

—**Voya:** "*Inherit Midnight* is *39 Clues* for teenagers, and as such, is thrillingly successful. In action scenes, narrow escapes roll out in breathless bursts. This is for teens who like adventure, puzzles, and drama."

—**Booklist:** "This book is a thrill ride through time and space, revealing the secrets of a very messed-up family."

Praise for: *The Vanishing Game*

—**VOYA:** "A gripping mystery . . . impossible to put down. The reader races to keep up with the plot only to get walloped by a mind-blowing twist ending that turns the entire story upside down."

—**Library Media Connection:** "This book has twists and turns galore. Part corporate espionage thriller, part paranormal, there are also elements of mystery and romance."

YALSA Best Fiction for Young Adults List

To Rachel Bruner and Deserét Baker
for helping me bring the Chateau to life

Wander down the twisted halls,
Search the chambers and the walls.
Open doors with a skeleton key.
It's all for naught. You shan't find me.

The Ghost Child
Act I, Scene I

1
The Gate

Rule One: *Don't talk to strangers.*
Rule Two: *Be home before dark.*
Rule Three: *Stay out of trouble.*

My grandparents set those three rules my very first night at their place, and for a couple of weeks I did okay. Until the day I met Zef, when I broke all three.

Cheat grass stabbed my ankles as I stomped through weeds, the summer sun warm on my shoulders. I stared at the distant place where forested hills bled down into abandoned farmland, wondering again—as I had every day since coming here—what my mother had meant when she'd warned me to stay away from the Chateau.

I could still see Jules resting her hip against the fender of our old brown Saab and picking at the threads of her cut-offs. She was saying her goodbyes but also lacing them with promises that I'd be with her soon in New York. The last hug came too soon, and I tried to ignore the empty ache caused by the feel of her arms around my neck. Jules let go, her eyes sad because she was leaving me behind, but also a little excited about her upcoming auditions.

She opened the car door, ready to climb in, until her gaze drifted to the tree-covered hills. She turned thoughtful. "You'll make friends here, Kenley."

I glanced around the dairy where sweaty workers unloaded cattle feed. We were five miles from town and surrounded by nothing but typical Indiana fields. Besides, I didn't want to be here long enough to make friends. I'd wait for that until I got to New York.

"When you do," Jules added, finally turning back to me with a vague uncertainty, "those friends might want to take you to a place called the Chateau."

My eyebrows raised a bit. "What's that?"

"Just an old place that's been around for years and is falling apart. Kids sometimes go there and prank each other, but it's not safe."

She gave my arm a squeeze. "I don't want you doing that, okay?" For three seconds Jules looked like a real mother, in spite of her wild strawberry blond curls and tight tank top. "Promise."

Her strict expression was so unlike my usually carefree mom I wanted to laugh, but the bitter taste of getting left behind made it fade. I mumbled an agreement and then watched her drive off, finally going inside my grandparents' house.

For two weeks I shoved down thoughts of the forbidden Chateau, while remembering how Jules had acted casual but was betrayed by a tightness around her eyes. In spite of the boredom, I'd spent my time trying to please my strict grandparents and do what they asked. Until today, when everything changed.

The path ahead narrowed, though beneath the weeds I could make out shallow wagon ruts on either side. A long time ago, this had been a lane. Eventually, rusty barbed wire strung between two weathered posts blocked my way. Ancient trees stood on either side, so close even a bike couldn't get through. However, I was able to squeeze past, though a low twig scratched my leg.

Scraggly oaks crowded together, blocking my view of the hills, and I glanced back. How far had I come? All my flimsy reasoning was based on a few anxious words from my mom who happened to stare in this direction. Gnats swirled above the weeds as I stood there debating whether to keep going. But then the thought of going back to the ranch after what had happened earlier tightened my stomach, and I pushed forward.

In time the path widened, and I followed it around a

deep curve between trees which at last opened into a clearing. I gave an incredulous gasp, hardly able to believe what loomed ahead. Aged wrought-iron gates stood in front of what looked like a castle. Its walls were dark beige stone, the front covered with rows of tall, close set windows, shutters cast wide. Backed against a tree-covered hill, the faded blue roof matched the washed-out summer sky.

I hurried forward until reaching the gate. "I don't believe this," I said in a hushed voice, struggling to understand what this place was as my fingers curled around the fence bars. On either side, vines crept up thick stone columns. Tipping my head back, I studied the decorated top of the double gates. Swirls of dark filigree climbed to a central point high above, both ominous and lovely. Finally, I lowered my gaze, eyes again drawn to the castle that looked so out of place. For a couple of seconds I could almost pretend it had appeared here from some enchanted realm or other dimension, and that it might just disappear.

A faded sign hung from one of the crossbars. It warned of danger and showed a walking stick figure beneath a red slash mark. A chain was wrapped around the gate and attached with a lock. But then I noticed links dangled free at the bottom and picked one up. The twisted end was bright silver against the tarnished outer metal, as if someone used bolt cutters on it.

I pushed just a little and the chain slid away from one side. The gate didn't creak the way I expected, but made a quiet sigh that sounded like a sad whisper. A cloud slid across the face of the sun, and the air grew cooler on my neck. I looked back, sensing *something*, but not sure what. Empty patches of ground surrounded the scraggly oaks, and in the opposite direction from where I'd come was a road sparsely covered with gravel. Half choked with weeds, and falling away in places, a vehicle could travel along it, but the ride would be rough. It came from the general direction

3

of town, where those nonexistent friends my mother had imagined might live.

I shifted my weight and rubbed the scratch on my leg, knowing what I wanted to do but not sure I should. Then all the crappy bits and pieces from that morning came back to me. How I'd left the house in an upset rush, wanting to get away from my grandma saying, *"Goodness, Kenley! Such carrying on about a cell phone, of all things."* My grandpa had scowled because I'd been arguing with Jules on their landline after discovering my cell service had been cut off. As if he wasn't just as mad at my mother for forcing me on them!

I used my phone to snap pictures of the Chateau, since it was still able to do that. More than anything, I'd love to send a photo to my friends, but of course I couldn't. So instead I pushed the gate a little more until the bottom bar hit swollen roots. The opening was wide enough to slip through, and I stepped forward, drawn towards the Chateau. The closer I moved, the more massive it seemed, and that same question kept coming back to me: What was this amazing castle-like building doing in the middle of rural Indiana?

For the barest moment it seemed to murmur a reply that I'd been here before. Impossible, though, since if I'd seen this remarkable place even once, I would have remembered. The idea of exploring filled me with a fluttery sensation, but I hesitated just a little before finally banishing my grandparents' rules. This was the first excitement I'd experienced in two long weeks.

I started down the cobblestone walkway, passing a cracked fountain filled with weeds and then going up the front steps that led to tall double doors. Another chain wrapped around the decorative handles, still intact and padlocked. A sign hung from rusty nails on one of the ornately carved oak doors, a violation of what had once been a beautiful entrance. Like the sign on the gate, it warned against trespassing.

Moving from the porch, I walked past bushes with scraggly branches that blocked the windows until finding a bare spot. I stood on tip-toe to look through one of the many small panes, disappointed that the house was far more trashed on the inside than I'd expected. No furniture, just an empty room with layers of peeling wallpaper and an open door hanging from a hinge. Through that opening I could see into another distant room, glimpsing striped wallpaper that looked like faded brown ribbons.

I soon turned a corner and continued around the huge house, peeking inside any window I could reach. Everything whispered of past grandeur: ornamental wainscoting, a deep-set arch beneath a second floor balcony, a broken sideboard that had fallen over, and plaster walls shedding pale layers of blue and tan. Despite the empty rooms, I was intrigued and wished I could go inside, even though my pulse quickened at the thought. I was already trespassing, and coming here was the one thing Jules had asked me not to do.

A mental image of my mother caused a painful pressure in my throat. My whole life I'd heard her cutting comments about dairy life in this tiny Indiana town and how she couldn't wait to get away from her strict parents. That's why she never said stuff like: *Kenley, clean your room. Do your homework. No elbows on the table.*

Pretty much, Jules and I did whatever we wanted. Taco dinners at midnight, sleeping in when we could, and shopping at thrift stores because we were usually broke. I liked school for the fun of it and did okay, but studying for tests didn't matter. Jules said grades were just letters on a piece of paper. They didn't show the important stuff, like how good I was at drawing, balancing her checkbook, or re-sewing clothes to make them vintage chic. She refused to answer letters from the school and had never gone to a parent teacher conference. To Jules, life was about finding our joy and not letting others stifle us.

Now, though, everything had changed.

I touched the dead cell phone that felt heavy in my pocket. Alive, it had been my single link to the life I'd loved back in Branson, and to my closest friends, Dana and Kiefer. Now, it was merely a tiny corpse that looked life-like but couldn't text, make a call, or access the Internet. The feel of it against my hip was a constant reminder of how selfish Jules was acting.

Rounding the last corner, I saw a wide veranda at the back of the house. Curved steps led down to a flagstone path that wandered through what had once been a rose garden. Now, wild grasses choked the thorny brown limbs. Most of the bushes had died long ago, though green twigs still struggled to survive. One even sprouted a few wilted yellow roses. Beyond the garden was more overgrown property that backed against a wooded hill.

I climbed the steps to the veranda and tested the double French doors. Locked. The beveled panes of glass were all intact, though some had cracks. Cupping my hands on either side of my eyes, I leaned close. Inside was a huge, open room with square pillars between windows, the marble floor cracked and covered with debris. The walls had rectangular stains of smudged brown, showing where large paintings or mirrors had once hung. A chandelier dangled from a single cord, the tangled metal badly damaged, a few pieces of crystal clinging to it like frozen tears.

The more I studied the ruined ballroom, the more my earlier sense of excitement faded. Finally, I pulled back, shoulders slumping. It had looked much more enticing from the outside.

The breeze that had kept the day pleasant died away, the air growing warmer. Built-in benches ran along the length of the veranda. I sank onto one in a shady spot, leaning against the cool stone wall of the house. Digging my phone out of my pocket, I tested it, hoping Jules had paid to resurrect it. Nope. As if in a coma, it sat in my hand, vital signs still strong except for the one that counted.

What would my friends think when their texts and calls didn't come through? I remembered my earlier conversation with Jules, when I phoned her on the Strickland landline all panicked. Her voice had been apologetic, her excuses real but not any less annoying.

"I'm sorry, Kenley, I just don't have enough money to pay for your phone right now."

"But yours is working!"

She gave a guilty sigh. "Millie and Doug let me join their plan. I've got to have it for call-backs after auditions. How else can I get work?"

She started telling me about the roles she'd tried out for and also an audition as a back-up singer. Once she got a job and her first paycheck, we'd get a studio apartment and I could join her in New York.

"Why can't I come now?"

"There's no room, Kenley. I've told you. Their place is tiny, and they're being generous letting me crash on the couch."

"I could sleep on the floor. I wouldn't be any trouble."

Jules brushed this off, going on to say how it would all turn out if I was patient. She told of the fun we would have, but for the first time I took a good look at how Jules was the queen of painting optimistic pictures about our future. She always tied it up with hopes and promises that hardly ever turned out.

For most of my life, I'd bought into it, accepting her dream of success as we bounced back and forth between New York and L.A. It was true that my pretty and talented mother had a great singing voice and lots of stage experience, but so did a thousand other actresses. Two years ago we ended up in Branson, Missouri, the theatrical capital of the Midwest. We'd been happy there until the lounge where she sang and worked as a waitress closed, and she couldn't find another job. How had it all come undone so fast?

Turning off my phone, I put it in my pocket. I'd thought about running away, back to Branson, but what would I do after I got there? The apartment where we used to live was no longer ours. I couldn't stay with Dana because she had to do that every-other-week thing between parents. And though Kiefer's house had plenty of room, his mother didn't like him hanging out with friends from those "show business families". Ironic, since the theaters in Branson brought in the tourist buses that kept the town alive, including his family's string of gas stations.

I leaned my head back against the wall, eyes sliding closed. At sixteen, my life felt like it was at a complete dead-end. My hands went limp and I tried to ignore the heat behind my eyelids, the painful ache in my throat.

The faintest sound of chamber music reached me. I opened my eyes and it faded to nothing. I looked around the veranda, so bright with late afternoon sunlight it made me squint. No movement in the garden; no sound, either. Even the birds had stilled their chatter in the growing heat, so where had the music come from? I wondered if I'd imagined it.

Thinking I should leave, but dreading the thought of going back to the dairy, I closed my eyes for a few seconds more. My mind went to a drifting place, thoughts weighed down by unhappiness, until the music came back.

I opened my eyes, confused by how dim the light had grown. A tingling sensation ran up my arms, my breath catching in my throat. I was standing inside the ballroom.

2
The Stranger

"Imagine what this place must have been like a century ago," a voice whispered from behind.

I spun around but saw no one. A wave of dizziness swept across me. Everything felt off-balance, as if the floor had suddenly tilted and I might fall. A moment later it righted itself and the room began altering before my eyes. The debris on the floor vanished, polished marble gleaming beneath my feet. Paintings in ornate frames now decorated smooth plaster walls, and hundreds of crystals hung from an enormous chandelier, reflecting prisms of candlelight. Sound and movement overwhelmed me: chamber music mingling with voices, women in ball gowns and feathered masks, men in old-fashioned jackets, most of them wearing masks, too.

I could hardly breathe. "This isn't real."

The same voice spoke near my ear. "No, it isn't. But it once was."

I turned again and saw him. Tall, his hair slicked back, he wore a simple black mask. He didn't smile, though he did step closer.

A shiver passed through me. "I must be dreaming."

He shook his head and reached out, his fingers grazing my arm. "You shouldn't be here."

My eyes flew open and I stared up at a guy leaning close. His fingers pulled back from my arm and I squinted at his shadowed face, his head and shoulders fiercely backlit by the shimmering orange of the setting sun. It took a couple of seconds to realize he wasn't wearing a mask, and I was still sitting on the veranda.

I stood, bare legs peeling from the bench, my body

stiff from sitting so long. The guy kept staring at me. Trying to hide my disorientation, and how fast my heart thrummed, I turned away.

"You shouldn't be here," he repeated.

Ignoring his comment, I moved to the French doors. In the lowering light everything looked different. All was dark inside the house now, and I caught a brief glimpse of my mirrored image. My jaggedly cut copper hair reflected a darker amber, my eyes wide with confusion. I leaned in closer to the glass, squinting until I could see inside the ballroom. No masked dancers and no musicians—just an old place falling to pieces.

"But it seemed so real."

"It always does," the guy said with a hint of dark humor.

I turned and for the first time saw him clearly. He was about my age, maybe a little older, with a lean jaw and deep-set eyes. Eyebrows were straight slashes that gave him an intense look, though a full mouth softened the effect. His thick brown hair would have looked messy if it weren't for the sharp points of his sideburns.

He shoved his thumbs in the pockets of his long shorts, his stance casual enough, though his gaze wasn't.

A small ache throbbed at the base of my skull, and I felt shaky from the strange dream. How had I fallen into such a deep sleep, and why had the vision of masked dancers seemed so real? Neither of these were questions I could ask. Instead I said, "You live here?"

He shook his head. "Of course not. Nobody does."

"So you're trespassing, too."

His eyebrows drew in, making his gaze even more severe. "How long you been sitting here?"

That was a good question. The sun hid behind the hills now, the glow in the clouds dimming, and it felt as if a lot of time had passed. "Maybe a couple of hours," I admitted. *Maybe more.*

He blew out a slow breath. "You might feel sick for a day or two, probably have a headache. It won't last, though."

"What are you talking about?"

His comments seemed nearly as crazy as my dream, but before I could say anything else, he motioned to me and headed down the veranda steps. "Come on. Let's get you out of here."

I had no intention of going with him, though the shadowy darkness that spread across the garden made me dig out my phone and check the time. Dinner at the dairy was at six. Even if I ran all the way home, I would be late. My grandparents, the Stricklands, would not be happy and might even ground me, though I could point out how calling them was no longer an option.

"Are you coming?" He asked, impatient, and started to say something else when distant shouts interrupted us.

Two male voices mingled together, calling words that were hard to make out. I strained to listen. A hoot of angry laughter cut off, then another call of what sounded like, "Seth, where are you?"

The guy swore under his breath, bolted up the steps, and grabbed my wrist. He started dragging me after him.

I pulled back. "Hey, stop it!"

He pushed me against the curved stone barrier at the side of the veranda stairs. "Look," he hissed in a low voice. "You hear them?"

His tone made me flinch, and I nodded. "Who are they?"

He signaled me to lower my voice. "A couple of guy you really don't want to run into," he whispered. "Especially not here."

Something in the way he emphasized those last three words, and the uneasy glint in his dark eyes, made me believe him.

"Okay," I mouthed.

More yelling with a crazed, hostile sound, and this time louder. Whoever it was, they were getting closer.

I whispered, "Are you Seth?"

"Zef," he corrected, letting go of my wrist. "Stay low, and follow me. You fall behind, I'm not coming back."

With that, he turned and headed along the Chateau, moving in the shadows. Squeezing the phone that was still in my hand, I hurried after him.

3
Into the Dark

"Down here," Zef said in a low voice.

I looked around, having lost sight of him. It took a couple of seconds to see he stood lower than me, in a dark space between two overgrown evergreens. Stone steps led down to a shallow alcove at the back of the Chateau. Zef held aside a branch and I scooted under. He turned to a warped door that had an inset window with spaces for four panes. Two pieces of glass were missing, a third badly cracked. He reached through an empty square, working the door handle until it clicked, then forced it open. The weathered wood complained, and I worried that the guys chasing him might hear.

"Hurry," Zef whispered, stepping through the doorway.

I hesitated. What if going inside the house was more dangerous than running for it? Staring into the blackness that had swallowed him, a prickling sensation began at the base of my neck. I started to back up. Everything was quiet now. Those other guys had stopped shouting so maybe they'd gone away. I decided to head for the gate, my foot on the first step, when a gunshot rang out.

Sucking in a startled breath, I spun around and stumbled through the opening. Zef closed the door most of the way, stopping just short of latching it. I could barely see him in the dim light seeping through the empty panes. But then he moved away, and though I tried to watch where he went, blackness swallowed him.

He spoke softly. "We need to go, before Riker and Dean get up the nerve to come in here after us."

"After *you*. I don't have any issues with them."

"Right." His tone turned sour. "Except you're a girl. Alone at the Chateau. You want to go face them, be my guest. It'll give me time to get away."

My body tensed even more. I opened my mouth to tell him what a jerk he was but heard two more gunshots, this time closer, and the words died on my lips.

Outside the house an angry voice shouted a string of curse words, punctuating them with Zef's name. I stared into the blackness and a pounding impulse warned me to flee, but unable to see, how far could I run? A flitting shadow passed across the pale light seeping in through the tiny window, too indistinct to know if it was one of those guys.

Fingers brushed my shoulder and I flinched as Zef leaned near. "I can get you out," he whispered, his breath stirring the hair near my temple. "Trust me?"

Trust him! This complete stranger who seemed almost as dangerous as the unknown guys chasing him? I wanted to act cool, but fear held the reins of my racing pulse and I heard myself croak, "Okay."

I flexed my stiff fingers, for the first time remembering the phone I held, and flicked it on. The small amount of light didn't reach far, just enough to give me a muted glimpse of cupboards and counters that faded into dimness.

"No!" he hissed. "They'll see that!"

I shut it off and we were in the dark again. "We need to call the police. My phone isn't working, but I think it still has emergency mode."

"Shh." Zef held still, as if listening, and I did too.

No more shouting or gunshots, only a low creak that could have come from either outside or the house itself. Worried they were coming to the door, I started to back up and bumped into him.

When he spoke, I had to strain to hear him. "It's not a good idea calling the sheriff, since we'll get charged with trespassing. I'm not up for that, are you?"

I thought about it. "No, but it wouldn't be as bad as getting shot."

"Odds are, Riker won't actually shoot us. The gun is to scare me."

"He's not trying to kill you?"

"Probably only wants to beat me up. But if he's drunk… guess I don't know." His fingers found my wrist, encircling it. "Let's go."

"What, you have night vision or something?"

"No. Got this place memorized."

That shut me up. How many times had Zef been inside the Chateau? Before I could ask, we started moving.

He tugged and I followed, trying to ignore the awkward feel of his touch. We didn't go fast, and I made myself concentrate on what he was doing. Three steps, then stop, a couple more, stop again. Next, he guided me sideways. Several more steps forward until I heard his free hand brush against what must have been a wall. He scooted right and I went with him.

It felt crazy to follow his lead, worsened by the uncomfortable throb at the base of my skull. I wanted out. Away from him, and away from the darkness.

"All right," he said. "We're going through a door but then you need to stop, step left, and press your back against the wall. Do it just the way I say. If not, you'll fall into an open stairwell."

Not waiting for me to answer, he moved through the opening and I went with him. I shoved my back against the wall, my other hand brushing what felt like crumbling plaster.

"Good." Zef's voice was calm, though he seemed to be breathing a little fast. A downward tug on my wrist let me know he had moved lower. "The railing is rotted away. Slide your foot over until you feel the edge of the step, then go down."

"This is insane."

He gave a low laugh that sounded as if he agreed. I followed him as he moved lower, feeling for the edge of each step with my left foot the way he'd told me to, and always keeping my back on the wall. The stairs creaked under our weight, and I wondered if they were rotted, too.

"Is this safe?" The sound of fear in my voice embarrassed me.

We'd gone down at least three steps, and I didn't think he would answer, when he finally said, "Nothing in this place is safe."

"Where are we going?"

"To the larder. You always talk so much?"

Heat warmed my cheeks, the blush that too easily colored my face hidden by the dark. "Oh, right. I forgot how you hick farm kids never say more than five words at a time."

Zef didn't answer so I stayed quiet too, getting into a rhythm of sliding over and stepping down. The air began to grow cool and musty. I wanted to know how much farther but didn't want to be the first to talk. A minute later he stopped. "We're here."

Stepping forward, he stumbled over something, his fingers jerking free of my wrist. He mumbling cross words and shoved aside what sounded like a box. Apparently he didn't have everything in this place memorized.

"This way. There's an open door just ahead."

It was harder without him leading me. I inched forward with hands outstretched and felt my way through the opening. I took more steps, then heard him shut the door behind me. A dim light came on. Zef had his cell phone out and switched it to flashlight mode. I blinked, looking around a large room with no windows. Instead, it had rows of empty shelves. Many of them sagged, others fallen all the way to the floor. Rough wooden crates sat in random piles. Dust coated everything, and loose cobwebs hung in dim corners, nearly as dilapidated as the shelves.

I looked in the direction of the door. "Think they'll come down here?"

"Depends how much they've had to drink. Riker tends to be a little spooked by the larder when he's sober. Not that he'd admit it."

"What'd you do to make him so mad?"

Zef went to a crate and flipped it over. Underneath was an eight pack of plastic water bottles. "Other than being born, you mean?"

He set his phone on the crate and freed one of the bottles. I watched him unscrew the lid and take a long drink, then he tossed me one. "Riker is my older brother. Dean's a distant cousin."

For two seconds I could only stare at him like he was the dumbest guy I'd ever met. "Are you kidding me? We're running from your brother? You freaked me out about these guys, and they're your family!"

One corner of his mouth turned down. "Riker is a sociopath. Or, if you want the correct medical name for it, he suffers from antisocial personality disorder." He said the last three words like it was a joke.

"He's been in trouble with the law since he stole his first pack of cigarettes at thirteen. And Dean's hung around him so long he's just about as bad. Neither of them made it through high school."

"So?"

He took another drink before adding, "The last time they got expelled it was for bullying two freshmen girls. They went back that night and trashed the office. Caused thousands of dollars damage, though nobody could prove it was them. I don't even want to tell you what they did to the principal's car."

"When did that happen?"

"About two years ago. More recently, Riker's been in the county jail, and I'm the one who helped send him there." He moved a board aside with the toe of his shoe. "I knew he'd come looking for me when he got out, I just didn't know it'd be today."

My anxiety came back, but I tried not to show it. "So how did you get him sent to jail?"

He checked his phone like he didn't hear me. I glanced around the shadowy room, for the first time actually wanting to be at my grandparents' house. "Look, I've got to get home. I'm already late for dinner."

He gave a half-humorous snort. "I'd say that's the least of your problems right now."

"Oh yeah?" My eyes were drawn to a narrow arch in one of the walls. "You don't know the Stricklands."

"Actually, I do. We live down the road from them. You're their granddaughter, right?"

"How'd you know that?"

Another no-answer from him and I walked over to the archway. Light from my phone let me see into a small room lined with rows of short shelves. It was in better shape than the larder.

Zef followed me. "This is the wine cellar. What's your name?"

I glanced up at him. "Kenley. And you're Zef."

"Short for Zefram."

"Never heard that one before."

His eyebrows drew in. "You watch any of the Star Trek shows?"

"Not really. Only if I was channel surfing."

"My parents are big Trek fans." He seemed more embarrassed by this than his brother being a sociopath.

Something caught his attention and he looked over his shoulder. "Did you hear that?"

I listened, fearful of footsteps coming down the stairs, but all was quiet. Zef stared at the closed door. "There it is again. Do you hear knocking?"

I shook my head. "What are you talking about?"

"Crap. I didn't think it would start so soon."

A new thought surfaced with a tingling warning: he might be more dangerous than his brother, and I needed to get away from him. Since going back up the stairs wasn't an option, I walked to the center of the larder and scanned the walls. Maybe there was a second entrance. Moving away from the door, to the opposite side, I studied the shelves. They had less dust than the others, and oily fingerprints on the vertical boards, though that could have been there for years. Scraped into the floor was a worn mark that made a half circle, as if the entire shelf swung outward. I started pulling, but it didn't budge. Zef came and stood beside me, arms folded in a silent question.

"There might be a door behind here," I said. "Help me move this."

He didn't, and I kept tugging, feeling foolish but not wanting to give up. Finally he reached under one of the shelves and pulled down on a small lever I hadn't noticed. There was a click, like a latch unlocking, and the wall slid open easily and without a sound.

I gaped at it, then at him. "You knew about this?"

He nodded once, a glint of suspicion in his eyes. "Yes, but how did you?"

"Educated guess." I pointed to the fingerprints on the shelves and the curved mark on the floor.

"And that's all?" His tone said he didn't believe me. "I'd been coming here for nearly a year before I found this door."

"If you knew it was here, why didn't you say something?"

"Because I want to wait until Riker and Dean are gone."

Holding up my cell phone for light, I peered through the opening and saw a wide hallway. Shallow steps led up, and alongside them a concrete ramp. "Where does this go?"

The sound of running feet overhead startled me. "Please tell me you heard that," Zef said.

"Yes, of course!"

"Change of plans." He ran and snatched up his cell phone then headed back to me. "Time to go."

I slipped through the opening and he followed, grabbing a large handle at shoulder level on the wall and pulling until the odd door clicked shut. "Just so you know, we can't get back in this way, since it only opens from the other side."

"Does your brother know it's here?"

"I doubt it."

"But you're not sure."

We hurried up the steps. The long hallway had a closed in, earthy smell, and I noticed that in certain spots the stone walls crumbled away, roots thin as hair dangling from them.

My phone died, cutting our light source in half, and I shoved it in my pocket. My head began to hurt even worse, and I wondered how much longer until we'd get out, but didn't ask. Half a minute later a new sound directly ahead distracted me and I slowed. "What's that?"

Zef slowed too and glanced at me. "Come on."

I couldn't move, stunned by a skittering sound that kept getting louder. Squinting, I peering into the shadows ahead and saw movement. Finally realization hit me. It was the sound of tiny claws on stone.

I began backing up, a choked breath catching in my throat. Zef came to me. "What's wrong?"

"You don't hear those rats?"

He lifted his light to dispel the nearby shadows, but it only penetrated a few feet into the gloom. "There aren't any rats in the Chateau."

"You can't know that."

"In fact, I can. For one thing, there's no food for them to live on."

This made sense until something furry brushed past my ankle. I squealed and jumped. Zef grabbed my upper arms, forcing me to face him. The phone in his hand pressed on my arm, the light of it not reaching his features. "Listen, Kenley. Ignore it and just keep going."

Squeaking calls joined the skittering, and I turned my head to look at the hallway ahead of us. For the first time I got a clear look at the wave of rats swarmed over each other, their eyes and teeth glinting, dark bodies writhing. Their claws scraped the stone steps, sharper than knives, hairless tails whipping the air.

"They're coming!" I gasped, struggling to pull free.

His fingers only tightened on my arms, tugging me forward. *Didn't he see them?*

Knowing they would be on top of us, that they would bite and claw our legs, a sob crept into my voice. "Let me go!"

He didn't. I squeezed my eyes shut, body braced for the attack, as the shrill squeals grew into screams. Then, as fast as a switch being flipped, the sound cut off. I opened my eyes and gazed at the hallway ahead of us. The rats were gone.

4
Trouble

I stood outside the Chateau, gulping in warm summer air as Zef closed the double doors of the delivery entrance. The waxing moon had just risen, not quite full but still large enough to shed milky light across the property. Compared to the darkness inside, it seemed bright.

In spite of the mild air, my body felt clammy and chilled, my temples throbbing as if I'd been in a race. Zef came to stand beside me. "You okay?"

I turned to face him, trying to keep my voice steady. "I saw rats. And then they... disappeared."

He nodded, looking thoughtful but not alarmed. "It's the Chateau. Stuff like that happens when you're inside."

"What are you saying?" I squeezed my fingers into fists. "Because I don't believe in haunted houses."

"Me either."

I waited for him to tell me what he knew, but he kept silent. After glaring at him I stomped off, deciding I didn't have time for whatever game he was playing. To my surprise, he followed. I took off running along the side of the house and rounded the corner to the front. Zef caught up with me, easily matching my stride, even when I increased my speed. We neared the fence and through the bars I saw a white pickup where the overgrown road led in the direction of town. A little ways from it, and parked at an odd angle as if the driver had skidded to a stop, was a dark red car.

We slowed, both of us breathing fast. "The pickup's mine," he said between breaths. "I can give you a ride home."

Not sure at all about this, I slipped through the gates

and almost tripped on something, seeing the cut chain had fallen to the ground. Zef was halfway to his pickup when I heard, "No, no, no!"

His windshield was splintered in cracks spreading out from several large depressions. There were also dents on the hood. Glancing back at the red car, I saw a metal baseball bat propped in the driver's seat. I looked back across the shadowy property of the Chateau, worried Riker and Dean might show up.

Zef splayed his hands on the pickup's fender. "Damn him! I just got this windshield replaced. Took me two months to earn the money to pay for it." His hands slid forward. "And look what he's done to the hood."

I wondered how this could upset him more than what we just experienced inside.

"I'm sorry, Zef." I meant it. A trashed pickup, a nasty brother and cousin, and Trekkie parents who thought naming kids was a joke. He had a rough deal, but so did I. And I wasn't waiting for those guys to find us.

"I've gotta get home," I said over my shoulder and took off.

Home. The dairy wasn't home, just a place where my grandpa only cared about cows, and where I was forced to do chores with my grandma—a distant woman I'd mentally nicknamed G'ma. I jogged down the rutted path leading from the Chateau, pacing myself so I'd have the stamina to run the entire way.

Shadowy lines interspersed with strips of moonlight were scrawled across my path, disorienting as I raced along. Watching for roots and avoiding the deeper shadows that bathed the ground, I thought how different this place seemed during the day as wild fields merged with ancient trees. In the daylight, the land surrounding the Chateau had seemed enticing. Now, it felt like a trap closing in. Weeds scratched my legs and the rutted lane threatened to twist my ankle if I stepped wrong.

In time I grew disoriented, not sure if I was even going the right direction until I practically ran into the barbed wire strung between two posts. I squeezed past, hurrying through the abandoned fields. It seemed to take forever to finally reach the road, relief flooding me as my feet hit solid asphalt. I took off running, finally able to move faster. I sprinted past a tall blue silo that had five white spots high up, pranks from when my mother was a teenager and her guy friends had filled eggs with paint. In time I passed a field green with corn, houses in the distance dark smudges behind glaring floodlights.

As I ran, I thought about my realistic dream of being in the ballroom, and also my escape from the larder with Zef. The more I tried to sort it all out—including my delusion of rats—the more unbelievable it became.

Even though my heart pounded and my breath came in ragged gasps, I didn't stop running. Not until I rounded the bend that merged with the road leading back to the dairy. I bent over, hands resting on knees, panting and trying to ignore the pounding in my skull.

The drone of an engine startled me. I looked back at a white pickup heading in my direction, wondering how he'd gotten here so fast when the road to the Chateau led in the opposite direction, back towards town.

The pickup stopped. Zef leaned across and opened the passenger door. "Get in. I'll take you home."

Not: *Would you like a ride*, but instead a gruff order. Glancing ahead, knowing he could drive me back to the dairy much faster, I still hesitated. Rule one came to mind: *Don't talk to strangers.* Was Zef still a stranger after our experiences tonight? Probably. But more important was that I had questions only he could answer. I climbed in and stared at the windshield covered with cracks that looked even worse from the inside.

He must have read my expression as we took off. "I know. It's got to be replaced. Can't fix the dents in the

24

hood, though."

"At least he didn't shoot your tires."

Zef shrugged. "Guess there's that."

"He's mad because you got him sent to jail." At least that much I knew.

He paused before explaining, "I have a part-time job at the Simmons Auto Parts store downtown. A couple of weeks ago, Riker came in. I knew I needed to keep an eye on him."

He slid his hands up the steering wheel, fingers squeezing it. "He tried walking out with a set of wrenches, but I followed and we got in a fight outside the store. The owner, Mr. Simmons, stepped in and Riker elbowed him in the nose. After that, the sheriff tackled and cuffed him."

"How does any of that make you the bad guy?"

Odd shadows drifted in and out of the pickup as we drove. "To somebody like my brother, everyone else is to blame."

He slowed the truck as we neared a two story house set back from the road. I'd noticed this home when walking past this morning in my search for the Chateau. It was older but well kept, with tall trees in the yard and surrounded by barley fields. At the moment, the most noticeable thing was a sheriff's car parked in the driveway.

Zef leaned forward a little to look through my window. "That's all I need. Bet he's talking to my parents about Riker."

"You live there?"

He nodded, concern in his eyes as he accelerated.

"Does Riker live at home?"

"Not since he was eighteen. I'm not sure where he's staying now. Either with Dean or the new girlfriend I've heard he's got. After I drop you off, I'll have to see what the sheriff wants."

"Are you going to show him what Riker did to your truck?"

A frown touched his lips. "If I do, they'll want to know where it happened, and my parents won't like hearing I was at the Chateau. Though they'll notice the damage soon enough and I'll have to explain. Just rather not do that in front of the sheriff."

We drove by a pasture full of cows belonging to the dairy. "They don't want you going there? Why not?"

Braking in front of the driveway that led to my grandparents' place, Zef turned to study me. Three-quarters of him was hidden in shadow, making it impossible to read his expression. "Kenley, know something? You ask more questions than any girl I've ever met."

He reached across me, opening the pickup door. "The Chateau is dangerous. Stay away."

I climbed out and slammed the door, stomping up the long drive that passed under a metal arch declaring: *Strickland Ranch*. I heard Zef make a U-turn but didn't look back, hoping I never ran into him or his crazy brother again.

5
Double Trouble

I hurried toward the Strickland compound where three houses sat in a row, each separated by large lawns and vegetable gardens. In my mind I called it *Land of the Js*. My grandparents, Joe and June, had decided to name all their kids with the same letter. Mom's brothers, Jed and Josh, worked the dairy with Grandpa. They were both married, and Jed had two little kids, Jill and Jaden.

A breeze picked up and my nose wrinkled at the sour stink. No matter how long I stayed at the dairy, I'd never get used to the smell. I jogged up the porch steps and through the front door, hearing voices in the kitchen. Inside the house it smelled much better, the remnant of Grandma's cooking making me suddenly hungry. My stomach soon reminded me I'd skipped lunch.

Entering the kitchen, I was surprised to see Grandpa Joe sitting at the table. Always around sunset, he and my uncles started milking the cows. My grandma had the phone to her ear, talking in a worried voice until she saw me. "Thank goodness! Kenley, where have you been?" Speaking into the phone she added, "Julie, she just came in. Do you want to talk to her?"

My grandpa didn't wait for my mother's reply. He folded his arms across his large stomach which always seemed to battle the suspenders that held up his pants. "I hope you have a good excuse for this, young lady."

Until that exact second I hadn't thought about an excuse. Having Jules for a mother meant I was used to telling the truth, since she was the least strict adult I knew. But standing there in my grandparents' kitchen, with its mint green walls and white cupboards, I knew I needed one. The only thing I could think to do was: a) apologize and b) hold my hand out for the phone. I did both, but hearing Jules dismayed voice on the other end made me realize this wasn't the best idea, either.

"I know you're upset," she said, more emotional than I'd heard since the lounge closed and she was out of a job. "But running off is really foolish, Kenley. And dangerous."

"I didn't run off."

"Where were you, then?"

Aware that both grandparents were listening, I started making up stuff. "I went for a walk in the woods and got lost. You know how the trees all look the same. I must've gotten turned around." Even to me it sounded lame. "Then I fell asleep." The truest part so far, despite the omission that it was on the Chateau's veranda. From the corner of my eye I could see they weren't buying it.

I let out a slow exhale. "It's not like my phone works and I could call home."

"So that's what this is about?" my grandpa boomed, putting one of his large hands on the table. "You trying to scare your mother into getting your phone working?"

"No, of course not!" I studied his meaty features and thin sandy hair as my grandma came to stand beside him. Her face was plain, her short hair shot through with gray. For a couple of seconds I was distracted by how completely ordinary they were. It wasn't the first time I'd marveled at how Jules—with her beautiful eyes, perfect soprano voice, and thick strawberry blond curls—had come from them. They didn't sing, or daydream... or do anything impulsive and fun. And neither of them was good looking.

I turned away, talking into the phone. "I'm sorry, Jules. When I woke up the sun was setting. I knew I'd be in trouble and tried to get home as fast as I could. It took longer than I thought it would." Except for omitting huge chunks of info, this was pretty much the truth. At least it sounded better.

"Okay, Kenley. Just don't do it again, all right? I've got an audition tomorrow, and if it works out, I'll be able to come get you soon."

"Sure."

Even though it sounded hollow, I hoped she was right. More than anything I wanted to believe she'd get a big part and a big salary, whisking me away to a New York apartment.

We talked a little more and I studied the cow cookie jar with a cracked ear glued back on. It had been around ever since I was a little girl, the glue a yellowed line. I kept staring at it, hoping my grandparents would stop watching me, but they didn't. I hung up and faced them, a throbbing pressure at my temples.

"You're grounded," my grandpa said, just like that. No more questions, no chance for me to work it out with them, just his rigid way of dealing with rule-breaking.

I shoved a hand in the pocket of my shorts, fingers brushing my useless cell phone. "Grounded from what, exactly?"

He just looked at me, the crease between his shaggy eyebrows deepening, but I kept going. "It's not like I have any friends here. Or a car. And now I don't even have a phone to talk to my friends back in Branson."

"Enough about that blasted phone!"

My grandma put a calming hand on his arm but it didn't have much effect, since he added, "Go to your room."

His raised voice made me jut out my chin. "I don't have a room. Do you mean go to the sewing room?"

He stood, the chair sliding back with an unhappy grunt, and I left the kitchen, heading up the stairs. I didn't stomp or slam the door, since I didn't want to give him a reason to come after me. Despite my tough face-off with the old guy, my heart thumped. In the kingdom of *unfair*, Joe Strickland was the ruler, and now I was an unfortunate subject.

I kicked off my shoes and plopped on the narrow bed, settling in with my back against the wall and knees pulled up. The bed was like a boat in a sea of fabric. Stacks of folded material sat in orderly piles everywhere, including on shelves, the sewing machine table, and even in boxes under the bed. It was crazy how much G'ma had collected, though I grudgingly had to give her credit for organizing it so completely by color.

Once upon a time this had been Jules room, back when her name was still Julie and she'd spent hours in front of the mirror singing into her hairbrush. These days all that remained were the faded daisy wallpaper, the bed shoved in one corner, and a beat-up dresser: two top drawers for me, the bottom two packed with thread and yarn. And, of course, my mother's senior picture hung on the wall, a faded blue and gold tassel dangling along the side of the frame.

Right after graduation, she and her friend Lucy headed to New York to start their acting careers. Lucy didn't stay long, but my mother got her first role and soon married my dad, Keith Barrett, an aspiring playwright. As I studied the busy patterns of stacked fabric, I wondered how different my life would be if my father hadn't died in a car accident when I was four. I rested my head on my palm, wishing the pounding would stop.

A quick knock made me look up. Not waiting for an answer, G'ma opened the door and came in the way she always did. This time, though, I didn't resent the invasion of privacy since she carried a plate of spaghetti.

"I thought you'd be hungry."

She held it out to me, her eyes scanning the sewing room. "I can clear out more of the fabric and put it in the shed."

I took the plate. "No, you don't have to. I didn't mean what I said."

It sounded so sincere that I wondered if I was finally

getting the hang of lying. Shoving in a mouthful, I thanked her for the spaghetti with the worst table manners, except I was on a bed so maybe it didn't matter. Even reheated it tasted great, and I admitted to myself that despite the stuff I didn't like about being here, the food was always good. I never brought this up to my grandma, though.

She dragged over her sewing chair and sat down to face me, which was when I realized the spaghetti came with a price. "Kenley, I need to know where you've been for all these hours."

Now I chewed like a dainty princess, as if talking with even a little bit of sauce in my mouth was unacceptable. It didn't work because she waited. I thought about the Chateau and everything that happened. No way was I willing to discuss it, but then I remembered Zef. News of anything in this little town traveled fast, so if he told his parents about me—or worse, the sheriff—it would get back to the Stricklands.

"I met someone."

The look on her face was almost worth the confession, and I took another large bite of spaghetti to hide how it made me want to smile. Deciding I had nothing to lose, since I was already grounded, I added, "His name is Zef."

The worry in G'ma's eyes faded. Not what I'd expected. "Oh, you met Zefram Webb?"

I shrugged. "He didn't tell me his whole name, but how many Zefs can there be? Anyway, we were talking and it got late. He gave me a ride home."

This didn't seem to bother her. She even smiled. "Zef hires on with us when we harvest the alfalfa. He's a hard worker. His parents are good people who've been through a lot."

For once, I was interested. "They live just down the road, don't they?"

"Yes. His mother, Beverly, inherited that acre where their house now sits, though the land around it was sold off long before she was born."

"So they're not farmers?"

She shook her head. "Miles teaches science and math at the middle school. Beverly works part-time from home these days, since her health doesn't let her do much else. And Zef has a little sister named Kes who's eleven or twelve. But it's Riker, the oldest boy, who about broke that family. He's been trouble since he was young, and over the years his parents tried everything. Last we heard, he was in jail."

I didn't correct her or explain what I already knew. My grandma's gaze drifted to the picture of Jules with the graduation tassel. "It's hard on a family when a child chooses a wrong path. People always think you're to blame."

I lowered my fork. How could she compare my mother's decision to pursue an acting career to Riker's life of crime? I felt that familiar pressure inside, the pounding at my temples increasing. I wished she'd just leave.

She stared at the plate. "Is that all you're going to eat?"

"My head hurts. Can I get some painkiller?"

"You probably got too much sun."

Just go away, G'ma, will you? "Nope. Me and the sun are friends."

She gave me that same confused expression I saw a lot, so I said, "I like being in the sun."

A couple of seconds ticked by, and I wondered how our conversation could get any more stilted until she added, "Maybe you should start wearing a hat."

No comment.

"Though I must say, you're the only redhead I've ever seen who doesn't have even one freckle."

I shrugged. "Jules says it's a gift from my dad. She calls it my golden peach complexion."

Grandma's mouth turned a little sour. Now what was it she didn't like? My talking about my dad?

"Kenley, it's disrespectful to call your mother by her first name. Do your friends all do that?"

I thought about telling her the story of how my mom had taken me to a theater party where I pretended to be one of her friends, calling her Jules the way they did. Afterwards, we'd laughed about it and somehow it became an easy habit we both liked. But as I studied my grandma's eyes, I realized she'd never get it. Instead, I folded my arms and pressed my lips together.

This didn't stop her from starting up a monologue about how kids should call their mothers "mom" and also how Julie was my mother's real name, not Jules. Then it dribbled over into more stuff about respect, so I stopped listening. Inside my head was a constant drumbeat spelling out the single chorus: *I hate it here.*

She finally took the plate and left, but came back with a glass of water and a couple of painkillers. "We should turn in. Tomorrow is a busy day."

It was 9:30. And to the people living the dairy life, every tomorrow was busy.

I hate it here. I hate it here. I hate it here.

6
Boxes

A rooster screeched off-key, underscored by the drone
of news radio coming from the kitchen directly beneath my
bed. Pans clanked on the stove. A blender whirred. I turned
on my side, not bothering to check the clock as mornings
here always began at five. Pulling the covers over my head,
I begged sleep back. During the night I'd been awake for
hours, unable to sleep because of my headache and also
analyzing everything that happened.

Voices joined the kitchen noise as family and dairy
workers arrived for breakfast. Finally the sounds died down
and I drifted off. When I next woke, too-cheery light
seeped around the blinds. A mild remnant of yesterday's
headache remained, so I closed my eyes and lay still, letting
my thoughts drift in a hazy blur.

I began thinking about my dream of the Chateau's
ballroom, and was drawn into a daydream where I added
details: women in beautiful gowns and men with stiff white
collars beneath old-fashioned jackets. Couples danced to
haunting music, others talked in quiet voices. Most wore
masks, and many of the women held gold or silver fans.

My mind snagged on that. Had I dreamed about the
fans, or was I making it up? Of course, the whole thing had
to be made up. But I kept the fantasy going, wondering
what I was wearing. I hadn't even thought of that and
mentally looked down at a dress of heavy satin. It hugged
my waist then billowed out in ivory folds. My hands
smoothed the softness, candlelight shimmering it with
touches of gold. The image seemed to grow in richness:
layers of netting beneath a full skirt, fitted sleeves that
ended above the elbow and flared out in a wide ruffle of

soft lace, a velvet ribbon tied at my throat above a square neckline inset with more lace.

My eyes slowly opened. Sitting up, I grabbed my art bag hanging on the corner of the bed and dug out my sketch pad. When the pencil touched a clean page, I experienced my usual sense of anticipation.

I began lightly sketching an oval for the face, curves for the neck, arms and body, last of all the flow of a wide skirt. My pencil easily captured the lines of the dress, adding in details of lace that edged the square neckline and flared above the elbows. The picture rapidly formed. I shaded the folds of cloth and bodice curves, as if I could actually see the effects of candlelight. More quickly than I would have thought possible, the gown was drawn. I held the drawing away from my face to study it, impressed with how fast it all came together. Usually, when I drew, I needed to erase. For me, it was a slow process of sketch and re-sketch until I was satisfied.

Not wanting to stop, I kept working on the scalloped edges of lace and included the toe of a shoe peeking beneath the wide hem. Last of all, I fleshed out the arms, one softly bent behind the back, the other resting on the full skirt. Drawing the facial features was hardest, self-portraits always a challenge. I went to the mirror above the dresser and stared at my reflection, working back and forth between mirror and paper. I drew wide eyes beneath smoothly arched brows, an average nose, and the full curve of my mouth. When I was done it seemed a little generic—*Kenley or not?* Reaching up, I tried to smooth my thick, jaw length hair, its wild strands not cooperating. I gave up and started sketching it anyway. My red-gold hair fell across my forehead and I copied the lines, but it didn't look right with the old-fashioned dress. Heading back to the bed I plopped down and this time did erase, at last penciling in an upswept hairstyle with curls trailing behind. Better. Not me, but at least it fit with the period dress.

In the distance the rumbling growl of a tractor engine started. I went to the window and looked out across the dairy as the morning sun sent out bright rays. Black and white cows stood in rows at feeding troughs, their tails lazily swishing away flies. Beyond the dairy buildings, fields of grain spread out carpets of green and gold. As usual, the outside world beckoned me to leave the stuffy house and go walking. But to where? Though the Chateau intrigued me, it didn't seem smart to return.

Before I could decide, I noticed my grandma weeding tomatoes in the garden and then remembered I was grounded. My plans for a walk deflated. I put away the sketchbook and headed downstairs to the kitchen, the speckled linoleum cool beneath my bare feet.

Breakfast was long gone, but a loaf of homemade bread sat on the counter. I cut a piece and put it in the toaster, then grabbed the landline phone and called my friend Dana. She answered with a little hesitation, not recognizing the number but figuring it out when she heard my voice.

"Kenley! What's going on? I tried calling you ten times yesterday."

A renewed sense of isolation rushed back. I began to explain about my disconnected phone, and Dana's reaction was what I needed. "But it's so unfair! And you don't even have a computer there, either, so you can't send emails."

"Yeah, I know. It's like I'm cut off from everything."

"Doesn't your mom get how tough this already is for you?"

I appreciated Dana saying exactly what I had been thinking. We chatted a while longer, topics changing, and as I nibbled on toast she talked about the upcoming horror movie-fest in Kiefer's basement. She also told me how she'd applied at a pizza place and had an interview next Monday.

"That's great, Dana. I'd love to get a job. But when I

ask around, the first thing they want to know is how long I'll be here."

I didn't add the rest, that in spite of the many times Jules and I were forced to be frugal until we had rent money, I'd never been so broke.

"How long will you be stuck there?" Dana asked.

That was another worry. I could just imagine the summer slipping away and school starting. Would I have to enroll at the local high school, *home of the Mustangs*?

The screen door banged as my grandma came in, peeling off garden gloves and eyeing my pajama bottoms. Apparently, still wearing them after ten wasn't appropriate. I wandered into the living room with the clunky handset still to my ear, wishing I could take it upstairs but knowing the outdated beast wouldn't get reception that far away.

"Gotta go, Dana. You guys have fun tonight."

The sound of how much I wanted to be there must have been in my voice, since she sounded sad when she said goodbye. Even though I wasn't really into horror films, it was always a blast to be with my friends in Kiefer's basement, eating licorice and watching out for popcorn being thrown at each other when someone in the movie screamed.

I returned the handset to the kitchen and saw Grandma waiting for me. "Kenley, I've been thinking. What you need is a project."

Right to the point. I shoved the last bite of toast in my mouth, hoping she didn't think pulling weeds was the project I needed.

"We should make a quilt together."

I swallowed. "I've never made a quilt."

Her eyes turned a little steely. "Julie told me you sew. Or at least alter clothes, isn't that right? So this should be easy for you, mostly straight stitches. Get dressed and meet me out in the shed."

The sewing room stacked with fabric came to mind.

"Why are we going to the shed?"

She reached the back door. "Because that's where your baby clothes are stored."

This made even less sense. "Uhh... Grandma, how long am I grounded?"

Pausing, as if thinking, her head gave a single nod. "Until the quilt's done."

I hustled upstairs to change.

A few minutes later I headed to the storage building they called the shed, thinking how it was anything but. Two stories high, nearly as big as my grandparents' house, and with three giant garage doors, it loomed behind my Uncle Jed's place. I crossed the asphalt parking area, where there were always a minimum of two pickups, and brushed away the ever-present flies that swarmed everything. "Go find the cows," I muttered, entering the side door and shutting them out.

Inside, the floor was a massive concrete slab beneath rows of equipment that included lawn mowers and table saws. Tons of hand tools were neatly organized on work tables, and standing metal shelving along one wall held all sorts of containers from plastic bins to rows of fruit-filled jars.

Shoved in one corner was the furniture that Jules had dropped off—along with me. The flowered couch, navy recliner, and coffee table that had once filled our apartment's tiny front room now looked small and sad, as if they felt misplaced too. I wanted to straighten the tipped shade of the floor lamp, pat my headboard we'd so carefully repainted bright aqua, and pass on the hollow promise to our stuff that they'd soon be on their way to an apartment in New York.

Instead, I headed for the wooden slat steps leading to the second floor and found my grandma looking over a bunch of cardboard boxes stacked on metal racks. She'd already opened some, and as I watched she pulled out a large one and dropped it to the floor. "Julie should've labeled these better."

A few had words scrawled in black marker, most didn't. I asked, "Why are we looking for my baby clothes?"

She didn't even glance up. "It's called a memory quilt. We're going to cut up your childhood clothes."

This sounded like a lot of work, and not something I was excited to do, but I still helped her check the boxes. One held some of my old school papers, another my mom's yearbooks and high school things. Finally Grandma found what she was searching for, a whole stack of baby and little kid clothes that looked permanently wrinkled from spending years smashed in a box. Since I didn't remember wearing them, it wouldn't be much of a memory quilt. But being grounded left me with even more boring hours than usual, and when it came to projects I preferred sewing to weeding.

I folded in the flaps of the boxes while my grandmother decided how they should be restacked. I'd almost finished closing them all when the contents of a small box grabbed my attention. It was filled with assorted notebooks, typed pages held by hinge clips, a stack of theater programs, and published plays bearing my father's name: *Keith Barrett*.

"This is my dad's stuff."

She stopped to glance down and nodded, then picked up the box of baby clothes. "Let's go."

I grabbed the smaller box and when she raised her eyebrows, a defensive note lined my voice. "It's okay for me to look through this, right?"

"Of course."

Back in the sewing room, my grandma set up her long cutting table and ironing board, which left almost no space to move around. She picked up a baby dress of pale green with tiny orange flowers on it, shaking it out. "I made this for you. My first grandchild."

Her voice sounded wistful and it surprised me, as she'd never seemed the sentimental type. She handed me a rotary cutter and a four inch plastic square. "Use this as a template, and make sure you avoid any stains or snags. The fabric blocks also need to be ironed."

"You're not staying?"

"I've got to start lunch."

"Oh." Mealtimes were a major production with lunch happening in shifts as everyone who worked at the dairy came in to eat.

"Once you've got enough squares, we'll pick fabric for the strips that go between."

I worked for almost an hour, my stack of fabric squares unimpressive as I wondered if this grounding was going to turn into a life sentence. Blowing the bangs out of my eyes, I sank down on the bed next to the box of my dad's stuff and decided to take a break.

With my back resting against the wall, I skimmed the titles of his plays, a tingling excitement growing inside me. For most of my life, my dad had been a blurry memory. Sometimes I would look through our old photo album, studying his long face that was a little homely and a little handsome all together, just to remind myself of him.

Studying his pictures always brought back the barest echoes of recollection: *His low, sandpapery laugh. The time he'd knelt beside me, a ladybug on my arm so soft it tickled. Sunlight turning his auburn hair copper, and someone saying, "She's sure got her daddy's coloring." Sitting high on his shoulders, my hands on top of his head, feeling like a stilt-walker... Hiding in a dark place, eyes squeezed shut. Orange tiger lilies reflected in the shiny wood of his coffin.*

Back then, as an almost five-year-old, sadness hollowed me out until I was empty. Weeks passed and it felt like sleepwalking until one day my mother came home with a blue balloon tied to a long yellow ribbon.

"Just so you know," she explained. "We can't keep this."

Taking my hand, she led me out onto the sidewalk in front of our apartment. "Kenley, this balloon wants to be free. Making it stay with us until the air finally goes out means it'll never be able to fly."

She bent down, her eyes seeming to hold all the love in the world. "Do you want to help me let it go?"

I nodded.

Mama handed me the string and we counted to three. My fingers held tight just a little longer, then I opened them and felt the wisp of yellow ribbon slide across my palm. Two seconds more and the balloon was soaring. Up it went, my eyes tracking it the whole time.

Her voice was sad but strong. "Kenley, we have to let your daddy go, too."

I held my breath, unable to stop watching the balloon as it drifted in the cloudless sky. Finally, it faded to nothing.

Blinking, I let out a slow breath as if I was still that little girl from long ago. I listened to the sounds of my grandmother working in the kitchen and the mooing of far-off cows. My eyes focused on a puff of steam seeping from the forgotten iron, my small stack of fabric squares next to it.

Turning to the box beside me, I lifted out one of my father's plays and started reading.

7
What I Found

Exhume my bones, unearth my teeth,
Dig secrets from the ground.
Be cautious of the truth you seek,
Lest you curse what you have found.

The Ghost Child
Act I, Scene IV

During the long days of being grounded, I kept thinking about the Chateau. I even sketched it from a picture on my phone, adding more details each time I went back to the drawing. Why had my mother never talked about this place? Her childhood stories were filled with tales of pranks with friends, the excitement of acting in school plays, and even running for local dairy princess. But she'd never said anything about the huge, castle-like building in the middle of nowhere. And though I could pretty much talk to her about anything, this was one topic I didn't dare bring up.

Instead, when she called I told her about reading my father's plays, which she thought was cool. I said, "My dad must've been smart. In the box, there are notebooks full of research."

"Oh yes, very smart. He had this way of analyzing stuff most people don't usually even think about. You take after him that way."

I liked the comparison. "Another thing I never knew, he started a book. I think it was going to be a historical novel."

"Yes, that's right," she slowly answered, as if pulling

up a memory from long ago. "He talked about someday wanting to get a book published."

I thought of the thin stack of manuscript pages clipped together and a shallow sigh escaped me. "Guess he never got the chance to finish it."

Because he died. Those unspoken words caused a break in the conversation and Jules changed the subject, which wasn't a surprise. We didn't talk about the accident that took my father's life, or the days of sorrow that followed. She only wanted to talk about good memories. Like the story of how they met—her first acting role at the same theater where he worked as an assistant director. Or about the day I was born, her still wearing a period costume from the *Sweeney Todd* cast and him all in black from helping out backstage.

She also liked to tell about the day he sold his first play, when I was just six months old. They'd both been thrilled. It was those published plays, I knew, that had helped us get by after we lost him. The twice-yearly royalties were an anticipated bonus letting us catch up on past-due bills and then go shopping. Sadly, with each year that passed, the checks kept getting smaller. When they did come, we always went to dinner. For dessert we ordered his favorite: warm blueberry pie with vanilla ice cream.

I looked out the sewing room window at the darkening sky, recalling my most recent conversation with Jules. She'd sounded upbeat and hopeful, even though nothing much had come of her auditions so far. Mainly, it was because she'd run into Anthony, a guy she dated a couple of years ago. I'd liked him okay, since he was funny and invited me along on a few of their restaurant dates. But it ended when he was offered a chance to direct a traveling theater company and Jules had accepted the job in Branson.

Plopping on the bed, I stared at the folded memory quilt I'd finally finished. Today I'd done the last of the yarn tying then hemmed the edges. The whole project had taken me eight long days. The look of it turned out all right and I told G'ma it was awesome, even though I really thought it had way too many pink squares.

Just then, she knocked and looked in, telling me goodnight and encouraging me to turn in soon. I nodded just so she'd shut the door, then glanced at the clock. It was barely after nine, and I thought how I'd never get used to their *early to bed, early to rise* routine.

With a sigh, I grabbed the box with my dad's stuff inside, thumbing through his published plays until realizing I'd read them all. I decided to choose one of his projects that were the beginning scenes of new plays, each held together with black binder clips at the top.

I picked the title I liked best, *The Ghost Child*, and lay back on the bed. It began with a description of the first setting when the curtain rises:

At RISE: (An old-world room with faded wallpaper and aged furniture that speaks of lost grandeur. Early evening.)

(DERRICK, a thirty-something real estate agent dressed in appropriate 1940s apparel, checks his watch.)

(HOLLY enters. She is DERRICK's wife. Her posture is tense, as if hiding frayed nerves.)

HOLLY
You're sure they'll come? And that they're willing to buy?

DERRICK
(Tersely.) I already told you. Can't you just trust me about this?

HOLLY
Because whether they do or not, I won't stay in
this Chateau one more night.

Chateau? That single word jumped out at me and I sat
up. I began reading through the pages and scrutinizing each
word of the story. Two new characters were introduced,
Ned and Janice Baxter, a couple pretending to be interested
in buying the old mansion. In a following scene where they
were alone in the sitting room, the dialogue hinted that after
many years Ned had returned to the area where he once
lived, eager to secretly investigate the Chateau because of
something eerie he'd seen there when he was a boy.

The more I read, the more I sensed that the setting—
and possibly the story itself—had actually been inspired by
the real Chateau. Which meant my father must have found
it, too.

I could hardly stay seated on the bed, a thrumming
vibration coursing inside me as my mind flitted along all
the possibilities of what that meant. I read more dialogue,
where the character Derrick joked about the Chateau being
built miles from civilization. That clinched it.

Flipping the page, I experienced a sinking sensation.
The paper was blank, as were the six pages following it.
What had I expected? This was clearly a first draft and
even had several typo corrections and changes written in
pen. I thoughtfully returned it to the box, which I slid under
the bed before clicking off the light.

I climbed under the sheet, lying in the dark and just
thinking. In time I dosed off, but my sleep was fitful. I'd
wake, and then my mind would gear up, creating all sorts
of images of my father visiting the Chateau, maybe even
exploring it. What had he seen, and how much did he know
about it?

When I next awoke, it was in a groggy haze. Staring at

gray shapes in the early morning light, for several seconds I couldn't figure out why everything seemed wrong. Then I understood. This was my grandmother's sewing room, not my bedroom back in Branson, and the comfort of briefly believing I was still in our old apartment dissolved.

I clicked on the small lamp, blinking at stacks of material and the sewing machine. The clock showed it was still early enough that even my grandparents weren't awake. In that moment, I felt desperate to escape. I dressed quickly and went down to the kitchen, art bag slung across my shoulder. I grabbed an apple and cookie, then searched the pantry for the juice boxes my grandma kept for my little cousins. A sound of footfalls overhead interrupted, and I hurried to the back door. I didn't want to ask if my being grounded was over only to have them tell me it wasn't. In my mind, finishing the quilt was good enough.

I slipped outside, the June air cool as I headed away from the house and passed beneath the *Strickland Ranch* archway. Dawn ran a pearly bead along the edge of the hills, the gray sky melting to a shade of blue I wished could be captured in an eyeshadow palette. I hurried down the empty road, staring at the pale moon that hung low in the sky, thin as rice paper.

Excitement from finally escaping the ranch plucked at the tightness inside me, and I smiled until noticing the house where Zefram Webb and his family lived. I thought of everything that had happened at the Chateau and knew it wouldn't be smart to go there again. Both Jules and Zef had warned me to stay away, but after reading the first pages of my dad's partial play, I had to go.

The narrow path I followed tapered to an end at an uncultivated field surrounded by trees. I turned around, not sure how I'd gotten on the wrong trail. Backtracking, I searched for the barbed wire strung between weathered posts but didn't see it. As the sun inched up and turned the clouds to copper, I stopped and dug in my art bag only to remember I hadn't gotten one of the juice boxes. The trees around me looked the same, so did the fields, but I'd been letting my thoughts drift and must have made a wrong turn. Going back, I eventually found a fork in the path and took it, but soon it veered off in the direction of a wide cornfield and I again stopped. Tall weeds tickled my thigh and I brushed them away, finally deciding I needed to go all the way back to the main road.

I stomped off, kicking up dust. The first time I'd looked for the Chateau it hadn't been that hard to find, so why did it now seem elusive? I reached the road and started walking along the pavement when it hit me. I'd turned off too soon on a narrow path that appeared almost exactly the same as the one I should have taken.

In time, the posts strung with rusted barbed wire came into view where they stood guard among scraggly oaks. I hurried forward and squeezed past one. More sure now, I moved faster, my art bag beating out a rhythm against my side. And then—just as it had before—the Chateau rose up from between towering trees, offering the same striking view as before with its pale blue roof and darkened windows.

Sunlight slid across the grounds and colored the face of the Chateau. The gate's chain was still in a heap on the ground. I was ready to slip inside until remembering the vision of rats swarming down the long service tunnel. Why I'd seen that, and what it meant, was the most curious thing about this place. Just to be on the safe side, I decided to limit my exploring to the outside. At least until I knew more about it.

I followed my same route around the house, peeking through the many windows. It looked the same as before. The air slowly grew warm, my legs tired from the long walk. Reaching the veranda in back, I climbed the steps and leaned close to the windowpane in one of the French doors. The sight of the wrecked ballroom caused a renewed sense of sadness. I hated seeing it in ruins, like Cinderella's dress torn to rags. I sat down on the bench and again rested my back on the wall.

The rose garden beyond the veranda looked in even worse shape as light detailed thorny brown limbs held in painful poses. My thoughts wandered back to reading my father's unfinished play, and also to Jules, wishing I could tell her about it. I had to admit that our last conversation had left me feeling homesick for her. What would happen to us if she didn't find work?

The morning breeze rustling tree limbs, and the lazy drone of bees, sounded restful. I closed my eyes, letting out a slow sigh. I should've stayed in bed.

Paintings in ornate frames decorated smooth walls, and an enormous crystal chandelier reflected prisms of candlelight across the marble floor. Music mingled with voices, both pleasant and discordant. Women in shimmering ball gowns and feathered masks waved gold and silver fans and smiled, men in old-fashioned jackets courting them.

I looked down at my satin dress, fingers brushing its soft folds. Across the room was a massive mirror in a gilt frame. Moving past clusters of people, I went to it. The girl in the mirror wore a pale mask, her red-gold hair styled with curls in back. Kenley or not? I reached up to take the mask away.

"Don't do that," a voice said, and I looked up at a reflection forming behind my own. Tall, with hair combed back from his face, he wore a simple black mask. He leaned into me, as if sharing a secret. "Want to see something no one else knows about?"

I hesitated a little until he smiled. The friendliness of it, the sheer invitation of becoming some sort of conspirator with him, made me smile, too. "What is it?"

"You'll see." He held out his hand. "Trust me?"

At that moment I did trust him, in fact longed to go with him! I slid my hand into his and he led me through the ballroom. Dancers parted and drifted away like watery images distorted by a pebble tossed in a pond. The music quickly faded to nothing. "This way," he said, his voice threaded with an excitement that I began to feel too.

We ran down a wide hallway lined with candle sconces and open doorways, passing a library on the left and a great room to the right. The satin of my dress rustled across the floor, our footsteps echoing in the quiet as his fingers squeezed mine.

We hurried through the center gallery and I glimpsed paintings before we entered the grand foyer. We reached the curved stairway and slowed. "It's so dark," I whispered.

Above us, all was black. Even the candlelight flickering from the wall sconces seemed unable to penetrate the gloom. The eagerness of moments ago vanished, replaced by growing dread. "I don't think we should go up there." I hardly recognized my voice—child-like and frightened.

"There's nothing to be afraid of."

His words were a lie, and I knew it. "But you're scared."

He didn't deny this, only tugged on my hand. I pulled back, trying to break his grip, but he wouldn't let go. "You've got to come. You must see!"

Cold darkness drifted down the stairs. I tried to turn away but couldn't, my heart racing. "What's up there?"

"A secret trap." His words faded to a whisper. "Third door on the right. And don't forget to knock."

A rapping noise invaded my awareness, a sound that

started and stopped like an irregular heartbeat. Blinking, peering past deep shadows and nearly blinded by a slanting beam of sunlight, my eyes focused on a million manic dust motes.

Finally making sense of my surroundings, I sucked in a choked breath. I was standing inside the Chateau.

8
Intruder Alert

I spun around, heading for the French doors leading to the veranda, my thoughts dancing more crazily than the dust motes as I tried to work out how I'd gotten here. For a few seconds I was afraid the doors wouldn't open and I'd be trapped. However, the handle moved beneath my fingers and I stepped outside, gulping in the warmer air. I turned to peer into the ballroom and studied the angles of shadow and light. The sun was much higher now than when I'd been sitting on the bench, which allowed a thick beam to slide through a window on the east wall.

Finally pulling away, I looked around the veranda and across the dead rose garden—all the same as before. But what about the doors? The last time I was here they were locked, so this morning I hadn't even thought to test them. But they must have already been unlocked, since I ended up inside. Still, how had I done that when I'd been sitting on the bench? Had I fallen into some sort of trance and then entered the Chateau? So far as I knew, I'd never sleepwalked in my life.

Common sense told me to head home fast, and I was halfway down the veranda steps before I paused to think. The ballroom dream had seemed so real and ended too abruptly. I couldn't help but wonder what was upstairs, even though this whole thing had to just be a fantasy brought on by my infatuation with the Chateau and the discovery of my father's play. But as I stood there, the morning sunlight comfortable on my shoulders, I said to myself, "I'm not going to let some dream scare me. After all, this is just a house."

I reentered the ballroom but left the door slightly ajar.

Walking purposefully across the debris-covered floor, I passed through the slanting ray of light, the air current sending the motes into an even wilder jig. I'd barely stepped into the dim hallway when a rapping noise started then stopped. Breathing a little faster, because I'd felt certain the knocking had only been a part of the trance, my ears strained in the silence. I had just about convinced myself I was dreaming again, this time with open eyes, when once more it picked up. Louder this time, it seemed to be coming from the room on the left. Quietly moving forward, I reached the open doorway and peered in.

Heavy oak shelves lined an entire wall, and floor-to-ceiling arched windows let in muted light from beneath a wide eave. On the far end of the room, near a shadowy place and with his back to the door, a boy stood facing the wall. The fingers of his left hand ran lightly across peeling wallpaper, the knuckles of his right tapping.

I studied his dark brown hair trimmed neatly at the nape in opposition to the top part that was messy, as if he'd shoved his fingers through it. A tan T-shirt, tucked into low slung jeans, stretched across his shoulder blades and the muscles of his back. Even though I couldn't see his face, I knew it was Zef.

Stepping through the doorway, I asked, "What are you doing?"

He spun around, mouth slightly open. His brows pulled inward. "Kenley?"

I took a couple of steps across the worn wood floor, noting the walls covered with peeling paper above chipped wainscoting. My vision dimmed and wavered a bit, and for a couple of seconds I glimpsed period furniture, paintings, and elegant watered silk of palest green. The floor and woodwork gleamed, the shelves lined with books. Two thoughts battled each other: disbelief, and also the tiniest idea of how a girl could disappear into a place like that. But then I blinked and it was gone.

Zef frowned. "How'd you get in here?"

I suppressed a shiver, my eyes scanning the room but now seeing only dust and debris. Realizing he watched me too closely, I said, "Through the veranda."

Fisted hands went to his hips. "Those doors are locked."

I put my hands on my hips in a mocking, copycat way, determined to hide the edginess plucking at my nerves. "No they're not."

Zef strode past me and out into the hallway. I followed him through the ballroom to the French doors, which he stooped to examine. He ran his fingers over the external keyhole and handles, then straightened and turned to me. "The keys to open this from the outside were lost long ago. Someone must have gotten in the Chateau another way and then unlocked them from inside."

His gaze said I was the main suspect. I shook my head. "Wasn't me."

He went out onto the veranda, looking around, then paced the length of it as I watched through the glass panes. A couple of seconds later he stooped to pick up a cigarette butt. He flipped it out into the garden and came back through the French doors, one of which he held open for me. "Did you want to leave?"

"No. Are you telling me to?"

"Yes."

I scowled. "Why do you act like you own this place?"

He didn't answer.

"What... do you?" I stared at him, internally fidgeting because I suddenly wondered if maybe he did, despite his statement about trespassing the first time we met.

"It belongs to the county," he finally said. "They took possession of it decades ago for unpaid property taxes."

His eyes studied me in a slow way, as if measuring what to say. "But if my family had the money to pay off the taxes, we'd own it."

I remembered what my grandma had said about the Webbs once having a lot of land, though now their house sat on the last remaining acre.

"Not that this place is worth anything," he added, heading back to where I'd found him.

I trailed after him. "Why were you tapping on the library wall?"

He stopped at the door and I almost bumped into him. "How did you know this is the library?"

I waved my hand in the direction of the room. "What else, with all those bookshelves?"

Zef turned and leaned against the door frame, eyes on me again. "I wasn't joking around when I told you this place is dangerous."

His serious tone sent a slight tingle up my neck, but I shrugged in a way that said I didn't care. "And I told you I don't believe in haunted houses."

"Dangerous isn't the same as haunted."

"If you're trying to scare me, it's not working. And since you don't own the Chateau, you can't stop me from looking around."

I turned and marched down the hallway to where it opened into a long gallery. In my fantasy it had been lined with beautiful paintings. Now, though, only rectangular outlines on stained plaster showed where they had once hung. That's when it hit me. I hadn't been in this part of the Chateau last time, so how could I daydream about a room I'd never entered?

Footsteps sounded behind me, and I sensed Zef catching up. I hurried through the arch that led to the main foyer.

"Where are you going?" he called.

I felt unnerved by the familiarity of the foyer and staircase until remembering how I'd looked through a number of windows while walking around the outside of the house.

Zef neared me but I headed in the direction of the staircase. "Kenley?"

"I just need to see something."

Trash and thick dust covered the foyer's marble floor, footprints throughout. I started up the steps when Zef moved in front of me, blocking my way. He backed up several steps, standing above with arms folded in the stance of a soldier on guard.

My eyes narrowed. "Really? You're going to physically stop me?"

He didn't budge and didn't answer, either, except to lower his chin and gaze at me like he had laser vision.

"Fine!" I dropped into a football crouch, knees bent and hands out in front. "I can take you."

His eyebrows lifted. Suddenly he laughed, a throaty sound full of amusement. The face that had been so stern this whole time turned boyish and he unfolded his arms. He glanced away and then back at me, shaking his head and chuckling a second time.

Finally he motioned to me, a smile still on his lips. "Come on then. If you're that determined, I'll show you around."

I hurried forward before he changed his mind. He ran his hand along the black metal banister that was oddly free of dust. "Besides, the second level is one of the safer areas, except the far west end where the floor's given way."

The stairs made two turns, the upper hallway forming a square balcony around the foyer below. On the opposite side from the filigree railing were rooms, and the first one I saw after reaching the top of the stairs was large. Double doors with decorated molding were cast wide, and four tall windows looked down on the fountain in front. A fireplace was topped with an elegant marble mantle, several deep cracks marring its surface. A destroyed Persian rug in shades of crimson and brown still covered the floor. Once, it must have been beautiful, though now it was filthy and so badly shredded I wondered if there might be rats in the Chateau after all.

"What's this room, do you know?"

Zef barely glanced in. "The master bedroom."

"It's bigger than my grandparents' living room."

He had already moved on to the next door as if bored, clearly trying to rush me through. The second room was only half as wide as the first, though still larger than any bedroom I'd ever dreamed of. The single door had come off its hinges and lay on the floor just inside. Striped wallpaper, alternating yellow and blue, covered the upper half of the walls just above wainscoting. It appeared in better shape than any I'd seen so far, though frayed lace hung at the windows, looking more like stringy cobwebs than curtains.

The next door down the hall was closed. *Third door on the right*, the dream stranger had said, and I touched the handle.

Zef had already passed it and glanced back. "That's just a service area."

"But it's where I'm supposed to look," I said, half to myself.

The door opened into a small, narrow room with no windows. To the left were shelves, most of them empty. A very old flat iron, aged to an odd shade of brown, sat on a heating plate next to a vintage ironing board, the wood split and warped. On the right side of the room, a narrow worktable was built into the wall. I took a couple of steps in, peering through the shadows, and at the far end of the room saw what looked like a recessed storage closet with no door. Long ago, it had probably held linens.

Zef used the flashlight mode of his phone to shine around the room. "See? Nothing here. Let's go."

I pressed my lips together, aware of Zef standing behind me. Giving one last glance around, my eyes caught on a small cupboard door set into the wall on the right, just above the worktable. I opened it and saw a dumbwaiter with a beat up metal tray inside. "Does this work?"

Zef yanked on a frayed rope, and with a loud creak the box inside moved a few inches. "Sounds like the pulleys are shot, so I wouldn't trust it with anything important. Can we get out of here?"

He shut the little door and I stared at it, mind busy. I wandered deeper inside, my eyes searching the walls until I reached the linen alcove at the far end. "Bring your light over here, will you?"

He came, though his steps sounded reluctant. "If you stay this long in every room, it'll take too much time to see the other hallways."

I snatched the phone from his hand and he made an annoyed protest. I didn't answer, too busy shining it around and examining the cedar-lined shelves and walls.

"Want to explain what you're looking for?" he said.

Until then I hadn't noticed how close he stood and glanced over at him, a smile tugging at my lips. "A secret trap."

I laughed a little, thinking I'd probably find nothing, but intrigued at how my mind had taken me on a strange adventure with clues I was only just putting together.

"You mean like a mouse trap?" He said it slowly, trying to decide if I was a complete nut case.

"No. In theater lingo, the word *trap* means a hidden opening. You know, like the trapdoors they use on stage?"

"You're looking for a trapdoor. In a linen closet."

I slid my art bag off my shoulder and knelt down. "Not a trapdoor, exactly."

In spite of saying that to him, I shone the light down, running my hand across the floor and regretting it when my fingers left streaks in the thick dust. I wiped them on my shorts.

"Most of the time, a trap is a secret opening an actor can pass through to make a sudden appearance. Or an exit.

Sometimes, though, it's just part of the stage equipment. Like a corner trap."

"And what's that?" he asked.

"A small opening, usually at the side of the stage. It's fitted with a door or sometimes just a flap, so things can be handed through it in a way the audience can't see."

Zef crouched beside me, his face mostly hidden in shadow. "Oh, right. You'd know all this stuff because your mom's an actress." His words were thoughtful, not what I'd expected.

I gave him back his phone and probed the side of the cedar wall beneath the bottom shelf. Something gave slightly beneath my fingers, like a latch releasing, and a small square fell open.

Zef shone his light onto a tiny wooden door hinged at the bottom and with a pressure latch at the top. He turned to me. "How did you do that?"

I couldn't tell if he was upset or excited, my own mind whirring. "I just pushed on it."

We both bent down and looked inside, so close together his shoulder bumped mine. He wiped away cobwebs and angled the light to reveal a small lever. "Why don't you move back? Maybe I can turn it."

I scooted out of the way and he reached his hand inside the secret trap. He worked at it until the muscles in his upper arm bulged. Finally we heard the protesting screech of rusted metal giving way, followed by a series of clicks and a whirring noise from the other side of the wall. The back of the alcove, shelves and all, swung away from us. Zef stood, and so did I.

Heart thumping, I stared into the lightless opening, shocked at what we had just done. Zef pushed the closet wall until it swung slowly wider, hidden hinges making a terrible squeal. Dust rained down in ribbons and then billowed into the room. A little of it got stuck in my throat, and I coughed. He rubbed his eyes and blinked a few times before pointing his light at the floor. Metal steps descended inside a narrow spiral staircase. Without even glancing at me, he moved down.

"Hang on, will you?" I said between more coughs. "How do you know that's even safe?"

He didn't answer but went lower, and I thought it a bit funny that I was the one giving the safety lecture this time. From the flitting beam of light, I could tell he was studying the back of the hidden door.

"Come look at this."

I tested my weight on the stairs then stepped down next to him. The stairwell was so narrow I had to turn sideways for both of us to fit. On the back of the door was a metal weight attached with a rusty chain that ran around a couple of pulleys.

"It's a counterweight mechanism used to release the door. Simple but effective." He sounded pleased, and in the backwash of light I could see him smiling.

I peered into the complete blackness beneath us, seeing nothing beyond the next couple of steps. "But where does this go?"

"Down. Want to come?"

His invitation was unexpected since he'd been trying to get rid of me from the moment I got here. Not waiting for an answer, Zef went lower into the stairwell until the dust-covered top of his head disappeared from view. I listened to his feet clanking on the metal stairs, the sound fading as a tingling sensation crept up my neck, a restless flutter in my stomach.

My thoughts wove themselves and then unraveled. I wondered about the stranger in the dream who had urged me to come here, and the fact that there really was a secret trap and I'd found it. I worried about what lay in the darkness below. I also thought of Jules far away in New York, leaving me stuck in a place where nothing exciting ever happened.

Reaching back into the closet, I grabbed my art bag and headed down the steps.

9
Down the Rabbit Hole

"I hope you're not claustrophobic," Zef said as he stepped off the bottom of the stairs and into a very narrow passageway.

As we'd climbed down the metal steps, I tried to suppress a growing anxiety. No reason to let him know that, though. "Nope," I lied. "I'm loving this. Where do you think it leads?"

He shrugged and I peered around his shoulder. The light from his cell phone barely cut into the gloom ahead, and I wondered how far down we were.

He started forward. I followed behind, since the passage wasn't wide enough to walk beside him. The air smelled dank and sour, and what looked like creeping mildew edged the blocks of stone that formed this hidden hallway. The floor was covered by rough cobbles that weren't comfortable to walk on, but unlike the rooms upstairs, it was surprisingly free of dust.

"Zef, what if this dead ends?"

"And the door upstairs gets shut and we can't get out?" His voice held a teasing note.

"So we'd be trapped down here?" I tried to be casual, but my tone came out a little squeaky.

He laughed and the sound echoed back to us, which meant the passageway must go on for a long ways. Despite the coolness coming from the surrounding stone, sweat prickled the inside of my arms.

"Anyone ever died in this place?"

His steps slowed and he looked back at me, though the way he held onto the light I couldn't see much of his features. He seemed to be studying me. "Yes. You don't know?"

"Know what?"

A whisper came from behind. *"Keep going."*

I spun around, peering into the blackness. "Who's there?"

No echo this time. In fact, it seemed as if my voice had been swallowed by the shadows. I bumped into Zef, not realizing until then I'd backed up.

"No one's there," he said.

I blew out a breath, ready to keep going, but Zef didn't move. He stayed facing me, the light from his phone shining on me more than him. "Tell me how you knew about this hidden passage."

I raised my eyebrows. "I didn't."

"But you found the secret trap."

"Because I was poking around, is all. You saw how it fell open when I touched it."

He slowly shook his head. "When we got to the service area, you said it was where you were supposed to look. And you knew right where to find the opening that hid the lever. How?"

I shrugged. "A good guess."

"I don't think it was a guess at all."

Not wanting to explain about the stranger in my daydream, I rubbed damp palms on my shorts. "Let's keep going."

"Sure. As soon as you explain."

I shifted the strap of my art bag to the other shoulder, even more irritated than when he'd tried to block me on the staircase in the front foyer. "You know what, Zef? Go ahead and act like a jerk. I'm getting out of here."

I stared at the gloom behind me, too late realizing he was the one with the light.

"It'll be slow going in the dark," he pointed out, brushing his fingers across his dusty hair. "Look Kenley, I need to know."

Facing him again, I folded my arms. "You *need* to know, or you want to? Because we all want stuff. Right now, I want out of here. The sooner I do that, the sooner I can get away from you."

His slight frown was barely visible. "Tell me, and I'll get you out."

"I hate stubborn guys!"

He wasn't the first obstinate boy I'd met, and I doubted he'd be the last. When he didn't budge, I finally let out a heavy sigh. "Fine! I'll talk. But in the meantime, we keep walking before the battery gives out on your phone."

Zef nodded as I glanced back, a new thought coming to me. "Though maybe we should turn around and go back the way we came. I mean, there might not be another way out."

"Of course there's is. Good old Henry wouldn't have built this hidden hallway without an exit."

He started walking forward and I hurried after him. "Who's Henry?"

"Henry Broderick, my ancestor who build *Chateau de Beauchene* back in 1890."

"That's the name of this place?"

"Yes. *Beauchene* means a place of beautiful oaks. I guess the trees looked a lot better when he built it. These days, most of them are dead or dying. But the county won't pay to have them taken down, since the land is worthless."

I thought about the amazing building above us. Despite being run down, it could be remodeled and turned into a massive bed and breakfast, maybe even a museum. "How can that be..." my voice trailed off as I heard footsteps. I glanced behind but saw no one.

Zef said, "Enough history for now. You were going to explain about the hidden trap."

Even though I'd agreed to tell him, I hesitated. "You'll think I'm nuts."

"No I won't."

I brushed what felt like a cobweb strand from my neck.

"You won't believe me."

He slowed a little and lifted his light, glancing back. "Yes I will. Nothing you say can surprise me."

"Yeah? Well, then let me start off by explaining I'm a logical girl. I like facts. Reality. Some kids hate algebra, but not me. Math has logic, and you know what to expect."

"But what you've seen and heard here doesn't make sense. It breaks all the rules of logic."

Chilled by the dank air, I rubbed my arms. "Yes."

"Go on."

"I fell asleep on the veranda and had a dream about the ballroom. It was like being there a long time ago. Old-fashioned music. Women in ball gowns, and everyone had masks. Someone told me to go upstairs and look for a secret trap."

"Someone?"

"A man. He wore a mask, too. See? Told you it was crazy."

He stopped and pointed his light at the ground ahead where broken stones lay in a heap. "Looks like part of the wall gave way here. We'll have to climb over."

He scrambled across and then looked up at the ceiling with a startled expression. I wanted to ask him what was wrong but the sound of heavy footsteps behind us distracted me. This time, they were accompanied with the sound of murmuring. I looked back down the tunnel, not sure if I saw movement in the shadows. The voice was indistinct, almost a growl, and I shivered a little. Whoever was back there, they were getting closer. What if Zef's brother, Riker, had come into the Chateau and found the service alcove open, the way we'd left it?

"What's wrong?" Zef asked.

"Footsteps," I whispered. "Someone's in the tunnel behind us."

Just saying it made the hair raise on the back of my arms. My heart raced like a chased rabbit, breath coming fast. Fingers encircled my wrist, making me jump. Zef had taken a hold of me, and he tugged.

"Come on, I'll help you climb over." His reassuring tone said he understood how unnerved I felt, which surprised me. I was torn between going with him and staying to face whoever was coming. That was until another sound reached my ears. A new chill ran through me at the scrabbling claws of rats.

"Nothing's really there," Zef said.

I tried to pull my hand away but he wouldn't let go, and I glared at him. "Are you saying you can't hear that?"

"No, I can't. Because whatever you hear or see, it's not real. You're hallucinating."

"What?"

"There's a combination of gases seeping from small fractures in the ground under the Chateau, and the lower we go, the more susceptible we are. This far down is probably the worst place to be. I should've grabbed some breathing masks but was too excited to explore after you managed to find that secret door."

The voice behind me was getting closer, talking over the growing noise of the rats, and I could hear his random words skewered with anger. For an insane couple of seconds I thought it sounded like my grandpa. The mental image of him squeezing his bowling ball stomach through the narrow passage, red-faced and panting, made me laugh. But when the sound bounced off the walls, I stopped.

"Gases? You're sure that's what it is?"

"Positive. The rats weren't real, remember?"

"Actually, the rats are back." I tried to say it calmly, but my throat was tight. My eyes scanned the darkness, waiting for them to appear.

"Whatever you think you're experiencing, it's just an illusion caused by the fumes."

"But it's not affecting you."

He looked grim. "Yes it is. I hear Riker upstairs. He's

screaming his head off and shooting out the windows. Is that what you hear?"

"No."

"Okay, then. Just climb over the rocks. We need to keep moving before both of us really lose it."

I scampered up the mound of debris, one foot sliding and my shin taking a painful hit. Zef steadied me until I made it over. Then he pushed me in front of him, holding the light high so I could see. My head buzzed at what he just told me, but I hardly had time to put it all together when we came to what looked like a door. It didn't have a knob or handle in the regular place. Instead, it was outfitted with rusted chains and a counterweight mechanism like the one on the back of the alcove door.

In spite of Zef's explanation, I still heard the squeal of rats and a hostile voice calling out. Both grew louder, my name repeated between swear words.

Zef grabbed one of the chains but it broke, the heavy counterweight dropping to the ground as rusted metal crumbled in his hand.

"Can't you open it?"

"I'm trying." His voice was as cold as mine was hot.

Manually moving the pulleys the latch finally unclicked and the door moved a bit.

"Kenley," a gruff, panting voice said from close behind. A shudder slid up my spine and tightened my scalp, but I refused to look back.

Zef shoved the door. It budged a few more inches. I joined him, throwing all my weight against it, tennis shoes scrabbling to get hold. With a loud screech, it finally slid open enough for us to squeeze through.

I stumbled into a shadowy room brought to life by Zef's light that began to wink like it might give out. Rows of dusty, slanted shelves and an arched entryway were familiar, but I could only focus on pushing the hidden door closed.

"That's not necessary," Zef said. "Nothing's back there, remember?"

Ignoring his advice, I leaned into it but didn't make much progress until he helped. The hinges again made that same screeching sound until the door clicked shut. The shelves fit so neatly into place that no one would ever believe it was an opening. Breathing fast, standing there and listening to *nothing* because no sounds—human or rat—now came from the other side, I finally looked around.

"Uh... this is the wine cellar."

"It is." Zef ran a hand across his forehead and let out a bitter laugh.

"What's wrong?"

It took him a while to answer. "Not what I was hoping for."

I could see he was upset but didn't care as my own frustration rose to the surface. "You could have told me, you know! About the gas and hallucinations."

A flush crept up my face, and I felt self-conscious because of the way my cheeks always got too pink. It wasn't enough to stop me, though. "When I woke up on the veranda that first evening and said how it all seemed so real, you said something like, 'It always does.' Because you knew! And then I was freaking out from the rats that disappeared, but you still didn't explain."

Zef shrugged. "I've learned the hard way not to waste my time explaining the Chateau to others. Trust me, I'm tired of being laughed at. Same as my grandpa."

"Why? What happened?"

He stared at nothing for a moment. "After having some creepy stuff happen here, he shared it with a couple of friends who weren't exactly loyal. They spread it all over town. Of course some of the old timers still hang on to the local legends about this place being haunted, but most said he was crazy. After that, my grandpa paid to have the Chateau examined and we finally learned about the gas."

He wiped his hands on his jeans. "And those kids who do believe it cause more trouble by sneaking out here to get high from the fumes. Others just want to goof around and frighten each other."

"Kids do that?" I remembered my mother's warning, which made more sense now.

"Sure. Riker and Dean were pros at it. They even started contests to see who could last the longest before getting spooked off."

I studied the dirty smudges on his face and the coating of dust in his hair. Did I look as disheveled? "I had a headache after I left here, and I'm guessing that's from the gas, too. You said I might feel sick."

"Yeah."

"So everything I saw, the ballroom and dancers, all of that..." *And the fascinating guy in the mask...* "It was just a delusion."

"Of course. How could it be anything else?"

"It couldn't." And yet this caused a wash of melancholy.

Zef shrugged like he understood. "That doesn't stop it from seeming real. Trust me, I've had enough experiences in this place to know how those vapors can mess with your head."

His brows drew in over dark, serious eyes as he continued to study me. "But that's not what's really important right now, is it? I'd say you're missing the key issue."

I lowered my chin and stared up at him. "What are you talking about?"

"You said the man in the mask told you about the secret trap. But how's that possible?"

He moved closer, bending his head a little to maintain eye contact. "He was just a hallucination."

For the first time in a long time, I didn't know what to say. I turned away and stepped through the archway into the larder. Just ahead were the stairs. "Bring that light, will you?"

I started going up, Zef following, until the creak of boards overhead made me stop. It sounded like someone was walking around upstairs, but then I reminded myself it must be another delusion.

I glanced back at him and kept my voice low. "You don't hear that, right?"

"Actually, I do."

He passed me on the stairs, though we both had to move carefully since there was no railing. At the top, he opened the door and looked around. We stepped into a large, empty room with morning light streaming in through wavy panes of glass. No one was in sight. We paused to listen, and I found myself almost holding my breath. I looked at Zef who shook his head. Neither of us heard any more footsteps. Instead, the house seemed too quiet.

10
Don't Drink the Water

The aged kitchen had been designed for utility with long, built-in tables, deep sinks, and cupboards from floor to ceiling. A huge antique stove of faded green dominated one wall, its silver embellishments tarnished to a dull gray. The last time I was in this room it had been dark. In daylight it was transformed into a vintage place where cooks and maids once worked.

Zef had asked me to wait while he checked out the rest of the ground level. Unfortunately, the headache from last week was making an impressive comeback, but at least now I knew why.

A moment later I caught a whiff of a dank smell. The kitchen was old and decaying, like everything else in the Chateau, but until now I had never noticed any odor except dust and years of unwashed grime. This was different, more like a muddy bog thick with rotting leaves, and as I stood there it grew more intense with each breath I took.

"One o'clock, two o'clock..." a childish voice said from behind me.

I whipped around, so certain that it came from nearby that I was more unnerved by seeing no one than if there had actually been a little kid standing there. I peered into the shadowy corners of the room and then studied the closed door on the far side of the kitchen, deciding that was where it might have come from. My mouth went a bit dry, but then I shook my head. This must be no different than what I'd experienced in the tunnel, just another manifestation of the gas fumes.

"Three o'clock. Four." Definitely a child voice, but something more to it, like toxic oil swirling on the surface

of water.

"No," I said with determination, more to myself than the hallucination as my hands hugged my elbows.

The doorknob jiggled and I sucked in a breath, frozen to that spot. It felt as if time slowed.

"One o'clock, two o'clock." The voice faded then swelled, as if carried on a breeze. *"Three o'clock. Four."*

It turned angry. Malicious, even. *"Whatever you do, don't open this door!"*

My eyes were riveted to the doorknob, waiting for it to turn. Or for the kid on the other side to say something else. Neither happened. Instead I stood there, seconds ticking by and sweat prickling my skin until the breath I'd been holding demanded release. I slowly exhaled, the headache tapping at my temples.

I repeatedly told myself this wasn't real, but that didn't stop a tremor from passing through me. "Prove it, then," I finally whispered to myself, forcing my feet to move.

I walked across the kitchen and reached for the doorknob. My fingers touched it but reflexively jerked back. For the briefest second I thought they'd been burned, until I realized the knob wasn't hot but icy cold. I heard giggling from the other side. Opening it fast, I shoved inward. Rusty hinges screeched, and I pushed the door all the way back so that no one could hide behind it.

The room was empty. No furniture, and definitely no little kid. Semi-circular, it had five walls inset with tall, narrow windows that let in dim light. Once, it had probably been a pleasant breakfast room, but now the glass panes were heavily streaked in layers of dried rainwater that looked like permanent tearstains. Another doorway stood across from me, and it was open. I walked there and looked out into a hallway. No movement, and no sound, either.

I headed back to the door leading into the kitchen, giving one last study of the room and my eyes focused on the dusty floor. I saw the prints left by my shoes, but there was something else. A few partial, child-sized prints seemed to be beneath them, though I couldn't be sure because of the scuff marks my own had made.

Finally, I went back into the kitchen. "Zef?"

I got no answer and wondered what time it was, remembering I'd agreed to babysit my younger cousins, Jill and Jaden, so Aunt Mae could get her hair cut. I glanced at the door leading into the overgrown herb garden and decided to give him only another minute before I took off.

Thirsty, I looked through my bag and saw an empty water bottle. I dreaded the long walk home in the summer heat with nothing to drink. The kitchen sinks, I noticed, didn't have regular faucets, instead outfitted with cast iron hand pumps. I stared at one of them, wondering if it worked. Grabbing the handle, I pumped up and down several times. It didn't take long before a gurgling sound preceded a gush of water. It was clear and cold, and I held my hands beneath the small stream. A residue of dust drained into the sink, showing just how dirty I'd gotten, and I started to rinse off my arms. Before I finished, the water narrowed to a trickle. I pumped again, which brought another stream, and cupped my hands beneath.

"No!" Zef shouted, running forward. He grabbed my waist and jerked me away from the sink, forceful enough to cost me my footing.

He steadied me, but I pulled away from him. "Hey!"

"Did you drink that?" He pointed to the water trickling from the pump.

I shook my head as he started throwing open cupboard doors. "What's wrong, Zef? It's just water!"

He grabbed a bottle from a shelf and hurried back to me, uncapping it. "No, it's not. It's loaded with toxic lead that killed Henry Broderick's wife and two of his kids. Hold out your arms."

He acted so alarmed that I did, standing there as he poured bottled water over my hands and arms, letting it splash on the floor.

"Henry, your ancestor who built this place?"

"Yes. And if it was strong enough to make them sick back then, who knows how bad it's gotten sitting in deteriorating lead pipes for more than a century. I warned you the Chateau is dangerous."

When he finished, he held out the bottle that had a little water still in it. "You're sure you didn't drink from the pump?"

I took it, pretending to be cool but worrying about what he was telling me. "No, just washed the dust off my hands."

I drained what was left in the bottle, shaken by how close I'd come to drinking the pump water but not wanting to tell him. He grasped the hem of his shirt and jerked it off over his head, then used it to wipe off my arms, though a dusty, sweaty shirt wasn't the best sort of towel. Zef, I noticed, had some impressive muscles, the kind that probably came from farm labor. Afraid my expression might betray my thoughts, I tried to cover it by saying, "Thanks. I didn't think the water could be harmful. It looked okay."

"Can't always trust stuff by the way it looks."

"Invisible gas. Poisoned water..."

He shook out his shirt and put it on again, heedless of the damp spots. "Come on. Let's get off the ground floor."

I followed him out of the kitchen, pausing to glance inside the breakfast room again. I thought about telling him about what I'd heard, but instead asked, "So why'd this guy Henry build a castle out here, in the middle of nowhere?"

Zef raised an eyebrow. "It's not *nowhere*."

"Okay... Rural Indiana then. It isn't exactly a place for castles."

He smiled a little. "True. And that's what his neighbors thought, too. Henry grew up not far from here on a small dirt farm. Left home at seventeen to find his fortune, which he did. Steel manufacturing and eventually railroads. He traveled to France where he met his wife, Estelle. They had three kids, and I'm descended through the oldest daughter."

"So he wanted to impress his childhood friends?"

"Or he just wanted to come home. I don't know."

We reached the foyer and Zef headed up the staircase. I followed, remembering what he'd said the last time we were here about upstairs being safer. "Oh, I get it. The second story isn't as dangerous because not as much of the gas reaches here."

"Right. The Chateau has what I call hot spots, places where the gas seepage seems to be worse. The larder and veranda are two of those. Plus anywhere there's a fireplace. Guess I can add the hidden passageway to the list."

I felt a little surprised Zef was now willing to answer my questions and wondered what had caused the change. I also decided to take advantage of it. "What kind of gas makes hallucinations?"

"It's not just one kind. About ten years ago my grandfather paid a geologist and a chemical surveyor to study the property. They found out that two minor faults intersect on this acreage, causing fractures in the ground, and that's where the natural gases leak from. The chemical tests showed it's a combination of alkaloids, decaying hydro-carbon deposits, and other stuff I don't remember. Let's go to the service area and check out the secret door again. I want you to tell me more about that trap."

I stayed on the top step. "I don't know anything else. Hallucination, remember?"

When he saw I wasn't coming he turned back. "I think you might know more than you realize. Your mom is an actress, right? Which is how you learned about stage stuff."

"So?"

"Remember when I said Henry's wife, Estelle, was from France? After they came back to America he told everyone she was a *comtesse* from French nobility. But our family's secret story is that she was really a *cancan* dancer working at a Paris theater when Henry first saw her. After they bought this land, they sent for Phillipe Moncharde, a famous French architect who was best known for the theaters he built across Europe."

"And Moncharde is the guy who made the Chateau?"

Zef slowly nodded, studying me with an expression that said his mind was taking two paths. "He designed it and started the construction, but local builders finished it. And he must've been the one who created the secret passage, though it's not on the blueprints."

"If it was on the blueprints, it wouldn't be secret."

"True. And now I'm thinking he used the same sort of tricks in the Chateau as from the theaters he built. If he did, then someone who knows about stages might be able to figure out more about this place."

"Are you asking for my help?" Definitely a turn-around. I tried not to laugh.

He didn't answer right away, his hand resting on the black iron railing. "Yeah, guess I am. I've been exploring the Chateau for months, and finding that hidden door today was the first real breakthrough."

"Breakthrough to what? Why have you been exploring, and what are you looking for?"

Zef rubbed the back of his neck, breaking eye contact and sliding back into that evasive mode of his.

I asked, "What time is it?"

He checked his phone. "Almost ten."

"I've gotta take off." I headed down the stairs.

"I really don't get you, Kenley," Zef called after me. "First, I ask you to leave and you don't. Now I ask you to stay and you won't."

The way that rhymed made me smile. "I'm babysitting my cousins, and it's the first paying job I've been offered since getting here. Need the cash, or I'd stay."

Once through the French doors, I inhaled the summer

air until remembering this was what he called one of the hot spots for gas seepage. After that I held my breath, hurrying around the side of the house and past the cracked fountain in front. By the time I exhaled, my head was pounding. The rest of the way, I covered my mouth and took shallow breaths.

I went through the gates, then passed under the giant, scraggly oaks. The morning sun angled through gnarled limbs, leaving wraith-like shadows on the ground. I turned back for one last glimpse of the Chateau. Despite knowing its ugly secrets, the beauty of the place still impressed me.

"This castle is all for you, Kenley."

The whispered words caught me off guard and I spun around, then turned in a full circle. I was alone. The trees stood far enough away that no soft voice could have reached me from someone hiding behind them, which meant it hadn't been real. Somehow, a shred of hallucination must have trailed me here—a warning of how far-reaching the effects of the Chateau's gases could be.

Looking back at it, I saw Zef head around the fountain and down the main drive. I stepped back into the shadow of a tree, watching. He passed through the gates and bent to pick up the chain. With his back to me, he wrapped it around the bars then took a padlock from his pocket and secured it in place.

I was ready to leave when a movement in one of the upper windows caught my attention: an indistinct blur of what looked like a person. I blinked and it was gone. Standing there, I wondered if it was another illusion or only the reflection of a passing cloud.

As Zef turned away from the gate, I slipped around the bend before he could see me and took off running.

11
Visitor

After helping my grandma with the dinner dishes, something that was becoming an unwelcome nightly ritual, I used the kitchen phone to call Dana, planning to tell her about the Chateau. Unfortunately, she was shopping with her dad and we had to keep it brief.

Next, I called Jules but it went to voice mail. I frowned. It had been a while since we'd last connected. Maybe, though, she was working. This new idea perked me up. Last time we talked, I found out she'd started applying for waitress jobs. Not what she wanted to do, though inwardly I felt relieved. It was a much more practical solution to our financial problems than her holding out for a part on stage. Once I joined her in New York, I could look for work too and together we'd get by.

In the sewing room, I went to the open window where the faded calico curtains stirred. Clouds gathered in gray clusters and released splatters of rain that cooled the air. On the large paved area in front of the storage building, my two little cousins rode their bikes. Jill was eight, Jaden six. My mother's older brother, Jed, married a lot later than she had. And her younger brother, Josh, and his wife Nora, were expecting their first baby. This meant that the age differences between me and my cousins was light years apart.

I hadn't minded babysitting Jill and Jaden, though the pay was a whole lot less than anticipated. Aunt Mae gave me seven dollars for being with the kids for two hours. Even though I didn't know the going rate for local child care, it seemed she'd given herself some sort of substantial family discount. Of course, since my grandma thought I should watch the kids for free, I was lucky to get any cash out of it.

The breeze made a sudden shift, blowing in from the dairy and bringing the heavy scent of cow cologne. I slammed the window shut and rubbed my temples. The headache stayed, though at least this time I knew its source: the gas fumes I'd inhaled.

I picked up my art journal and sat on the bed. It had been a while since I'd looked at my drawings of the Chateau, and I liked what I saw. The *History of Architecture* class I'd taken last fall had helped me develop my skills, and the added shading gave good dimension. Until now, though, I hadn't realized how well I'd managed to catch its forbidding aura. Yet everything Zef told me about the place brought a sense of disappointment. I may have been searching for answers, but the truth had sliced away the old mansion's mask of mystery. I penciled in the name *Chateau de Beauchene* beneath the picture.

The next drawing was the one of me in the ball gown, or rather the generic girl who looked somewhat like me. I studied the lace on the bodice and sleeves, the thick satin folds of the skirt. Closing my eyes, I remembered how silky it had felt beneath my touch. How real the masked dancers had looked, and the movement of the women waving their silver and gold fans in rhythm. Candlelight had reflected from hundreds of chandelier prisms as I'd stood before the mirror, my red-gold hair in cascading curls. And then there had been the shadowy man who seemed to know my inner thoughts. Yet none of it was real. I opened my eyes. Zef's explanations made sense, and I knew he was telling the truth, but I'd wanted a different answer—though I wasn't sure what.

I closed the sketch book and glanced around until my gaze rested on the box holding my father's stuff. I brought it over to the bed. It was a jumbled mess and I decided to organize it by putting the plays in one pile, research notebooks in another. Under those were random papers, an envelope with receipts, and a manila folder that had letters from his agent and publisher. One of the cardboard flaps on the bottom of the box was raised, and when I lifted it I found a small roll of unprocessed film. I picked it up, wondering how old it was. Probably twelve years at least, since that's when my father had died and this box was packed away.

I held it in a curved palm, like a fragile egg, wondering about the undeveloped pictures. My pulse beat a little faster as I imagined the possibilities, hoping most of all that they were of him. My dad, Keith Barrett, was eternally frozen in the photos stored in an album I'd often looked at. Getting new pictures of him would be a gift to both Jules and me, but where could I get it developed now that everything was digital?

A brief knock preceded G'ma opening the door. She wore a slight smile. "You have a visitor."

I stood and shoved the roll of film in the same pocket with the seven dollars. "Who is it?"

She'd already left and I stared at the open door, wondering who would bother to come see me and why Grandma seemed pleased. Then it hit me. *Jules!*

That's why I hadn't heard from my mother. She wanted to keep her arrival a surprise, and I found myself grinning as I hurried down the hall. A dozen ideas flooded me all at once, about how she must have gotten a job and found a place for us. Had she brought a trailer so we could pack up all our stuff from the shed? And would she spend the night or were we going to head out right away?

Halfway down the stairs I heard my grandpa say, "We've always had Holsteins, though I been considering adding in some Jersey stock."

"You've been saying that for years, Joe," my grandma commented.

My steps slowed.

A familiar guy's voice said, "Might actually be a smart investment, Mr. Strickland."

I caught sight of boots beneath clean but faded jeans, a hand holding a tan cowboy hat by his side, a plaid cotton shirt open at the collar. Two more steps and Zef's face came into view, his hair slightly damp and more neatly combed than I'd yet seen it. He looked up at me and smiled in a friendly way that struck me as *not-the-real-Zef*, though my grandparents didn't seem to notice.

"Hi Kenley. I was wondering if you'd like to go for some ice cream."

He said it with uncertainty, as if he didn't want to get rejected, and my grandma glanced at him with a touch of sympathy. Clearly she had no clue that his politeness was a cover-up. The Zef I knew had dragged me through a dark Chateau when we first met.

Everyone was looking at me as I shoved down my disappointment that my visitor wasn't Jules. "Ice cream?" I finally repeated in a non-brilliant way.

"If it's okay with Mr. and Mrs. Strickland." He turned to my grandpa. "I'd have her back by ten."

Have her back? What was I, a sack of potatoes he was hauling?

"Nine-thirty'd be best, Zefram."

"Yes sir."

Not waiting for me to make an excuse, Zef opened the front door as my grandma said, "Go on, Kenley. It'll be good for you to have fun with someone your own age."

Wondering what alien had taken control of her, I also struggled with the sting of knowing Jules hadn't come for me after all. I bit my lip, hoping it didn't show. How stupid to think my life could work out the way I wanted.

Next thing I knew, Zef and I were walking down the drive to where his white pickup was parked.

"Sooo," I said. "They just love you."

He raised a somewhat cynical eyebrow and opened the

truck door for me. I folded my arms and studied him. He'd even shaved, fitting the role of clean cut teen that my grandparents kept trying to force me into.

"What's going on, Zef?"

The shy, uncertain expression had long disappeared. "We need to talk."

I didn't move.

"How'd the babysitting go?" he finally asked in a slow drawl.

"Lots of Legos and Playdoh."

"How's the pay?"

"Not bad."

This lie must have been apparent because he smiled. "Not good, either, I'm guessing." He nodded at the pickup. "You have to be back by nine-thirty."

My fingers touched the film in my pocket. "I want to go to the drugstore."

He put on his cowboy hat and gave a single nod, all in one slick move. "Not a problem."

I climbed in.

12
History Lesson

Rain sprinkled the windshield of Zef's truck as we turned onto Center Street leading into town. For someone who said we needed to talk, he wasn't saying much. A square box sat between us on the seat. I glanced at it, then at Zef, and finally at the drops hitting the glass. "You got your windshield fixed."

He guided the pickup around a corner. "My dad helped. We also hammered out some of the dents on the hood, but most of them are there to stay."

I'd noticed that, too.

Zef glanced at me as if debating how much to say. "My dad went and had it out with Riker, telling him to back off or we'd press charges."

He pulled into a small city park and stopped next to an empty playground. The stormy breeze blew the swings as if invisible kids rode them. After turning off the engine, Zef removed the box's lid and took out a brown tinged family photograph that looked antique. He handed it to me.

"Henry and Estelle Broderick, my great-grandparents four times back. And those are their three kids. This was taken about eight years before he sold his steel mill and built the Chateau, so around 1882."

Not sure why he wanted me to see the photo, I still took it from him, interested. Henry was a large man with a moustache, bushy sideburns, and a round nose. Estelle was pretty, her hair pulled up and styled in tight rings around a bun. She wore a white blouse with full sleeves, a wide satin bow beneath her high collar.

"She looks a lot younger than him," I said.

"Ten or eleven years, I think."

He pointed to the children. "Arietta, their oldest. She's the ancestor my mother's line comes through. Next was Louisa, then Henry Jr. After their family had been living in the Chateau seven months, Louisa died from misdiagnosed lead poisoning, followed by little Henry and then the mother, Estelle."

Seeing the picture of this long-ago family made their unhappy deaths seem more real. "And the lead that killed them was in their water? How'd that happen?"

"A mistake during the building of the Chateau. The architect, Phillipe Moncharde, stayed for the first months of construction but went back to Europe before it was finished. A local contractor took over, and when the house was plumbed, he used lead pipes instead of copper. Indoor plumbing was still somewhat new, so either he was ignorant of the danger from lead, or he cut corners to pocket the difference."

"Horrible."

The young girls in the photograph had their hair pulled up in loops and tied with thick ribbons. They wore white dresses, full from the waist but short enough to show stockings and black high-button shoes. The little boy had on a sailor suit, his gaze penetrating as he looked out from the picture with a slight scowl. For some reason, my eyes kept going to him.

"They didn't know what was making them sick?"

Zef shook his head. "For some reason the mother, middle daughter, and little boy were affected the worst. Henry brought in physicians from as far away as New York, but their medicines didn't help. And that wasn't the only problem. The servants wouldn't stay, saying the Chateau was haunted."

I glanced up at the windshield. Heavier raindrops hit the glass, leaving circles the size of nickels. "Of course. Hallucinations from the gas."

"My grandpa once told me it probably wasn't as bad

back then as it is now, after so many years of the Chateau settling and the ground fractures spreading. But it still caused problems, especially for those working downstairs or stocking the larder and wine cellar. Henry kept hiring new help and upping the pay, but when his family started dying it scared most of them off.

"Why didn't he just take his family and get out?"

Zef pushed back his cowboy hat. "I've always wondered that, too. The only thing I can come up with is that after putting so much pride and money into building the Chateau, he wouldn't accept it had problems. Henry was a strong-willed man, logical and driven."

"Who scoffed at the idea of ghosts, I'm guessing."

"Yes. Though after Estelle died, he started getting paranoid. Maybe he wasn't willing to admit he was having hallucinations, but the gas had to be bothering him, too."

I pointed to the oldest girl, Arietta. "What happened to her?"

Zef took another old photo out of the box, this one of a couple in wedding clothes. "She married a local land owner, Mathias Fairchild, a widower with four children. Her father didn't want her to, but after her mother and siblings died, she left the house and refused to return. Henry was upset but in the end didn't stop her."

A third photo showed the couple maybe five years later. Arietta and Mathias sat together, a baby boy on her lap, while four older children stood around them.

"The little boy is Stephen," Zef said. "He was their only child together, as Arietta had lifelong health issues from the lead poisoning. She helped raise her stepchildren, and there are a lot of Fairchilds around here, including my distant cousin Dean."

"Riker's friend?"

He nodded and I remembered the night they chased us, shouting Zef's name and firing a gun. "They all that scary?"

He smiled but it held no humor. "Only some of them."

I picked up the family photograph of the Brodericks again, taken in happier times before moving to the Chateau. "After Arietta left, what happened to her father?"

"Henry shot himself."

Neither of us said anything for a few seconds, just listened to the rain hitting the truck. I stared at the play-ground swings that had stopped moving, now merely smudges of red and school bus yellow through the watery glass.

"It's so sad. The Chateau is beautiful. First time I saw that blue roof against the hills, it felt like magic."

My wistful tone showed too much, I realized, and I lowered my chin a little, expecting Zef to be sarcastic. He surprised me by saying, "It has that kind of look, doesn't it? Like you could step into another world."

The image of it came clearly to mind and I murmured to myself, "A deadly one, though. We never should have gone there."

I gave back the picture. "Now I get why you said the place is worthless."

He nodded. "Even if the lead pipes could be replaced, the gas seepage still makes it a hazard. No one can live there, and it can't be sold."

I looked across the park in the direction of the drug store, once again aware of the film in my pocket. After all this time, I hoped it could still be developed. "Thanks for telling me the Chateau's history."

"I have a reason. There's one more thing you should see."

Sorting through papers in the box, he pulled out a clear sheet protector with a letter inside. The paper looked very old, the spidery writing faded and nearly worn away in the crease lines where it had been folded.

Zef handed it to me. "This is part of a letter that Arietta wrote to her son, Stephen, not long before she died. The first part talks about his planned visit with his wife and kids, nothing important. But then on this second page, it gets interesting."

I tilted it to catch the gray light coming in through the side window and started reading the delicate writing.

Often, these last two weeks, I have thought about our conversation when you asked to know more about the Chateau. For a long time you have been curious, despite my warnings, and I have been reluctant to discuss it. Even after all these years, it is a painful subject. But as you are to inherit the building and property, there is something I have decided to tell you. There is a place within the Chateau I call the Hidden Room.

I saw it only once, not long after my family moved in. I don't think we had lived there even a week when I came down with a fever. The sickness didn't last long, but combined with the excitement of moving into our beautiful French castle, it must have caused me to sleepwalk—a tendency I often dealt with during my younger years.

It was late into the night when I awoke to find myself in a hallway. The Chateau was so huge, and my mind still unclear from the fever and a sleep draught my dear *maman* had given me, that I was quite bewildered. Trying to orient myself, I turned and saw a glimmer of light far down the hallway and hurried after it. I chased it around corners, never calling out, for I experienced a sense of anxiety until finally discerning it was my father carrying a lantern. He entered through a doorway to a room and after a little hesitation I went in after him. Papa, I saw, stood in front of a peculiar opening in the wall.

"Arietta?" he said, looking startled that I had found him.

I thought he would be strict until hearing, "Goodness, where are your slippers?"

He smiled as if he had a secret to share and told me to come with him. We went through the opening in the wall and into a narrow walkway. Steps led down to a windowless room. A tall safe sat in the corner, and shelves held perhaps two dozen other valuable items. Papa set down the case containing his prized pair of flintlock pistols and winked at me. "Just leaving them here for safekeeping. Remember, Ari, never put your fate in the hands of others, and that includes banks."

Before I could hardly look around, he ushered me out and told me to face the other way. I heard a sliding noise but didn't look back, and then he took me on a wandering course through the Chateau. By the time he deposited me at my bedroom, I felt even more confused. And in the morning, after my fever broke, I almost wondered if it was a dream.

I did not think about the room again until after the tragic death of my dear sister, Louisa. She and I were the closest of friends, and seeing her wither away in the grasping hand of death still haunts me despite the many years that have passed.

The day after her funeral I went into her room, just to straighten the coverlet on her bed and see to the caged budgies she adored. That's when I noticed the lovely little Degas oil painting, *Ballerina with a Purple Sash*, was no longer hanging on the wall beside her dressing table. *Maman* had bought it for Louisa's tenth birthday, and it was my sister's favorite.

I flipped the page protector over to the back of the letter. "They actually owned a Degas?"

An inexpensive poster of the artist's work called *Dancers at the Barre* had hung on my wall as a little girl and was still somewhere in the storage shed. I went back to reading Arietta's letter.

I did not tell my mother it had gone missing, as her own malady seemed to worsen with the loss of Louisa, and I could not bear to do anything but try and ease her suffering. Our housekeeper had no idea what had happened to the painting either, but when she brought it up to Papa, he seemed unconcerned. I wondered, then, if he had taken it to the Hidden Room, though I could not think why and dared not bring it up considering his distraught state.

As you well know, the mourning wreath did not leave our door. We lost my little brother next and then dear *Maman*. Two evenings after her funeral, the cherished Mary Cassatt painting of a mother and infant went missing from her private salon. This I did tell to Papa, but he only poured more brandy and said nothing. Perhaps he was still angry at me for wanting to wed your father, but Mathias offered refuge and kindness, and I could no longer bear life at the Chateau. I believe you know the rest of what happened.

"Poor Arietta. This is so sad."

"Keep reading," was all Zef said, and I blinked, finding my place again.

Three months after Papa's death, our estate manager, Edwin Plover, returned to the Chateau to catalogue my family's possessions for sale. I had him bring a number of items to my new home, but the majority of the furnishings, paintings, and other valuables were sent by a convoy of wagons to Chicago's largest auction house. It is from those proceeds that you will receive the bulk of your inheritance. As with your older half-siblings, you will also be given a portion of the Fairchild land from your father, but aside from some jewelry and other small items I am giving your sisters, the Chateau earnings are yours alone.

This is the reason I have chosen to tell you about the Hidden Room. I think that in the depths of grief my father concealed certain items of personal significance. According to the estate manager, two paintings were missing from the main galleria, including the beautiful garden landscape by Monet which my parents purchased for their anniversary. Mr. Plover felt concerned that thieves might have taken them. However, if this were true, why did they leave more valuable pieces untouched? And why, when Mr. Plover brought me *Maman*'s jewelry, were her favored cameo brooches and pearl necklace missing? They had less monetary value than the yellow diamonds and other jewelry pieces he returned to me. Considering my father's distraught state of mind

The writing must have continued on another page, which wasn't attached, but I'd read enough. I looked up at Zef with disbelief. "Those paintings... Degas and Monet!"

"You know them?"

"Impressionists. My mom gave me an art history book for my last birthday." My voice had turned a little breathy.

"I love art," I added, as if I had to explain this because maybe a guy in boots who owned a pickup wouldn't think it was cool.

Zef reached out, carefully taking the letter from me, and I realized my fingers had been squeezing it. He surprised me by saying, "Don't forget the Mary Cassatt painting. Probably not as valuable as a Monet, but still worth a lot."

"How much?"

He set the letter in the box and closed the lid. "Depends on size and condition. At auction, her best have sold in the twenty million range. One Degas oil painting went for a little under thirty, Monet's best work hit above forty."

"Million." I needed him to confirm this.

"Yes."

I blew out a long breath. "That is a lot of money."

He bit back a smile like I'd said something funny. I didn't care, my mind too busy jumping from thought to thought.

"So if those lost paintings and other valuable stuff are still in the Chateau... That's why you keep going there, and why you were tapping on the wall in the library like you were looking for something. It's also the reason you weren't happy when the secret hallway we found ended in the wine cellar. You thought it led to the Hidden Room."

It felt stuffy and I rolled down the window a few inches, welcoming the scent of rainy air.

"Yeah," Zef said at last, his fingers resting on the lid of the box. "And I don't have much time left to find it." His eyes met mine. "Will you help?"

13
Time Limit

We left the truck, heading along a wet sidewalk that cut through the park. The rain had moved on, leaving beads of water on benches and blades of grass.

Words from Arietta's letter kept circling through my head until her story began to seem unreal. I wondered if it was some sort of hoax. "What if it's not real?"

"Meaning…?"

"The Hidden Room." The convincing dreams of the ballroom came to mind and my steps slowed. "Arietta might have been hallucinating. My own fantasy experiences in the Chateau seemed pretty believable."

"I've thought of that, too. But there's a ledger from the estate manager detailing the missing items, including the paintings. If they were stolen and later resold, there's no public record anywhere of *Dancer with a Purple Sash* by Degas. Or Monet's *Garden at Eventide*. I've spent a lot of time searching the Internet, and none of that art has surfaced."

"They could just be in private collections."

He hunched his shoulders a bit. "All of them?"

"Hmm… Unlikely."

Without hardly realizing it, we'd both stopped walking, and I studied him. "I can't remember the name of Arietta's son, but didn't he search for the Hidden Room?"

Zef shifted his weight, thumbs hooked in the pockets of his jeans. "Stephen, you mean. I'm not sure, but I don't think so. All I know is he was a soldier in World War I and lost a leg. Besides, he probably didn't care much about finding the room since he'd inherited a ton of money. And back then, the paintings were worth only a tiny fraction of what they are now. When Henry and Estelle Broderick bought them in France, the Impressionist movement was new. A lot of critics slammed it, and at first those artists were lucky to make any sales."

"I read about that."

A drop of water from an overhead branch landed on the back of my neck and slid inside my shirt. I shivered and stepped away. "But according to Arietta, the other things in the Hidden Room were valuable too. What about Stephen's kids? He must've told them about the room."

Zef shrugged. "If he did, nobody passed it on through the family. Stephen had a son, George, and then three daughters. They all burned their way through the Broderick inheritance until the Great Depression hit. After that, the girls married and moved away. George stayed in the Fairchild house and tried to sell the Chateau, but no one made a serious offer. After that, he let the property taxes lapse and also sold off a bunch of land. His son was my grandpa, Franklin Fairchild."

"Your whole family tree thing is getting confusing."

"Then maybe all you need to know is that my grandpa was the one who found Arietta's letter in a bunch of papers. He paid for the geologist and chemical surveyor to determine what was going on with the Chateau. He also gathered research, including testing the tap water to learn that lead poisoning was what killed the Brodericks."

I turned this over in my mind, trying to ignore the lingering hum of excitement at the thought of finding the missing paintings. "He must've searched the Chateau."

"A lot, actually."

"Then if he couldn't discover the Hidden Room, it's probably hopeless."

Despite the storm having rolled away, the sound of distant thunder reached us. Zef glanced back at the clouds glowering on the horizon, a bit of blue peeking through. "I thought so too and was nearly ready to give it up, but then you found the secret tunnel. Which proved that Phillipe Moncharde, the architect, built hidden passages not marked on the original blueprints. And if he did, it also makes sense that Henry had him design a safe room for valuables."

"Do you have the blueprints?"

He nodded. "Last year, after my grandpa passed away, we were cleaning out his place. I found them, along with that box of stuff in the truck. That's when I decided, why not try?"

We started walking again and I asked, "Are your parents helping you?"

The slight frown that touched his features made me answer for him. "Oh... They don't know."

"Nope. And for now, I want to keep it that way. My mom hates the Chateau. Mainly because of how much effort and money my grandpa put into it, which only increased after my grandma died."

The path ended at the edge of the park and we headed across the street and entered the drug store. As we approached the photo counter, Zef slowed. A cute blond girl sorted through orders. Her fitted shirt showed the white silhouette of a longhorn's head topped with a pink crown.

Zef was just turning away like he was going to leave when she glanced up and he froze. They made eye contact, the kind that was awkward enough for even an outsider like me to pick up.

"Hey, Zef," she said in a low voice, ignoring me. She had huge blue eyes surrounded by lashes double-coated with mascara.

"Sierra." That single nod he tended to give. "How long you been working here?"

She smiled, a bit too forced, but showing dimples. "Since last month."

Long pause before he said, "Still practicing barrel racing?"

"Every day."

A couple of times her eyes flicked to me with silent dislike—for no reason at all that I could tell—and I experienced a renewed surge of wanting to leave for New York. This whole odd-girl-out only proved how much I would never fit in at the local high school.

"Sierra, this is Kenley," Zef finally said.

I took the roll of film from my pocket. "Can you process this?"

Her eyes pierced me from beneath those overdone lashes. "We don't develop film here anymore. Everything's digital."

Like I didn't know that.

Zef said, "Who can, then?"

Her gaze went back to his as if drawn by a magnet. "There's a photo lab in Fort Wayne we can send it to. Takes a week, maybe longer."

I filled out an order form while she and Zef talked in stiff tones about the upcoming rodeo. I slid the film inside the envelope and handed it to Sierra who seemed reluctant to take it. She went to the register and rang up $15.56. "You have to pay in advance."

I pulled the babysitting money from my pocket, hoping the seven dollars had somehow miraculously reproduced. Zef, reading my expression, took out his wallet and paid the difference.

"Thanks," I managed as we walked away. I glanced back at the camera counter where Sierra, who had been staring at us, turned her focus on a clipboard. "What's her problem?"

He opened the door for me and I added, "I'll pay you back as soon as I babysit again."

"Don't worry about it. You still using an old film camera?"

"No, I found that in a box of my dad's stuff. It must've been in there at least a dozen years, and I'm not even sure it's still good, but crossing fingers to get back some pictures of him."

"How old were you when he passed away?"

My surprise at his knowing my dad had died was quickly replaced by understanding. Being my grandparents' neighbor, Zef probably knew a lot about our family.

"I was four going on five. We lost him in October, my birthday is in December."

We walked past several small shops getting ready to close and he said, "Will you tell me what happened?"

Most times when other kids pried, resentment tightened inside me. But Zef had asked in a gentle way, the softness of his voice unexpected.

"A car accident. I don't really know the details."

His eyebrows raised a bit so I explained, "Jules doesn't want us to dwell on losing him, only on remembering his life with us."

Rays of the setting sun lit the underside of distant rainclouds. I studied the sky, squinting a little. "Were you serious about my helping you search for the Hidden Room?"

He didn't answer until I turned back. "Yes Kenley."

I folded my arms. "If we find it, I want a share."

"How much?"

"Twenty-five percent."

"Okay."

"Just like that?" He'd taken longer to respond to almost everything else I'd said, even the unimportant stuff.

Zef smiled in that subdued way of his, as if he held on to a secret joke. "Say we find a painting that sells for ten million dollars. How much do you get?"

"Two and a half." My pulse beat a little faster at the mere thought of so much money.

He leaned slightly toward me, his features lit with wry humor. "Right now you're thinking of a hundred ways to spend it, aren't you? A big house, cool car, lots of shopping. Maybe travel."

"Sure," I answered. Mostly, though, it would mean a complete change in the scrimping way Jules and I had always lived.

He added, "Even after buying all that stuff, you'd still have lots of cash left over. I can't imagine spending millions, so no need to be greedy about hanging onto what I don't even have yet. Besides, my problem isn't splitting the money. It's the fact that finding Henry Broderick's hidden fortune has a time limit."

"What do you mean?"

His humor disappeared and he looked more serious than ever. "We're coming up on the start of July, which gives us barely one month. Because August first, the Chateau is scheduled to end up as a pile of rubble."

14
Introductions

Zef and I sat across from each other in a booth at a burger place called Della Ray's, banana splits in front of us. I didn't even want one, but all he'd said was, "I told your grandparents I was taking you for ice cream."

I studied the melting pool of chocolatey mess in my bowl. "Okay, now will you tell me what's going on? Were you serious about the Chateau getting destroyed?"

He lowered his spoon and began to explain about a law suit against the county after a girl named Mandie Parkston died at the Chateau. "She wasn't from around here, just visiting cousins in the area. They took her to a party with some friends who crashed the gate."

"What happened to her?"

"Between the alcohol, and unknowingly inhaling the gas seeping from under the veranda, she was really out of it. She ended up on the roof and then fell."

A slight shiver ran up my neck, even though I'd never known the girl.

Zef ate another bite of ice cream. "The legal stuff went on for a couple of years, until six months ago when both parties reached a settlement. Her parents accepted an undisclosed sum of cash if the county also agreed to destroy the Chateau." He used air quotes to add, "So this can't happen to anyone else."

"And August first they're going to tear it down."

"Implode it, actually. Ever seen one of those videos on how big buildings are brought down from the inside by controlled explosives? A demolition team out of Chicago has been hired to do it."

I slid my bowl away. "Which means if the Hidden

Room exists, everything in it will be destroyed."

"Exactly."

Zef started to say more but stopped when a guy and girl showed up at our table. They looked a little older than us and also seemed an odd match. The boy's narrow face was framed with longish hair, brown beneath bleached streaks meant to be stylish. A thin mistake of a moustache rested atop a slight smirk, his eyes a pale blue. Not a bad looking guy, but not really attractive, either. The girl, though, was striking.

Her perfect skin had a creamy hue, and black hair fell in loose waves down to her waist. She wore bright red lipstick that actually worked on her, instead of failing the way it did for so many others. Her exotic eyes said she had a right to wear that color.

"Hey bro," the guy said, sitting down beside Zef and making him scoot over.

"Riker," Zef replied.

For a couple of seconds I just stared, trying to match him with the mental image I'd formed of the scary guy chasing us with a gun. For one thing, he didn't look much like his brother, and I'd imagined him bigger. Instead, he had a wiry frame and was shorter than Zef. No doubt he resented that, since he was the oldest.

Riker threw an arm around Zef's shoulders. "Saw you got your windshield fixed."

I watched Zef for some sign of anger, but he kept his face on an autopilot version of talking-about-the-weather. "Yep."

"Sorry, about that, you know. Though you've got no one to blame but yourself."

Was he kidding? Zef took his usual route of not answering, which made me wonder if growing up with a lunatic older brother had taught him to opt for silence.

Riker withdrew his arm from Zef's shoulder. "You know you're not supposed to be out at the Chateau."

As if bored with the topic, Riker focused his attention on me but spoke to his brother. "Who's this?"

Zef said, "Kenley, meet Riker, my brother."

"Heard you and Sierra broke up. See you're into redheads now."

I blinked, glancing at Zef's stoic posture. Suddenly the whole uncomfortable scene at the photo counter made sense.

Riker motioned to the beautiful girl who'd been left standing beside the table, her expression curious but not impatient. "This is Meena. Kenley, want to make room?"

I started to move over but she said, "Why don't I order something first?"

She headed to the counter and Riker leaned back, watching her. "We're together."

Zef nodded. "I heard. How'd you meet?"

"In the park. She was jogging and stopped near my bench to catch her breath."

"Where's she from? Not around here."

"Grew up in Akron. Went to college for a year, then a month ago got a job at Farley's Insurance."

Zef checked the time on his phone and looked at me. "I better get you home."

Riker raised his eyebrows. "She got an early curfew?"

I slid out of the booth as Zef said, "Yeah, she does."

I'd barely taken a step when Riker grabbed my wrist, pulling me back. "Good to meet you, Kenley."

"Let go," Zef said, suddenly looming over his brother. The neutral mask he'd worn during their entire encounter had disappeared.

Riker smiled, his fingers tightened on my wrist. "Or what, little bro?"

Zef leaned in. "Or I break your arm. Again."

I blinked, taken aback. As for Riker, his smile vanished. Before he could retort, I jerked free and headed down the aisle of Della Ray's, then through the door. Zef caught up with me and we climbed in his pickup. Darkness had settled across the valley as we took the road leading away from town.

"I'm sorry about Riker," Zef said, sounding unhappy. "He's got no understanding of personal space."

The truck's headlights glinted off fences and trees, and I wondered if it was easier for him to talk more openly in the dark. "You broke Riker's arm?"

He flexed his fingers on the steering wheel, as if they'd been gripping it too tightly. "Because he hurt Kes."

"Your little sister?"

Zef nodded. "There's a trampoline in our back yard. We've had it ever since I can remember. One day, Kes was jumping on it. I think back then she was in kindergarten, maybe first grade. I remember her wearing a yellow top and one of those fluffy pink dance skirts."

"A tutu."

"Yeah, a tutu." He smiled a little. "For some reason, she loved that thing and wore it until it became a rag and my mom threw it away. Anyway, that day she was on the trampoline with her stuffed animals. Riker jumped on and bounced her too high. She got scared and started screaming, but he wouldn't stop. Long story short, I shoved him off and it broke his arm. Just another thing he's never forgiven me for."

I blinked a couple of times, surprised by the visual picture he'd painted. "How old were you?"

"Ten. Riker was twelve. The thing is, when I have to deal with my brother, I usually keep it low-key. Trying to reason with him is a waste of breath. My parents have spent their lives talking to him, and all he's ever done is tune them out."

"That explains why you ignored what he said about your truck."

He let out a hopeless laugh. "Ignoring him has been a way of life for me. But sometimes…" his voice trailed off.

"I didn't like him grabbing you that way."

His fingers squeezed the steering wheel again, both of us quiet until I remembered what else I'd learned.

"Sierra was your girlfriend?"

He nodded.

"Guess that's why the whole scene at the photo counter was so awkward." I said it like a joke but he didn't smile.

"Yeah." That single word came out a low exhale.

"Mind if I ask why you broke up?"

He glanced over at me with those dark eyes, a disparaging tug at the corner of his mouth. "Let's just say she wasn't as interested in the Chateau as you and I are."

I gave him a blank look and he added, "Sierra is like a lot of kids who grew up around here, knowing about the Chateau their whole lives and thinking it's a worthless pile of stone. She resented my wasting time there."

"That's a lousy reason to break up with you."

Zef shrugged, like it didn't matter, but I could see a trace of unhappiness in his eyes. "Besides, I might've stood her up a couple of times because I was too busy searching."

"Oh."

We drove the rest of the way in silence until passing under the arch leading to the ranch. Zef braked and turned to me. The floodlight from the high pole edged the planes of his face. "I've got work and other stuff going on for the next few days, so I can't get back to the Chateau until next week."

He climbed out and came around the truck, opening my door. We headed to the porch and he added, "But I'll be there Tuesday morning. If you decide you want to help, meet me there. If you don't show, I'll understand."

With that, he walked back to his pickup.

15
Phantom

That night, I had trouble sleeping. It seemed as if the mystery of the Chateau was split into two parts: the dangerous surroundings where even a sip of water could hurt you, and a secret room filled with a lost family fortune. I thought of Arietta's letter and wondered what else was in Zef's box.

Sometime around one o'clock I gave up trying to sleep. Putting on my flip-flops, I went to the storage shed and made my way to our stack of stuff in the corner. I looked through boxes for my art history book but couldn't find it. After twenty minutes I admitted that Jules and I could learn from my grandma's organizational skills. Next time we packed, I'd do a better job labeling.

Nearly ready to give up, I reopened a box that held sweaters and dug down to the bottom. "There you are!"

The large book pulled free and I set it on the arm of our couch, then put everything away. Back inside the house, I climbed on the bed with pillows behind my back and the oversized book propped on my lap. It was at least twenty years old but full of glossy pictures. Jules had found it at a used book store and been super excited to give it to me for my birthday.

In the section under *Impressionists* I studied examples of Monet, Degas, and Cassatt, plus other artists. My fingers slid across a sleek reprint of the Degas oil painting, *Dancers at the Barre*, in a museum called The Phillips Collection. This was the one I had a poster version of, two vague ballerinas in filmy aqua skirts against a blotchy orange wall. Studying its details, and turning pages to see other Degas examples, I tried to imagine what *Ballerina with a Purple Sash* might look like. And how would the art world react to its recovery, along with the other lost masterpieces? It might not have the same impact as discovering a comet or a major medical cure, but it'd be close. I couldn't bear the thought of the Chateau being brought down on top of those treasured works.

The pictures began to look bleary, the book heavy on my lap. I finally set it aside and clicked off the light, scooting beneath the covers. My thoughts went to a drifting place just outside of dreaming where Zef's voice seemed to echo back to me. *If everything you saw was a hallucination, how'd you know about the secret door?"*

The end of June brought scorching heat, so I went on fewer walks. Instead, I helped my grandma organize her pale blue and yellow fabrics, which at least held my interest. She was full of excited plans to make baby quilts, since my uncle Josh and his wife, Nora, had just found out they were having a boy. This was their first, and G'ma was on a mission to make sure the new grandbaby had everything it needed.

I spent my free time drawing images from my hallucination of the ballroom, sketching the forms of ladies with fans and the men who courted them. I also read, listened to music on my phone, and used the house landline to call Dana. Most of our conversations weren't long since she'd not only gotten the job at the pizza place but was taking Driver's Ed. As for Kiefer, he and his family were vacationing in Orlando.

Despite the vow I'd made to stay close, I felt my Branson friendships slipping away, just the same as it always happened when I was forced to move. This time, though, the isolation seemed lonelier than ever.

Maybe that's why I couldn't stop thinking about the Chateau and Zef's offer to pay a twenty-five percent finder's fee for those paintings worth millions. What would it be like to have that much money? To not always shop at thrift stores, forced to redesign someone else's clothes to fit? I'd gotten my license at fifteen but didn't have a car, though Jules was always willing to let me drive our ancient Saab. For several minutes I mentally sorted through every make and color I could come up with before deciding on a Porsche Boxster. Convertible. Metallic blue.

More importantly, a big chunk of cash like that could pay for a New York apartment. And I'd be able to attend a great private school, eventually applying to the best art colleges in the country. Or Europe. As for Jules, she could audition until her heart was happy, no pressure to earn money.

Finally a guy from the photo counter called the house to say my pictures had come in. Grandma was too busy to drive me, but she arranged for Josh's wife, Nora, to pick them up.

Nora worked downtown as an office manager for a seed company, and I usually only saw her at Sunday dinners. I could hardly wait, wondering again if there would be pictures of my dad. Or equally good, shots of all three of us together.

Grandma came in from the garden and sent me to get the mail. I walked the long drive to the main road, and in the mailbox were two items, a grocery advertisement and an envelope addressed to me in my mother's flowery handwriting. I tore it open. Inside was a letter and a couple of twenty dollar bills.

It was hard not to smile and feel emotional at the same time as I slid the cash into my pocket. This was a sacrifice for Jules, and I knew it. Forty dollars meant two bags of groceries or enough gas in the old brown Saab to keep it going another ten days.

I sat down on the porch and read about how she and Anthony were dating again. He'd just gotten hired to work with a Shakespearian troupe performing *Much Ado About*

Nothing with the scenes set in the 70s. Best of all, it looked like she might be offered the part of Beatrice.

I entered the house, wanting to call Jules but deciding I'd wait until Nora brought the photos. They didn't come until after dinner, and when she finally handed them over I hurried upstairs. Shutting the door and sitting on the bed, my heart beat faster. I opened the photo envelope and slid out a glossy stack, sucking in a stunned breath. The picture on top showed four women in elegant ball gowns holding silver and gold fans. Their eyes stared out from behind masks, as did the men dressed in dark, old-fashioned suits.

I moved to the next picture. That same breath now stuck in my throat, my head suddenly woozy until I finally exhaled. This one was taken from further away, catching the struck poses of dancers in shadow with a brilliant chandelier over their heads.

The third picture shocked me the most. It was exactly like the one I'd drawn of the ivory satin dress with a massive skirt, square neckline, and lace flaring from the sleeves just below the elbow. A velvet ribbon was tied at the throat of a masked young woman who resembled me, her hair pulled up with curls cascading down in back. Behind her, all was dark.

Fingers trembling, I flipped to the next photo. It was nearly the same, except this one showed a little girl standing beside the now unmasked woman. A four-year-old version of me in jeans and a Tinkerbell sweatshirt gazed up with a shy, happy look as my hand touched her satin skirt.

The young woman in the dress was my mother, posing on stage with me standing beside her.

I tossed the photos on the bed and frantically fanned them out, glimpsing costumed actors, props, stage lights, and impressive sets. Many more were of my mother in different poses beside a tall man dressed in black.

Two thoughts struck me. The dancers from my ballroom hallucination were merely a recreation of costumed actors from the set of *Phantom of the Opera*, which I must have visited as a child.

Worst of all, not one single picture of my dad.

16
Broken Promises

I was dying to talk to Jules. I wanted to tell her about the pictures and also ask why she'd never told me she had a lead part in a stage production of *Phantom of the Opera*, but my grandma wouldn't get off the phone. For some reason she kept on talking in low, intense tones. Probably to her sister who lived in Cincinnati and had a grandkid in rehab. I wondered if G'ma was sharing her own plight of having Jules dump me here.

Back in the sewing room, I sat on the bed and glared at the stack of photos now resting atop my art history book. I couldn't get over the disappointment of no pictures of my dad.

My cell phone rang. I jumped and turned to stare at it. I'd kept it charged so I could listen to music, but since getting cut off, it hadn't made a peep on its own. Recognizing the ringtone assigned to Jules, I grabbed it.

"Mom?"

"Hey!"

"My phone is working," I said like a genius.

She laughed. "Yes, and we're on a new plan together."

"That's great." And though it was, I still felt too upset about the pictures to be excited.

"What's wrong?"

"That roll of film I found, the one I told you about last time we talked? I just got it back, and there isn't even one picture of dad."

"Oh."

I could hear her disappointment and felt mad at myself for ruining her surprise of turning my cell phone back on. Why was I messing up everything right now?

I sniffed and said, "It seemed so great that we might get a few shots of him."

"It's all right, Kenley."

"I hardly remember him." This came out quiet, like I was a little kid.

"You were really small when we lost him. And it makes sense you were hoping for more pictures, since you don't have a lot of memories with your dad."

I crossed the room to grab a tissue for my nose, annoyed it was running when I hadn't actually been crying. "The photos are of you and a bunch of other actors in *Phantom of the Opera*."

She didn't say anything and I wished I could see her face. "Jules, you never told me you were in that play, and I know every part you've ever had. Especially the leads. From the pictures, it looks like you're wearing the Christine dress."

I'd only seen the movie, since *Phantom* was one play we'd never gone to. During my whole life growing up, I'd been to all my mother's practices or dress rehearsals, watching from favorite sweet spots in the balcony. But I felt sure I hadn't seen her in this play, and as I thumbed through the pictures again, something else made sense.

"I don't think Dad took these of the dress rehearsal, because no one's singing. It looks like they're just standing around. And there's even a picture of me next to you on the stage. I must've been four, because I'm wearing the same Tinkerbell sweatshirt from our trip to Niagara Falls."

"Yes, I remember now." Her voice turned a little hushed. "It was a final costume check before the dress rehearsal. Sort of a blocking session showing me where I needed to enter, exit, and stand. Your dad brought you to see me in costume and he had his camera. The assistant director was the nicest lady. She took you right up on stage so he could get a picture of us together."

"And you played Christine?" I still couldn't get over

the surprise of never knowing this.

"Originally I was just in the chorus but also the understudy. The lead actress was the director's girlfriend, and after a huge fight he fired her. That was just a couple of days before we opened. Suddenly, the part was mine. I could hardly believe it. Even though it was way off Broadway, in Indianapolis, it was at a very respectable theater. I was thrilled."

"Why didn't you ever tell me?"

She let out a slow exhale. "It didn't last. I only performed the part of Christine for three evenings."

"What happened?"

"Your father died."

I put the pictures down. "Oh."

"I left the theater in Indianapolis, and after the funeral took you back to our apartment in New York. We stayed together and I didn't work for months, getting us by with the insurance money. That was the hardest time. Just you and me, dealing with our grief."

Both of us were quiet. I didn't know what to say and sensed Jules was struggling, too. She finally said, "I don't want to see those pictures. You can toss them or just stick them somewhere, it doesn't matter."

I hadn't meant to make her sad, especially when everything must be looking up for the first time in months, so I repeated back what she sometimes said. "Change of topic, okay?"

"Definitely."

"It's great to have my phone working again. I could hardly believe it when it started ringing!"

"I couldn't wait to surprise you."

"Well, it worked. I about jumped off the bed."

"I knew you'd be happy." The smile had returned to her voice.

"And thanks for the twenties. Sure you can spare that much?"

"Yep. Got an advance from Anthony, which is how I paid for our new phone plan."

"Oh! He offered you the job with his Shakespeare group?"

"Yes."

I sagged against the headboard, smiling for the first time since getting the pictures. "Awesome! How soon do I get to come to New York?"

"About that..." Several seconds ticked by. "There's something I have to explain. Anthony earned a grant from a foundation that supports arts in education. This means they pay for a small cast to tour rural areas and perform in assemblies at high schools and middle schools. We'll be doing a very pared down version of the play, forty-five minutes instead of two hours, and our first practice starts next week. This program offers a great chance for kids to get exposure to Shakespeare."

I was all for that, so long as I got to be one of those kids. "You'll let me come with you, right?"

She didn't answer and I hurried to fill the silence. "I can help with costumes and props, like I did with that indie production of *Into the Woods* when we were in California."

"I can't let you miss school."

I let out a skeptical huff. "We can home school. You know I'm good at studying on my own. Besides, when have you ever cared about grades? You always sign my report cards without even looking at them."

"I'm sorry, Kenley. Really sorry. I've talked it over with Anthony and we've looked at this every way we could. There are only two vehicles, the truck that hauls sets and costumes, and a van for the actors. Every seat is taken. Anthony is even doubling as an actor, playing the part of Don Pedro, plus driving the truck. If there was any way we could swing it, he'd be willing. There just isn't."

I swallowed, pushing down the ache that threatened to overwhelm me. "You promised I wouldn't have to stay here. Only for the summer, you said, until you found work."

"I know, it's just that I didn't realize how much harder it was going to be. Even the waitress jobs have dozens of people scrambling for them, and they don't pay enough for us to rent a closet. This is the only way we can make it right now."

I pushed off the bed, aware of heat flooding my face and no doubt turning it the color of a radish. "But we aren't making it, are we? You're leaving me here and going off with Anthony."

She stayed quiet and I scrambled for something else to change her mind. "Grandma and Grandpa are not going to want me staying that long. They didn't even want me to come for the summer."

"I just got off the phone with your grandma before calling you. She understands."

All the words went out of me. If I said anything else, I'd start to cry.

Both of us sat there—her in New York and me in freaking Indiana—phones to our ears but not talking. I waited for Jules to say something. She was the adult. The parent. Why couldn't she come up with a way to get us back together?

"You mean more to me than anything," she said at last. "I wouldn't do this if there was any other way."

Her voice sounded sad and desperate. This time my eyes did get wet.

"Okay. I get it." My voice came out flat-lined.

"It won't last forever."

"I gotta go, Jules."

This was a lie. There was no need for me to go anywhere, stuck the way I was in the sewing room. But she let me get off. I dropped the phone on the bed, hating it for a couple of seconds like it was the reason my life had come undone.

The air felt suffocating and I hurried down the stairs, slowing when I heard my grandparents arguing. "This is just like Julie," my grandpa said, deep voice drifting up from the living room. "When is she going to grow up and start being responsible?"

"We have to think about Kenley," G'ma said, her placating tone much quieter.

Unable to face them, I hurried down the stairs and through the front door as she called my name. I pretended not to hear, running down the long driveway and under the metal *Strickland Ranch* arch to the main road. The humid air smelled of cows, the setting sun burning out against a cloudless sky and offering nothing pretty.

My mind fumbled with the pieces that were all there waiting for me. Grandma's anxious phone conversation. Jules wanting to soften the blow with money and by turning my cell phone back on. Her uncertain tone as she chose acting and Anthony over the daughter there was no room for.

I walked past meadows and beside an irrigation ditch filled with slushing water. Darkness crept across forested hills and down to the farmlands, signaling frogs and crickets to start their noisy mashup. After a while I stopped walking. In a wide pasture, cows turned to gaze at me with sad eyes that seemed to say, *you think you've got it bad.*

"Oh shut up," I grumbled.

Finally, I headed back to the ranch since there was no place else to go.

My grandparents weren't in the living room, but my relief at not having to see them ended when I went in the sewing room. Grandma stood at the shelves, pulling out more baby fabrics. She looked at me.

"Sorry, I can leave. I don't mean to always be in here."

"You have a right to, Grandma. It's your sewing room."

She put down the material and stepped closer. "I've

decided to clean out your Uncle Josh's old room and make him do something with all his trophies and sports stuff. Then we'll either move your bed in there, or turn it into the sewing room and let you stay up here."

I tugged at a thread on the hem of my shirt, and she handed me a pair of scissors. "Cut it, don't pull."

I snipped the thread, not knowing what to say. My grandma filled the silence. "We don't mind having you stay on, Kenley. Maybe it's time you got a chance at stability. Your mother assures me you're a good student, so we'll expect top grades from you. The high school here isn't big but they've got some first-rate teachers and programs."

She seemed to be waiting for an answer.

"Go Mustangs," I finally said.

G'ma must have totally missed my sarcasm because she smiled and patted my arm. After that, she took her fabrics and left the room. I went to the window and looked out at the dark sky with its winking stars. Being alone never felt so deep.

17
Unmasked

Fall leaves, in a dozen layered shades from amber to gold, covered the ground. Others hung from black tree trunks and shivered as the breeze encouraged them to tumble earthward. I shivered too. My daddy bent down and zipped my lavender sweatshirt with Tinkerbell on the front, then pulled up the hood. "That's better."

"Where are we going?"

He winked at me. "I have a surprise for you. Something really wonderful."

We started walking along the trail again and I skipped a little, trying to think what kind of surprise it could be. A small stream crossed our path and Daddy swung me over. The trees grew even thicker, bright limbs above our heads cutting out all but a glimpse of sky. After a while my legs felt tired and I started to complain.

"Not far now," he said, leading me to a place that looked down across the edge of the hill. He pointed to a stone castle with a blue roof. "Isn't it magnificent?"

I didn't know that word but nodded anyway. "Mag...niv...zen."

He smiled, his warm fingers giving mine a slight squeeze. We walked down the narrow path that zigzagged to the base of the hill. Soon I could see the huge castle even better, its stone walls filled with dozens of windows, peeling shutters cast wide.

"Does a princess live here?"

"Hmm..." A familiar sound of amusement entered his voice. "I believe so."

The Disney princesses danced in my thoughts and I

smiled up at him. "Which one, Daddy? Which one?"

He guided me between thorny brown stems taller than my head. "I'm not sure, but from the look of these bushes it might be Sleeping Beauty."

Excited to see her, I hurried forward until we came to the castle. We went up the steps and across a wide porch that Daddy called a veranda. All I could think about was the princess, and I wondered if her dress would be pink or blue, or magically change color.

We stood outside for a long time as he tried to unlock the glass doors, muttering that it hadn't been this hard the last time he was here. I looked back across the gnarled bushes we'd come through, where a handful of dead roses clung to prickly stems. The breeze picked up and I shivered again. A click drew my attention and he said, "Got it."

He opened one of the doors and we walked inside, where shafts of light sliced through deep shadows. I looked around the big room with a sinking feeling. "Oh."

"What's wrong, Kenley?"

"This place is bad. A princess doesn't live here."

"Not now," he said, standing in a spot where a streak of shadow fell across his eyes like a mask. "But once upon a time, a princess must have danced here in this ballroom, don't you think? Try to imagine what this castle looked like a hundred years ago."

He moved to kneel beside me, the shadow mask suddenly gone. "Close your eyes and I'll help."

His fingers gently covered my eyes, his hug comforting as I leaned back against his shoulder. "Long ago, my little princess, this room was clean and perfect. Splendid paintings and mirrors covered the walls. A chandelier hung from the ceiling with a thousand glowing crystals. Music played and ladies wore beautiful dresses." He whispered in my ear, "Can you see them?"

At first I couldn't, but then swirling images began to fill my head, making me a little dizzy. I nodded behind his hands and when he took his fingers away, I opened my eyes. Everything was just the way he'd described.

"I see the dancing ladies! They're like the ones last night, in Mama's play."

He laughed. "Yes... Very good. Now you know the secret, Kenley. This castle is all for you."

For a few seconds it was magical—the two of us in that ballroom—but then the happiness in his gaze drifted away and he stood. Shadows seemed to swallow him and when he spoke, his voice had become a bare echo filled with sadness. "It can't last, though. It was never meant to last."

The scene changed and I found myself in another room, this one with scalloped draperies and soft organ music. Speckled tiger lilies reflected in the shiny wood of his coffin.

My eyes opened and I struggled to sit up, disoriented by the buttery light seeping in beneath the curtains. The sheets were tangled around my legs and I shoved them off, getting to my feet. Heart thudding, body damp, I made it to the window and parted the curtains, squinting as I looked out. The dairy breakfast was long over, my grandpa and uncles already at the long milking shed where black and white cows formed continuous lines.

I headed to the shower and let water flow over my head, waiting for it to wash away my agitation. My mind whirred with the truths that came together. I dried my hair which fell into a thick sideswipe across my brow. My fingers tugged at the jagged pieces of jaw-length hair, a style Dana had helped me cut during my last week in Branson. For once, my usually too bright face looked washed-out, hazel-green eyes wide as they stared back at me. I put on eyeshadow and lip gloss, starting to look more like the Kenley I knew—the girl who usually had a good grip on reality.

Back in the sewing room, I stuffed my water bottle, sketch pad, phone, and the envelope of photos into my bag then headed downstairs. I could hear Grandma in the kitchen doing dishes. Though I wanted to grab something to eat, I didn't want to talk right now or have her rope me into canning jam.

I left the house at a jog, and reaching the main road turned in my usual direction. I passed Zef's house, which had a flag flying in front, and eventually the narrow path I usually took to reach the Chateau. Instead of going there, I kept on running until my side ached. The warm air forecast another hot day, but for now the breeze felt pleasant.

Ten minutes later I reached a narrow dirt road that wound between two cornfields. I'd come here once during my first week, back when I kept wanting to escape the ranch and before discovering the Chateau. The lane was wide enough for a pickup but eventually dead-ended at an irrigation pump next to a deep canal. A plank bridge spanned the water and from there a path wound up into a forested hill.

I crossed the canal and started on the trail, setting a quick pace that soon left the fields behind. The tree branches overhead were heavy with green, while in my dream the falling leaves had been orange and gold. My pace slowed as the path grew steeper, and I listened to chittering birds and the rustling sound of a small animal in the underbrush.

After a lot of twists and turns, I began to wonder if my dream had anything at all to do with these woods. It didn't seem familiar. I paused, trying to decide if I should go back, but pushed on a little further, coming to a stream that trickled over mossy stones. It was a startling moment of *deja vu*. Years ago, my father had swung me across the water. This time, I leapt it.

My breath came faster, and I hurried along the trail for another twenty minutes until the trees thinned out near a ledge jutting from the hill. Looking down, I saw the Chateau. Morning light silvered the windows, turning them to mirrors, and made the blue roof appear more faded than usual. A stone path cut through the wildly overgrown back property and met with the veranda. From this angle, the rear of the building looked much different than the front.

I held onto a nearby limb to steady myself. The dream was real.

A dozen years ago I'd come here with my dad. And if he'd taken me through the woods, then he must have also taken me inside the Chateau. This insight drew me forward. My feet hurried along the steep path that now wove back and forth down the face of the hill, my hands bracing against tree trunks so I didn't fall. The trail was overgrown in spots, as if no one had walked here in a long time, and I thought of Arietta Broderick. Had she once followed this trail, escaping the Chateau whenever she could? I imagined her with long skirts and high-button shoes.

My toe snagged on a root and I barely caught myself on a tree trunk, but not before a branch poked me in the head. Finally I reached the base of the hill and started across the back property, searching for the stone path.

A small arched bridge had no water flowing under it. Instead, damp brush and weeds clogged what must have once been a stream. It ended in a marsh filled with cattails and foul-smelling mud, and I tried to picture what kind of pond was originally there. Not far from that sat a windowless gardener's shed, the door secured with a rusted padlock.

At last a path appeared that cut between tangled growths, and I stepped over fallen limbs and ugly weeds that had shoved up between the flagstones. Soon I had a clearer view of the long, sharp thorns covering the dead rose bushes, and I walked cautiously to keep from getting scratched. Many of the bushes nearly reached my shoulder, brittle leaves still clinging on stems. To a little girl who was only four, it could have seemed like the tall briars around Sleeping Beauty's castle.

This was the way my dad brought me. I never saw the front of the Chateau until discovering it after coming to the Strickland Ranch, which was why I hadn't recognized it. In some small way it had seemed familiar, like the barest tug of a long-ago memory, but not enough for me to piece together that I'd been here as a child.

I walked up the veranda steps and tested one of the French doors leading to the ballroom. It opened easily and I stepped inside, the air cool. For just a second I had the feeling I might see the smiling stranger who—behind the mask—was actually my father. I stood still, waiting in the silence and hoping for something to happen. I even closed my eyes, trying to conjure up the odd chamber music and murmur of dancers.

Eventually I opened my eyes, seeing nothing but stained walls and the beat up chandelier hanging by its pitiful cord. I tried to get rid of the prickling sensation on my skin by rubbing my arms, finally moving into the main hallway. The empty library was on the left and I passed the sitting room next to it, going to where the hall opened into the gallery. Rectangular stains on the plaster showed where paintings had once hung, and my thoughts returned to the missing art pieces. I stepped closer, fingers brushing against a large square outline on the north wall. Had the Monet hung here?

"Hi Kenley."

I jumped and spun around, staring at the guy who stood with his head tipped a little to the side, a white facemask hanging around his neck and his backpack hanging from one shoulder.

"You walk like a danged cat, know that, Zef?"

He smiled in that almost-laughing way of his. "I thought you might come."

I looked back down the hall, catching a glimpse of the ballroom through its open doors. For a couple of seconds it seemed there was movement in the shadows, though when I blinked it was gone.

He stepped closer. "You okay?"

"Huh?"

Zef plucked something from my hair and held out a leaf. I motioned in the direction of the veranda. "There's a trail across the hill, and it ends at the back of the property. You probably know that."

He nodded. "You came that way?"

"Yes." I thought about saying more but instead stared past him.

"Come on."

He went to the grand foyer and started up the stairs. "Let's not talk on the ground floor where the gas can get to us."

"Oh. Right."

I hurried up the steps and went after him into the huge master bedroom where four tall windows looked down on the fountain. Two of the panes were shattered, glass everywhere.

"I don't remember them being broken."

"They weren't." Zef pointed to a couple of rocks in the corner. "I moved those. This morning I found them in the middle of the room."

"So someone's trespassing?"

He raised an eyebrow. "Other than us, you mean? It's not the first time somebody's broken out windows, but most of those are on the west side, where the fence is closer. And it hasn't happened recently, especially after the county started giving stiffer fines to kids if they got caught here."

"How much?"

"Not sure. It used to be fifty bucks, but three years ago after that girl Mandie died here, it went up. I've heard if you get a ticket, it's now around four hundred dollars."

My mouth went a little dry. "That's a lot. You ever gotten a ticket?"

"Nope. And we won't, as long as we're smart. You have to make a lot of noise for someone to notice we're here and call the sheriff. Keggers and racing cars get calls from the farmers, not what we're doing. Now, want to tell me what's going on?"

I folded my arms and looked at him with a silent, *I don't know what you mean.*

Zef smiled like he had a crystal ball and knew all. "You took the long trail across the hill to get here. Nobody does that when it's hot. And you're acting distracted. So what's up?"

My eyes dropped to my bag and I took out my art pad. I flipped past drawings of the Chateau until finding the sketch of dancers in the ballroom.

I handed it to Zef who said, "You drew this?"

"Yes."

"You're really good." He sounded impressed.

"Thanks."

"One of the first times I saw you, that's what you were doing. Sitting on a tree stump and drawing."

"Look at the costumes, Zef. And the background."

"Is this the ballroom?"

I nodded. "That's what I saw when I was sitting on the veranda the day we met. I'd fallen asleep and dreamed of dancers in old costumes. I didn't know about the gas, of course, that it was making me hallucinate. Once you explained it, I thought it was all made up."

He seemed confused. "It wasn't?"

"Yes, of course. But there's more to it. Remember my dad's lost roll of film?"

I took out the photos and handed him the top two, the

ones most similar to my drawing of the dancers. "This is what inspired it."

"Wow."

I reached out and flipped forward in the sketch pad to the drawing of the girl in the dress, then matched it up with the photo. "My mother, Jules. She was in *Phantom of the Opera* when I was little." I plopped another photo on top. "And that's me standing next to her on the stage."

"How old were you?"

"Four, almost five. I must've started kindergarten the next year."

"So, a long time ago you saw the people from the play and when the gas hit you, it recreated them in the ballroom. That makes sense."

"But I never remembered going to that play. Or coming here with my dad, even though I'm sure we did."

Zef flipped forward in the sketch pad, studying my drawings until I felt a little self-conscious and took it back. I held up the photo of me standing beside my mother.

"The play was performed at a theater in Indianapolis. My dad and I must've been staying at my grandparents' place, with Jules coming home between practices."

"And your dad found the Chateau."

"Yes, though I already assumed that because of something I found in his box of writing. But then this morning I had a dream about how he brought me with him. Actually, I think it was more than just a dream. I'm pretty sure it was a memory."

Zef studied me with a serious gaze that made me a little flustered. I put the photos back in my bag. "What I can't understand is why I forgot about this place when the dream was so detailed. He called it a castle, and I thought a princess lived here."

Instead of teasing me, the way I thought he might, Zef stared out the broken window and said, "Little kids forget stuff."

He turned back and shrugged, eyebrows drawn together. "I can hardly remember kindergarten. I think we sat on a rug when the teacher read books. And this one girl licked her glue stick."

For the first time that day I smiled, and he did, too. "Besides, Kenley, you were even younger than kindergarten, right?"

"Yes." I fiddled with the clasp on my bag. "It's just that I think the reason I know what I do about the Chateau is because of my dad. If he was exploring here, then he must have found the secret trap."

An intrigued expression touched Zef's eyes. "And shown you where it was. That's how you were able to go right to it and spring the latch."

"Except I don't remember. Maybe his bringing me here happened so long ago, I forgot about it."

"But your subconscious didn't. And if your father discovered other stuff about the Chateau, maybe he showed you that too."

Neither of us said anything. Finally, he tugged at the breathing mask hanging around his neck. "So, you still up for finding the Hidden Room?"

I didn't know why, just then, my pulse quickened and a prickling sensation crept up my neck. But before I could wimp out, I met Zef's gaze and slowly nodded.

18
The Dark Hall

Zef handed me a white breathing mask like the one still hanging around his neck. "Whenever we're on the ground floor, we wear these to keep us safe from the gas."

I slid the elastic band over my head. "Got it. Now what?"

"I give you the basic tour."

For the next half hour he showed me the ground floor. This included the rear foyer with a storage area between it and the kitchen, a huge pantry that had a second door leading to a service area across from a dining room ten times bigger than my grandma's. He showed me what was called the first conservatory. It was once used for music lessons and classroom study and still held a couple of old school desks. Beyond that were several guest bedrooms, three massive storage areas, and an open motor court with a section Zef called the *porte cochére*. This was basically a covered entrance large enough for vehicles to pass through and let passengers off at an interior courtyard.

The facemask muffled Zef's voice as he said, "When the Brodericks built this place the horse and carriage were just getting replaced by early automobiles, so I'm not sure what Henry kept in the motor court."

"The Chateau is even bigger than it looks from outside. How'd you know what all these rooms are?"

"I have the blueprints, remember?"

A second hallway with multiple turns led to the servants' quarters. Beyond that it split three ways, one hall leading to more rooms and a service staircase, another going past one of three entrances to the large study and then ending at the rear foyer. Part of it was blocked off, and

Zef explained how a section of the collapsed roof had caused a cave-in clear down to a storage room on the far side of the larder.

The third split eventually came out at the smaller second conservatory, just off the front of the ballroom, which had lots of windows and a glass roof. This room was full of dusty, long-dead plants, the foggy windows streaked with water stains.

Zef tugged at his mask. "Let's go upstairs so we can get these off."

On the second floor, we sat down on the top step and he pulled out strawberry flavored Snapple from his backpack, offering me one. "They're not cold anymore."

I opened mine and drank, thirsty enough that I didn't mind it being lukewarm. My gaze wandered down the wide marble stairs to the foyer. "No wonder Arietta was confused about where her father's Hidden Room might be."

"And we haven't even gone through the second floor."

I thought about the small, jutting windows that formed a row along the lower rim of the roof. "Or into the attic. What's up there?"

He stared across the foyer. "A lot of junk and a big hole in the roof."

"Guess I didn't realize how tough finding the lost room would be."

"My grandpa was smart. Had a Masters of Engineering. He spent hours searching before his health went downhill, and he couldn't figure it out. And I've put so much time into this place my friends have given up on me."

I thought about how Sierra had broken up with him. "Why's it so important to you?"

He didn't answer and I studied his profile with its strong lines. The abrupt edge of his brow and straight eyebrows gave him a penetrating look, the generous shape of his mouth a contrast. I thought how it would be interesting to sketch him, until he turned to look at me.

"Maybe for the same reasons you've got."

The artist in me had been so caught up in studying Zef that I didn't answer. He leaned back and said, "If we find those paintings, and the other stuff in Henry's Hidden Room, the money will change my family's life. Plus I don't like the idea of this place coming down on top of what my grandpa used to call our heirlooms. He said they were part of our history."

His expression turned cautious, as if he felt exposed by admitting this. I put the lid back on my bottle. "I agree with your grandpa. That night after reading Arietta's letter, I couldn't sleep and looked through my art book. Finding even one of those Impressionist paintings would be incredible."

"How, though?" A discouraged note crept into his voice. "Your figuring out the secret trap proved that Phillipe Moncharde designed at least one secret passageway. But it also shows how good he was at hiding the entrances. I'd searched that service room before and never noticed it. Same with the door on the other end of the tunnel in the wine cellar."

My teeth tugged at my lower lip as I thought about this.

He leaned forward, resting his forearms on his knees. "If you're right that your dad actually brought you here and showed you the secret trap, how'd he solve it in the first place?"

I studied the small dome in the vaulted ceiling above the grand foyer. Its carved molding, in faded shades of gold and coral, was still beautiful. "I'm guessing because he knew a lot of stuff about the stage."

Looking back at Zef I added, "You're the one who said the architect probably used the same techniques on the Chateau that he did when he built his theaters. From what Jules has told me, if my dad wasn't writing plays, he worked as a stagehand behind the scenes. He'd done that for years."

"When he brought you here, do you think he showed you anything else?"

Instinct told me he hadn't, but Zef had a hopeful gaze that made me shrug. "Maybe. What about the blueprints? Can I see them?"

"Of course. They're out in my truck."

He took off and I wandered down the second story hallway. I looked in the now familiar master bedroom with its broken windows. Outside, the breeze had picked up, coming through the empty panes to clear out the stuffiness.

I walked to the service area with the secret trap but had barely stepped inside when I heard knocking. Going back into the main hall, I looked around but saw nothing. I stood still and listened, though now the Chateau seemed unusually quiet. It struck me as odd how such an old house didn't have more creaking, or at least the soft settling sounds that come when air turns drafty.

After passing more rooms, I turned a corner and peered into deep shadows. This part of the house, away from the open railing of the balcony above the main foyer, was lightless. A few antique wall sconces still clung to flaking plaster, their glass chimneys long lost. Mostly, there were bare spots where the lamps had been torn away. My footsteps slowed and I leaned in, peering through the darkness. Gloomy now, at night it would be black unless kerosene lamps constantly burned.

I didn't know why, but this section of the house started to creep me out. For one thing, it smelled bad, like mold or something rotten. It felt colder, too—a dankness that sent a shiver through me.

My phone buzzed, making me jump because I'd gotten used to not having it. It was Jules, and I almost answered but didn't. If she asked where I was, I'd either have to lie or listen to her flip out when I told the truth. Instead, I waited, letting it hum away with her special ringtone.

I was still upset at Jules—and hurt and just all-around mad—but I also missed her. Disobeying her about coming here felt wrong. But not as much of a betrayal as her refusing to find a way for me to join the troupe.

My phone fell silent and I slipped it in a pocket, ignoring the beep that said I had voicemail because the tapping started up again. This time it sounded louder, and I felt certain someone else was here, probably another person looking for the lost room. This pushed me forward, but despite my determination to see who kept knocking, I found my steps slowing—my feet almost refusing to obey.

I thought about calling out to ask who was there, but that was what stupid girls in horror shows did right before they got chopped. My fingers shoved aside the facemask bugging my neck, and I realized it hadn't done what it should to protect me from the gas fumes. The tapping had to be a hallucination.

Forcing myself to keep moving forward, refusing to give in to the rush of adrenalin that dried my mouth, I wasn't prepared for the cold fear that hit me like a wave. I stopped walking. In fact, it was all I could do to stand there as every nerve in my body pulsed a warning: *Don't go down that hallway!*

Breathing fast, I leaned over a little and rested my hands on my thighs. For a couple of seconds I thought I might be sick and I waited for the nausea to pass. When I straightened, a slight movement in the distance drew my focus. Squinting, trying to make out the shadowy form that looked like a person, I took a step back.

He stopped... I felt certain it was male. Large, with a misshapen head, his face was scored by deep, unnatural wrinkles. Bloodshot yellow eyes, with small black pupils, bulged from beneath a heavy brow, and I recoiled from the sight of rotting flesh and pointed fangs. I turned and ran.

19
Malice

Not real! My mind screeched as I ran, my art bag slapping against my hip. Turning a corner, sensing I couldn't outrun him, I slipped into an unfamiliar room. I stood between two doorways missing their doors, my back against the narrow piece of wall. After waiting, I turned my head to peek around the doorframe, then quickly pulled back at the sound of plodding feet.

The footsteps stopped and my ears strained in the silence, sure someone was standing just outside the first door. I clamped my lips together, breathing silently, my mind racing. I tried to analyze what I'd seen. The bizarre face had to be a mistake, or more likely a hallucination from spending too much time downstairs with a faulty breathing mask. Seconds ticked by as I got my courage together to peek again, fairly sure the hall would be empty.

I had just about convinced myself to look when a new noise startled me, a low growl that grew in intensity. It made my stomach knot as I scanned the shadowy room for another way out. It held nothing but a deep closet and two small windows that let in a little bit of streaky light. With my back against the narrow wall, if I bolted out the door on my left, it would lead straight to the dark hallway I'd run from. The one on my right might reach the stairs to the grand foyer. But could I keep ahead of whoever was out there and make it down the steps fast enough? Unless, of course, it really was just a hallucination…

The growl changed to an aggressive snuffling like a wolf or dog, and a prickling of sweat formed along my hairline. I forced myself to leap through the door and sprint for the stairs. He came after me, dirty fingernails reaching for my arm as I dodged him. My feet flew across the floor, widening the space between us, until the toe of my shoe snagged and I stumbled. It gave him the edge he needed to ram my side, herding me into another room. I staggered away, turning to face the guy.

The hideous grin didn't move, the fangs fake. Phony black hair stuck out the top of a rubbery mask, his own hair hanging in lanky strands down his thick neck. He wore a black T-shirt faded to gray, salty sweat stains under the arms.

I stared at him, determined not to show how much he'd shaken me. "Very funny."

He didn't say a word, his indistinct eyes studying me from behind the mask, which caused a whole new sensation to crawl up my spine. I wondered if I knew him, though nothing about this guy seemed familiar, including his beefy arms and a roll of flab around his waist.

Why didn't he say something or move? Deciding not to let his freakish mask make my nerves tighter, I started for the door. He stepped in to block me and let out a nasty chuckle. Reaching to the back of his waistband he removed something and held it up—a knife with a thick black handle and steel blade.

He lunged forward and I scurried back, choking out a scream. He advanced again, stabbing with the knife and aiming for my stomach. I jerked my art bag around in front of me, not that it was much protection. Again he attacked and I jumped sideways, hearing him slam the wall as I ran for the door. He came after me. I sensed his hand raised to plunge the knife in my back and felt a whoosh of air as he brought it down, something grazing my spine that might have been knuckles.

I reached the doorway and nearly collided with Zef. "Knife!" I cried.

My warning came too late, and the blade plunged into Zef's chest. I screamed.

The blow knocked Zef backwards, but he reacted with an uppercut to the guy's jaw and then slugged him hard in the stomach. He fell and the knife clattered to the floor. I ran to Zef, fingers touching his chest. No blood yet, though I knew it would start to bloom in seconds. But I couldn't see a slice in his shirt, either, though I'd seen the knife go in. His calm eyes met my panicked ones and he touched my hand that was still on his chest.

"I'm fine." He sounded angry, not hurt, and bent to pick up the knife.

Putting the tip on his palm, he pressed down and I watched the phony blade slide up into the handle. "It's a trick."

The guy sitting on the floor let out a howl that took me a bit to realize was laughter. Zef glared at him and rubbed his chest in a way that showed the fake blow had still hurt. "Dean, you stupid jerk, take off that mask."

Dean. Zef's distant cousin and Riker's friend, one of the two guys who chased us through the Chateau that first night.

He peeled off the mask, revealing an ordinary face with a lump-of-clay nose and smirking mouth. The mask dangled from one finger before dropping to the floor. "Got this stuff last Halloween. You seen Riker?"

I glanced in the direction of the hall. That was all we needed.

Zef folded his arms. "What're you doing here?"

Pushing to his feet, Dean walked over to us. "I could ask you the same thing. Your mom and dad know you're here?"

For someone who didn't look very bright, he'd punched the right button. Zef scowled but kept quiet. Dean smiled at me, showing teeth with major gaps. "Shoulda seen your face."

I called him a bad name that probably shocked an Indiana country boy like Zef, but it only made Dean laugh harder. His eyes traveled down my bare legs then back up. "This your new girlfriend, Zef? Heard Sierra dumped you. She's with Charlie Pepper now."

His laughter cut off and he took faltering steps away from the dark corner of the room. "What was that?"

Zef and I glanced at each other, since we hadn't heard anything. Turning back around, Dean folded his arms and leaned his shoulder against the door jamb as if trying to act cool. A drop of sweat trickled down his forehead.

"How long you been hiding here?" Zef asked.

Dean's eyes went to the floor and he leapt forward, stomping down. He repeated this a couple more times. "Damn roaches!"

He began squashing bugs, even though nothing was there. It turned into a bizarre bug killing dance, feet thumping and flab jiggling. Finally, he seemed to have killed off all the imaginary roaches and just stood there, breathing fast.

Zef motioned to me, "Let's get out of here."

Dean looked up from the floor and moved to block the doorway leading to the stairs. "You should stay."

His words held more intimidation than invitation, making Zef glower. "What do you want, Dean?"

A sly expression settled on his features. "What d'you think? A share of what you find. Only fair, considering how your grandpa's family ripped us off."

Zef let out a sour chuckle and rubbed his hand across the back of his neck. "Oh yeah. It's always about how bad you Fairchilds got treated."

Dean's mouth made a mean smirk. "You're not the only ones looking now. Riker and I can search this place just as good as you."

"Be my guest. In the meantime, I hear more roaches coming."

Dean backed into the hall. I stepped over the mask, then paused to pick it up. As we passed him, I threw it at his chest. "You should wear this. You're more attractive with it on."

Anger lit his eyes. He stood there holding the mask against his fat stomach, his dopey face now hostile.

As we left, his voice followed us into the hall. "Next time I see you guys, I'll have a real knife!"

Neither of us looked back, though I could still sense his glare on our backs.

Zef and I headed out of the Chateau and down the veranda steps. He pulled off the breathing mask hanging around his neck and shoved it in his backpack. I put mine in the art bag.

"I'm sorry, Kenley. When I got halfway out to my truck and saw Dean's car, I ran back as fast as I could."

"That guy is a major creep." I shrugged, like Dean's prank didn't matter, but I still felt shaken. "What did he mean about your grandpa's family ripping off the Fairchilds?"

A pinched expression touched his face. "Remember Arietta's letter to her son? How she told Stephen he would inherit all the Broderick money?"

"Yes."

"His older half-siblings, who were Arietta's step kids, only got a portion of their father's land and money. Which wasn't that much after it got split five ways. From what my grandpa was told by his father, they were really unhappy when they didn't get a share of their little brother's big fortune."

"But that was years ago."

"Yeah, well, my dad says Dean's lazy family has a long tradition of holding grudges."

I noticed he was taking the long way around the west end of the Chateau. "Where are we going?"

"I want to show you something."

We passed the steps leading down to the kitchen door, where Zef had brought me inside the first night we met.

Beyond the far wing of the house stood a large gazebo that must have been white but was now mostly rust. Zef led me to the wrought-iron fence marked at intervals with stone pillars, the black bars overgrown with weeds. "It's along here somewhere…"

He pushed away dead vines until finding what he was looking for and released a latch. A portion of the fence swung outward, revealing a gate that wasn't noticeable when closed. I leaned in to study the recessed hinges and the way the iron bar across the top had fit neatly into the rest of the fence.

"That's cool. How'd you find this?"

"I didn't. My grandpa showed me." We stepped through and he shut it. "From now on, when we meet here, let's use this gate."

After what had happened with Dean, I wasn't sure I wanted to come again.

Zef added, "If we use the hidden entrance, then I can leave the chain on the front gate. I unlocked it for you, since I didn't know you were going to get here from the back of the property. Once it was open, that made it easy for Dean to get in."

We walked along the outside of the fence and had just reached the front corner when a dark green pickup peeled out, spewing gravel. Zef stepped back, not wanting to be seen, and I copied him.

"Dean?" I asked.

"Yep."

The pickup took the corner fast then disappeared behind giant oaks. We headed around to the front and Zef locked the chain on the gate as my phone beeped. Kiefer had sent Dana and me a selfie. He stood in front of a parade at Universal Studios with crazy characters in huge Uncle Sam hats. A sign on the float said, *Happy Independence Day!*

For the first time, I focused on my phone's date

display. "It's the fourth of July," I said, following Zef to his truck. "Nobody at the ranch said anything. Do the Stricklands even celebrate it?"

"Dairy life is tough," Zef answered as we climbed in. "Cows don't understand holidays. They've got to be milked twice a day."

"Are there fireworks in town?"

He shook his head and started the engine. "You have to drive to Fort Wayne for that."

I thought about Jules still in New York, where they had an amazing pyrotechnics show. She and Anthony were probably going to go watch it, while I sweltered here and listened to crickets chirp. It made me angry all over again.

Zef glanced at me. "I want to show you the blueprints. But I also think we need a break from the Chateau. You all right with going somewhere else for a while?"

Five minutes ago I'd been ready to tell him I didn't want to keep searching. But a mental image surfaced of last year's fireworks in Branson, where I'd gone with a big group of friends. Kiefer had sung along with the patriotic music, off key and making us laugh. Dana brought caramel corn and Cokes. A boy named Barry kissed me.

I also thought about my dad's unfinished play, and how the Chateau had given me a tenuous link to him. Air came in through the open window, ruffling Zef's hair. He slowed the pickup and looked over at me, our eyes locking as he waited for an answer.

"Okay," I said at last, and he turned in the opposite direction of the dairy.

20
What Zef Knows

We spread out a picnic blanket and sat beneath a weeping willow near a large pond. The smooth surface of the water mirrored sky and twisted green limbs. I hadn't even known there was a place like this and drew a slow breath, enjoying the smell of nature untainted by the sour dairy odor. "It's beautiful here."

Zef unfolded the blueprints which weren't blue at all, but instead an aged tan color. He sat back on his heels and gazed across the pond. "I come here sometimes, if I want to be alone."

The way he said it made me wonder if I was the first girl he'd brought here. I studied the cattails along the far bank. "Wish I could come here when I get tired of being in my grandparents' house. It's too far to walk, though."

Zef's eyes studied me. I focused on the blueprints, silently asking myself why that intense stare of his kept flustering me.

On the large top sheet he pointed out the different hallways and rooms I'd seen during our tour of the ground level. Everything was labeled in small but precise print, and it helped me get a clearer understanding of the Chateau's layout. In the bottom right corner was the name of the architect, Phillipe Moncharde, in fancy calligraphy with a small star between his first and last name.

The second page was of the upstairs floorplan which had the same insignia. I put my finger on the service area between the master sitting room and second bedroom. "You're right. There's not a thing here to show any sort of secret entrance. It's got the dumbwaiter drawn in, and the linen closet, but that's all."

He flipped to the third sheet. "This is the lower level. It shows the larder, wine cellar, and all the storage areas, but no secret tunnel."

"Mind if I take pictures? Then I can study them tonight, maybe memorize how the Chateau is laid out."

"Go ahead."

While I worked he pulled a small pack of M&Ms from his backpack and shared them, the closest thing I'd had to a meal since last night. I used my phone to snap photos and said, "Dean was sure freaked out about those roaches."

Zef smiled. "Kind of surprising he could move that fast."

"I think he's got a good career in pest control."

We both laughed and I added, "Would've been nice to have him take care of my rats."

"That gas can sure make you see stuff that seems real, can't it?"

Neither of us were laughing now, and I nodded. "I can understand why some people still insist it's haunted. What's the scariest stuff you've seen?"

He thought about this. "It's a tie. Either the time hands broke through the floor and grabbed at my legs, trying to pull me down into a grave..."

I made a visual shudder. "Or?"

"Or blood seeping from the walls."

This time I actually did shiver. "You win."

"It's not always terrifying hallucinations. Sometimes I've heard beautiful singing. And I've seen the rose garden in full bloom. It was pretty amazing."

"Ever wonder if being exposed to the gas is killing off our brain cells?"

He shifted his position on the ground. "I worry about that sometimes. But my grandpa was still sharp until the end, even after all his years of searching. Besides, it's not like I'm going to spend much more time there."

My phone rang. It was G'ma. "Kenley, where are

you?"

She wasn't much for niceties, always straight to the point. I looked around. "Umm... I'm sitting by a pond with Zef."

"Oh. I wish you'd start telling me when you're leaving. Your Uncle Josh emptied out his old room, and I thought we could move your things in there today."

For a couple of seconds I wondered why I'd been so excited for my phone to get resurrected, considering it kept me on a tighter leash. I tried to muffle my sigh. "Okay. I'll come home."

Zef motioned for me to give him the phone. I questioned him with my eyes, but all he did was reach for it.

"Uh, Grandma? Zef wants to talk to you." I handed it over.

"Hello, Mrs. Strickland. I'm sorry I didn't ask before now, but would it be okay if Kenley came to my family's Fourth of July barbecue? It's at two."

He paused to listen then said, "No, my mother won't mind. She's been asking to meet Kenley."

His mom knew about me?

"Yes ma'am. I understand."

Another pause.

"Sure. Do you want me to call if it goes longer than that? Okay... Thanks, Mrs. Strickland."

Zef disconnected and handed my phone back. I shook my head. "Maybe I should pay you for lessons in *How to Suck Up to Adults*, 101."

His lips gave a sarcastic twitch. "It worked, didn't it? If you're ready to go back to the dairy, just tell me."

"Nope, I'm good."

I bent over the blueprints again and heard him chuckle, not like he was amused but more in the way of, *what-to-do-with-a-girl-like-you?*

Soon I was caught up in studying more details of the

Chateau, flipping back and forth between the pages and trying to make the floorplans mesh with the places I'd seen. Zef explained some of what he knew, sitting close enough that his knee touched mine. I glanced sideways at him as he talked, studying the line of his jaw, how his bottom lip was a tiny bit fuller than the top, the slight way his Adam's apple moved as he talked. He had a nice voice, low but strong.

It occurred to me that there might be quite a lot more to Zefram Webb than the good looking but moody exterior of a guy who only spoke when he had something to say. It made me think of the glassy pond, reflecting sky and trees but not giving a glimpse of what lay beneath.

Zef showed me the rooms he thought didn't have a hidden entrance because he'd checked the walls with a stud finder. "If a door was framed by the builders, it probably wouldn't have two-by-fours running through it."

I adjusted myself into a more comfortable cross-sit. "This whole thing we're doing is kind of weird."

He looked up. "What do you mean?"

"Us agreeing to be partners and search the Chateau. Because even though we're working together, we don't know hardly anything about each other."

"That's not true. I know a lot about you."

I raised my eyebrows. "Like what, exactly?"

He seemed to think for a bit. "You're stubborn and headstrong."

"Gee, thanks."

"Good at math but like art better."

"Obvious."

"You're really talented at drawing."

"Thanks again." This time without the vinegary tone.

He shifted his weight to lean on one arm, tilting his head slightly and studying me. "When you sit outside and sketch, you don't notice anything going on around you. It's like you step inside your own world. If you're really focused, you sometimes catch the corner of your bottom lip between your teeth."

Staring at him, I wondered how closely he'd been observing me. As if reading this, he shrugged and gave a small smile that didn't last long. "When you go for walks it's in the same direction as cars drive. Which isn't safe, by the way. Especially because you don't pay attention, like you're daydreaming or arguing with someone inside your head."

I wanted to come up with a snarky comment but failed. In this light, his eyes were a chocolaty brown color with a dark amber ring around the outside edge.

Zef's brow puckered a little, like he was going over a mental list. "You don't like country life. Staying at the dairy makes you sad. Or upset. You've got a Missouri driver's license but wish you had your own car."

"How do you know that?"

"The day you came here, I was helping unload cattle feed for your grandpa. I saw you drive up in a brown Saab with Missouri plates, your mom in the passenger seat. Let's see... what else? When you don't want to answer a question you break eye contact. If you're trying to make up a lie, you glance down and a little to the side. And you act outgoing so probably make friends easy. But inside, you're actually kind of shy. Maybe that's why you blush easier than anybody I know. Your cheeks go a peach color, like right now. Even your lips get pinker."

He paused and looked down, his fingers absently tugged at the fringe of the picnic blanket. I brushed the back of my hand across one cheek, which felt too warm, quickly lowering it when he started to raise his head.

"And you're brave."

This surprised me more than anything else. "Why would you think that?"

"You didn't know Dean's knife was fake. When you thought he stabbed me, you screamed but didn't run away.

Instead, you tried to see how bad I'd been cut."

He glanced down at his chest as if reviewing it all, including the way I'd touched him. I said, "You're brave, too. You threatened Riker for grabbing my wrist."

Zef began folding up the blueprints. "Yeah. And I doubt repercussions from that little incident are over."

He stood. "Ready to go?"

I got up too, brushing pieces of stray grass from my bare legs. "Where?"

"My family's barbecue."

"Huh? You mean they're really having a Fourth of July barbecue?"

"Of course. I didn't lie to your grandma."

"Oh… So your mother has been asking to meet me?"

Zef gave a sheepish smile like I'd caught him. "Okay, so that I lied about."

I grabbed the blanket and went with him to the truck. We climbed in and he said, "How do cheeseburgers and potato salad sound? I think that's what's on the menu."

"Good, actually. I'm starving."

"I could tell."

"How?"

"Because of the way you scarfed those M&Ms. Plus your stomach growled."

I folded my arms as he started the truck. "It's like hanging out with Sherlock Holmes."

Zef didn't answer, but I could see he thought what I'd said was funny.

21
The Webbs

As he drove, I scrolled through the pictures I'd just taken. "One thing I don't get is why Henry Broderick thought he needed to build such a big place, when there were only five in his family. And the servants, of course. Still, the Chateau is ridiculously huge."

"Do a search on your phone for *Chateau de Lévesque* in the Provence area of France." He told me how to spell it and I found a bunch of pictures.

"It's the same... or close. The roof looks a different shade, I think."

"It was built by Moncharde for a wealthy marquis maybe thirty years before he designed ours. I think Henry and Estelle Broderick toured that one in France, and then hired the same architect to recreate it here in Indiana."

I scrolled through pictures of the inside, seeing the French chateau was in much better shape. A text from Jules interrupted me. She asked if I wasn't returning her call because I was mad. I replied that I was on my way to a barbecue with Zef but could talk tonight.

Her answer: *No worries. We'll chat later.*

My earlier guess was right. She and Anthony were going to watch the fireworks, while I was stuck in Podunk-land, USA.

We passed the narrow trail I'd taken to reach the Chateau and I asked Zef, "Why do you drive there instead of walking? It's not that far from your house, but the road leading in from town is a lot farther away."

"Because if I took off on a walk and was gone most of the day, my parents would know what I'm doing. But when I leave in the pickup, they think I'm going to work or seeing friends."

"But you don't really see your friends anymore." Maybe it was my turn to be observant. "You spend all your time searching the Chateau, which even made Sierra break up with you. Do you regret it?"

He didn't answer as I slid my phone in my pocket. "It's just that I miss my friends back in Branson. I know what it means to be lonely."

"Sometimes I do regret it," he admitted. "Especially because none of them have ever understood, including Sierra. Or maybe especially Sierra."

His eyebrows drew into a scowl. "A bunch of people in town started calling my grandpa a half-baked crackpot. They made fun of him for wasting his time and money on the Chateau. And of course kids pick up stuff from their parents, especially those who don't have enough brains to think for themselves."

This gave me more insight to Zef and I turned to him. "Which means finding your lost family fortune would let you rub it in their judgmental faces."

An ironic smile touched his lips. "Not the way I would put it, but yes. Redeeming my grandpa's good name is important to me."

"So if we do find it, what are you going to do with your share? Buy a new truck?"

"Probably."

"What else?"

He tapped his thumbs on the steering wheel. "Take my parents and Kes on a trip someplace exotic, like Hawaii. And after I graduate, go to Cornell or Northwestern." He glanced at me, hesitant but then adding, "Though the first thing I'd do is pay off all my mom's medical bills. Then get her into one of those university hospitals where they've got good specialists."

I remembered my grandma saying Beverly Webb struggled with some major health issues. "No wonder you're trying so hard to find your family's lost fortune. Makes my spending plans seem shallow."

He smiled a bit wryly. "There's other stuff I want, you know. Like taking flying lessons."

"Do they even have planes around here?"

"On the far side of town there's a small hangar and a landing strip. I think it would be cool to take off and fly somewhere whenever I wanted, then come back home."

I thought about it. "If I could do that, it'd be a lot easier staying in this town."

"Meaning?" He raised an eyebrow and I studied him.

"Your parents ever regret not naming you Spock?"

Instead of bugging him, the way I thought it would, he laughed.

Several cars were in front of Zef's house, but he found a place to park and looked over at me. "The thing is, Kenley, talking about what we'd like to buy or do is kind of a waste, because twenty-five percent of nothing is still nothing. And after today, we have only three weeks until that demolition crew shows up and starts wiring the place."

I think we both felt a little down as we headed along the walkway. Wafting smoke from backyard grilling crossed the fence. "Who are the other guests? More family?"

"No, friends who work at my dad's middle school."

He led me inside and I looked around the front room, immediately liking what I saw. It was decorated in an early Americana style with folk art prints and braided rugs on a hardwood floor.

"This is cool, Zef. Not what I imagined."

"What did you think it'd be like?"

"I don't know. Something with Star Trek posters, maybe."

Voices came from another room and Zef guided me through a dining area and into the kitchen. A woman with short, dark hair sat at the counter cutting up cantaloupe.

Across from her, a girl knelt on a bar stool, her long hair in a ponytail. They both stared at me with the same curious brown eyes.

Zef introduced us and his mother smiled. "Of course, you're June's granddaughter. I went to school with your mom. How's Julie doing? Still acting?"

I nodded, interested in the contrast between Zef's quiet nature compared to his outgoing mom. "She goes by Jules now."

"Is she on Broadway?"

"No, getting ready to tour with a Shakespeare troupe." I didn't add that they would only be performing at school assemblies, which sounded anything but glamorous. A new worry arose. What if her troupe actually ended up coming here, to the high school where I'd start in the fall? Even though Jules was good at acting, who wanted their mother to be center stage at a school assembly? I really needed to help Zef find that secret room.

"How long are you staying with your grandparents?" she asked.

"Not sure. Until the Shakespeare tour ends, I guess."

"So you'll be going to school here?" She smiled, like this was a good idea.

"Looks that way."

Zef was watching me, and I enjoyed saying something he didn't already know. He headed off more questions by leading me outside. "So you're staying here for the school year?"

I lowered my voice. "Unless we find what we're looking for."

The Webbs had a huge back yard with what seemed like a mile of grass and trees, and a trampoline in the middle. Out on the deck, a dozen people started getting in line at the pot luck table as Zef took me over to meet his dad. Miles Webb wore a *Grill Master* apron and held tongs. He was tall, with dark blond hair and a friendly smile. I got right away he was a teacher, since he had the comfortable look of someone who spends a lot of time around kids. If he was surprised Zef brought a girl to the barbecue, it didn't show.

We filled our plates and sat on chairs farthest away from everyone, though that didn't deter a broad-shouldered man from stopping by and asking Zef if he was going to turn out for football this year. "Thinking about it, Coach," Zef said.

"The team missed you last year."

When we were alone I asked, "Why didn't you play last year?"

He dug his fork into potato salad. "I had other things to do."

Meaning the Chateau, of course.

"Can I ask something? You said your mom is sick, but she looks okay. Not that you can always see when someone's sick."

It sounded lame enough that I wished I'd kept quiet, though he didn't seem to mind. "Some days are better for her than others. About three years ago she came down with Epstein-Barr, and that led to an immune deficiency and chronic fatigue."

Zef stopped talking as Kes approached and took the empty seat. He asked how dance camp was going. She gave him all sorts of details I thought would bore most big brothers, but he just listened. I took a bite of cheeseburger, watching him joke around with his kid sister and getting a different view of him.

As we ate, random bits of dialogue drifted our way, but when it suddenly got quiet I looked up and followed Zef's gaze. Riker had just stepped out on the deck, Meena's hand in his. Zef's mother put down her plate, hurrying over to them. She hugged Riker and smiled at Meena as they were introduced.

I asked, "Did you know he'd be here?"

Zef shook his head. "I don't think he's been home since he got out of jail."

He watched Riker and Meena at the food table. She wore tight shorts and a red tank, her dark hair pulled up. "Wonder what she sees in my brother."

"Maybe it's that whole nice girl falling for a bad boy thing you hear about."

He frowned slightly. "She doesn't look that nice."

They made the rounds, Riker acting friendly to everybody he met. They ended up coming over to us. He ruffled his kid sister's hair and talked to Zef like a normal brother, not the same as the guy I'd met at Della Ray's.

He smiled at me. "Good to see you again, Coppertop."

Like I'd never heard that one before.

Riker and Meena ended up at a cedar picnic table halfway to the trampoline. I wanted to ask Zef why his brother seemed so different today, but with Kes near stayed quiet. Once we made our escape and were out in his truck, it was like he read my mind.

"Every so often, Riker pulls off being a nice guy." His voice didn't sound happy about it. "He controls his behavior and puts on a good show. But it usually only lasts long enough to get my mom and dad's hopes up."

"What happened to him?"

"Nothing happened." His tone went from unhappy to cross. "Everybody always thinks it's the parents' fault when a kid ends up being emotionally disturbed. But sometimes it's just a fluke, like maybe he got wired wrong. Doesn't matter how normal a family is, there's not much they can do to change a kid like that."

I laced my fingers together. "It couldn't have been fun growing up with him."

The crease between his eyebrows softened. He didn't say anything else as we drove back to the Chateau.

22
What I Heard

Zef gave me a tour of the upstairs, and I kept checking the blueprint photos on my phone. It wasn't as confusing, but when we headed to the dark hallway in the west wing, my steps slowed.

He looked back at me. "Don't worry, Dean's not going to jump out at you again. His truck is gone, and he wouldn't walk here all the way from his house."

I hadn't even thought of Dean. My eyes explored the hall, taking in the threadbare carpet runner and broken wall sconces clinging to peeling plaster. Before, it was filled with a heavy gloom so thick I could hardly see. Now, despite shadows at the far edges, it wasn't dark.

Zef moved cautiously. "We can't go far. Up ahead is where the roof caved in and collapsed two levels of the floor. Make sure you stay away from there."

"What's beneath it?"

We stopped at a closed door. "One of the underground storage areas."

"How come you didn't show me that when we were downstairs?"

"Because I don't go anywhere near that if I can avoid it. The way the floor is broken up, it's the worst of the hot spots."

He turned the knob and the hinges moved soundlessly, as if they'd been oiled. We stepped inside and it occurred to me that the floorboards in the Chateau never creaked.

"What's wrong with this place?" I whispered to myself.

My heartrate picked up, even though there was nothing unique about the room except for a marble fireplace with a cracked mirror above it. Heavy draperies coated in dust blocked out the light from the window, and it was gloomier than the other rooms we'd passed. In one corner was a pile of spindly wood from a piece of destroyed furniture. The walls next to it were stained with streaks of water damage.

Zef reached into his backpack and pulled out a stud finder. "While we're here, I want to check a couple of these walls."

I watched him for a while, then walked over to the fireplace. The marble mantle was chipped, and above it hung a mirror covered in dark spots, especially around the edges. A crack ran through the glass and up into the gilt frame, making a slight offset in my reflection. I rubbed a smudge from my chin then took a couple of steps back as my eyes refocused on the reflection behind me.

My head jerked and I bit down a gasp, unable to make sense of the elegant striped loveseats, ornate lamps, and porcelain vases. At the far end of the room, on the edge of a rich Persian carpet, sat a child's rocking horse.

I spun around, gaping at the dilapidated room where Zef used the stud finder, his back to me. Returning to the mirror, I expected to see the same bright images as before. Instead, all it revealed was the rundown reflection of where I stood.

Zef put the stud finder back in his bag. "Didn't think I'd actually find anything there, but it was worth checking."

He came over to me. "So, where do we look now?"

I swallowed, not wanting to tell him what I'd seen... not sure what that even was. "How should I know?"

"Maybe your dad showed you another secret trap. That's what we're trying to find, right?"

"I really don't know anything about the Chateau. You're the expert."

My voice had gotten sharp, but I couldn't help it. "Just because I found one trap doesn't prove anything."

Zef studied me. "Kenley, you all right?"

I didn't meet his gaze, wanting to distract him from observing me so closely. "What's under that pile of wood?"

"I'm not sure." He walked over to it, crouching down and tossing aside a few pieces.

I wiped sweaty palms on my shorts, hot despite how cool the air in the Chateau was. A noise from the hallway startled me and I went through the door, staring into the shadowy hallway and listening. My mind tried to piece together what I'd heard, to peg it as animal or human... and to decide if there'd actually been a noise at all.

The air seemed heavier with each step I took, weighing me down. It grew colder too, prickling against the flesh of my arms and legs as I moved along the murky passageway. The sound came again, this time sharper, and I recognized it: a crying child. A little kid was up here alone. This freaked me out and I rushed forward.

"Where are you?" I called, passing through darkness so deep it seemed to seep from the walls. The sobbing increased, filled with such terror that it struck me to the core and made my heart thump. All I could think about was finding that poor kid.

Several more steps and the floor unexpectedly slanted downward, the boards turning spongy beneath my feet. I could feel it giving way and cried out, arms flailing but touching only air. In that one dreadful moment I sensed myself dropping into a pit.

Hands grabbed my waist, jerking me back so hard we both fell. "What are you doing?" Zef said, his voice angry and scared at the same time. "Are you insane?"

I sat up, peering at him through the gloom and listening past the throbbing pulse in my ears. "There's a little kid out there. Didn't you hear the crying?"

He clicked on the flashlight mode of his phone, pointing it down at the floor—or what was left of it. I felt my stomach drop. Jagged boards beneath a frayed carpet runner hung in midair around a gaping hole. The darkness inside swallowed the small beam of light. Overhead, the ceiling also had a large hole where the attic floor above us had given way beneath the weight of the collapsed outer roof. A splintered beam covered in chunks of plaster stuck through the opening, looking as if it could break loose without notice.

Zef blew out an anxious breath. "There's no little kid up here, Kenley."

For the first time I noticed how close together we were on the floor, and how he still had a hand on my waist. In the dim backwash of light, his eyes looked worried.

My gaze returned to the hole that reminded me of an ugly mouth with jagged teeth, and I suppressed a shudder. "But I heard crying. I'm sure of it."

I squinted at the passage on the opposite side until my eyes adjusted, finally able to see that it came to an abrupt end. I called out, listening for a child's voice but answered by silence.

He helped me up. "I only heard you shouting, that's all. Nobody crying."

"Which means what? That I imagined it?"

He guided me away like he still felt nervous we might fall. "I don't know."

"A hallucination? But you said the gas doesn't reach the second floor."

"Maybe I was wrong. It's not like I know everything about this place." He glanced back. "Or maybe there's a cat up in the attic. I've heard they can make crying sounds."

I stopped myself from saying how dumb that idea was. We walked back down the hall to where light seeped in through open doors, and I tried to shake off the anxious feeling. I couldn't. It didn't matter that what I'd heard wasn't real, because I could still feel the grief of those sobs reverberating inside my own chest.

Zef distracted me by holding up a filthy notebook with warped pages. "Look what I found under that pile of wood."

I took it from him and studied the water-damaged suede cover before opening it. Blocky writing was scattered throughout the pages, much of it faded to weepy smudges of ink that were no longer readable. However, much of it was still legible, and as I studied the familiar printing my heart started beating even faster.

Finally I said, "This is my dad's handwriting."

23
Settling In

"Are you sure that notebook belonged to your dad?" Zef asked for the third time as we drove along the rough dirt road leading from the Chateau back towards town.

I just looked at him.

He shrugged. "Okay."

"But it makes no sense for it to be stashed under those pieces of broken furniture, does it?" I flipped another page, making out some words that blurred away into nothingness, a frustrating puzzle that might be impossible to decipher.

Zef drove the pickup onto an asphalt road that was a lot less bumpy.

"The Chateau sometimes makes people do stuff that's not rational."

A small tingle crept up my neck but I ignored it. "At least this notebook is proof that my dad did explore the Chateau."

The sun hung low on the horizon when we pulled up in front of the dairy. We exchanged phone numbers and he said, "I'm working tomorrow and mowing our lawn Thursday morning, so I can't make it to the Chateau until Thursday afternoon. You want to meet then?"

"Sure. Text when you're ready, and I'll see you there."

After checking in with G'ma, I shut the door of the sewing room and sat on the bed, eager for a closer look at the notebook. I began at the front, studying the warped pages that had yellowed around the edges.

Soon I began to see that the words on the first pages had the most water damage, the ink blurred and unreadable. It left me with the same sense of disappointment as when I got back the developed film and there were no pictures of my father. But then I turned another page and there was only a little damage, the ink clear enough to read:

> *Eye of a needle,*
> *Noose made of thread,*
> *Stitch the lips closed,*
> *Bind up the head.*
> *Open the graves*
> *And welcome the dead.*

> *The Ghost Child*
> *Act II, Scene I*

Heart beating faster, I scooted to the edge of the bed. These were additional notes for the play my father had started writing! Reading the words over again, my fingers gripped the notebook. The rhyme brought to mind my own experience in the Chateau's kitchen when I'd heard a haunting child's voice:

One o'clock, two o'clock, three o'clock, four. Whatever you do, don't open this door.

What had my father seen at the Chateau, and what had inspired him to start writing this play? I wondered if he had learned about the Broderick family's tragic history and how three of them had died, including the little boy.

I turned another page, seeing notes that were probably from the early phase of his creative process. And then there were more verses written for *The Ghost Child*, each darker than the last.

A knock at the door made me jump, though it was only G'ma telling me goodnight. I echoed it back to her, though sleeping was the last thing on my mind as I turned more pages. The writing and verses grew difficult to read where the watery ink had faded to nothing. I grabbed a pencil and tried to scribble in what was missing, guessing at words. It became an intriguing puzzle. After several successes, I couldn't stop. I went through more pages, memorizing parts, until sometime around midnight my vision grew too blurry to keep going. Finally, I closed the notebook and slipped it inside my art bag.

Under the covers, my mind drifted to the edge of sleep, thoughts still lingering on my father. A scene slowly emerged, like half a daydream, both dark and hazy. I could see the outline of him kneeling by the pile of splintered wood. "It's not safe," he whispered, shoving the notebook beneath the broken pieces and glancing back at me. "Maybe they won't find it here."

I opened my eyes, studying the shadows in the room that seemed to drift closer. Had I been with him twelve years ago when he'd stuck the notebook there? It was hard to know. I repeated his words in my mind, wondering what he'd meant. Was there real danger in the Chateau, or were the fumes just getting to him and he didn't know it?

My own gas-induced delusions seemed very real, so his might have too. I wished he was still in my life and that I could ask him questions, but this line of thinking only caused a familiar creeping sadness to come over me.

The next morning, after I showered and scrounged breakfast, Grandma called me to my Uncle Josh's old room on the ground floor. "Time to get you moved in here," was all she said.

The only things left were a dresser and a desk with a chair, none of the pieces in the greatest shape. The walls were painted a typical shade of *I'm-a-guy* blue. Not my favorite. Taking down the stiff plaid curtains was number one on my list.

I told myself to look at the room with the optimistic view I'd learned from Jules whenever we moved into a new dump. Okay... so the closet would give me more room for my things. I'd even be able to bring in most of my clothes that were still stored in boxes. Best of all, I wouldn't be living over the kitchen, which meant I could sleep in. At least until school started.

My grandma and I agreed it was easier to bring in my own bed from the storage shed than haul down the one from upstairs. I was happy to see the aqua headboard I painted six months ago, though it didn't look that great against the boring blue wall, especially with my purple floral bedspread and the pink memory quilt.

Using a utility wagon, I hauled all sorts of stuff in from the shed, losing myself in arranging furniture. I also found my old poster of the Degas painting, *Dancers at the Barre*, and put it above the bed to cover all the nail holes where Josh's 4-H ribbons had hung. The color of the ballerinas' skirts matched the headboard, almost like it had been planned.

After lunch, my grandma came in with a stack of fabrics, letting me pick which one I wanted for the new curtains. I decided on a bold paisley with aqua and purple, kind of ugly by itself but it would pull in the colors from my bed. I finished putting everything in place, including plugging in the fake Tiffany lamp bought at a garage sale. Grandma came back with the finished curtains and tie-backs. It had taken her less than an hour to sew them.

When they were hung, we stood in the doorway and looked around. "What do you think?" she asked.

"It's definitely eclectic. At least that's what my mom would say."

She glanced at me with uncertainty. "What's that mean?"

I tried to remember how Jules explained it. "Um... kind of like when everything clashes, but in a good way."

Her mouth slipped into the slight frown she often wore. "I guess it does clash."

I folded my arms, studying the room with a critical eye. "But the curtains you made tie it all together. It works."

A bit of relief touched her face, making me realize how

hard she was trying. My grandma wasn't anything like Jules. Mostly, her life was a spin cycle of cooking and cleaning, with a little bit of sewing thrown in. It didn't slow down and it hardly ever changed, and maybe she was just doing the best she could.

On impulse, I gave her a hug. She wasn't the hugging kind of grandparent and it took a second for her to squeeze back.

"Thanks Grandma."

She patted my arm. "I'm glad you like it."

I stepped back, feeling a little awkward and a little good about the whole hug thing.

She smoothed her apron. "I'd better go check the roast."

Alone in my new room, I sat down on the chair that had a wobbly leg and rearranged the stuff on the desk. I'd meant it when I told my grandma that the room turned out good, and in a lot of ways it was a relief to finally have my own space again.

What I hadn't said—what I didn't want to admit even to myself—was how dejected it also made me feel. Because more than anything else, this room exuded permanence. It sent out a silent welcome beacon saying I could be here a long time. And that was the last thing I wanted.

24
Night-capade

During the following week, Zef and I were only able to meet at the Chateau twice. In part, this was because my grandpa was hanging around the house more. In a freak cow-related accident, his foot had gotten stomped on by a hoof. My uncles took over his work at the dairy while he healed, and with nothing much to do, he seemed to have set a goal of giving me more chores. One morning I slipped out the front door, hoping to meet up with Zef, and saw him sitting on the porch reading the *Tristate Livestock News*. He sent me right back inside to help my grandma can apricots. Two days later he made me help her can green beans.

I asked Grandma why she called it *canning* instead of *jarring*, since everything was in glass Mason jars. She didn't understand the joke and looked confused. After that I gave up teasing her and wondered if Jules might have been left on their doorstep and nobody told us.

The two times Zef and I made it to the Chateau, we didn't have success. The only good thing was that I started getting more familiar with the floorplan because of the blueprint pics on my phone.

The following week we met on a Monday afternoon, and Zef insisted we explore the secret passageway I'd discovered. I didn't want to and pointed out that it wasn't like anything Arietta described in her letter.

"But there might be another doorway hidden in the wall somewhere," he said. "Last time we hurried through so fast, neither of us would have noticed."

He argued with me for a while until I saw how stubborn he could be and gave in. This time, when we climbed down the narrow staircase, we wore our facemasks. Though it was still dank and creepy inside, at least I didn't hallucinate about rats or other unpleasant stuff. Zef brought a strong flashlight too, stopping to check the walls all along the way.

We found nothing, and by the time we made it to the wine cellar I was grumpy and ready for sunlight. He'd packed a picnic lunch and we ate beneath the willow by the pond. I leaned my back against the trunk, studying the water lilies and sensing how Zef was more discouraged than he let on. I knew how he felt.

That evening, after helping with the dinner dishes and watching TV for a while, I went to my room and shut the door. I sat on the desk chair with the wonky leg and stared at the Degas poster, a growing sense of hollowness emptying me. In the beginning, my experiences at the Chateau had given me a dreamlike sense of enchantment. I remembered the illusion of the ballroom, concocted from early childhood memories and creating a fantasy that felt otherworldly. But maybe there wasn't a secret room at all, and no paintings or other valuable stuff. For a few minutes it just seemed like a big prank, with me and Zef too dense to get it.

I grabbed my art bag, ready to do some sketching, but instead pulled out my father's notebook. With all the chores and everything else, I hadn't gotten back to it. I looked through more pages, saddened that so much of his writing had been lost by water damage, and again wondered why he had left it under that pile of wood.

After a dozen blank pages, more writing appeared with a new heading: *Chateau Descriptions*. These were easier to read, probably because they were closer to the center of the notebook and had less damage. My dad wrote about the different rooms and hallways, his crisp details letting me see it all clearly in my mind. At first it was interesting, but the paragraphs went on for pages, some of them with distorted water spots. I began skimming.

How many times had he explored the Chateau, and how much had he simply written from memory? I started to close the notebook when a piece of writing at the bottom of a page caught my attention.

> An interesting find was beneath the shelves of an open closet in a small service room. I discovered it when my flashlight crossed something familiar...

I turned the page, disappointed the next sentences were too faded to read, though the words beneath them were still clear.

> ...a secret trap, like the kind master architects built into old theaters. An amazing discovery! It took some effort to turn the lever inside, which made a terrible noise, but then I heard clicking and the shelves swung inward. It was a secret door leading down to a narrow tunnel.

The words blurred, but not because of water damage. Instead, it was as if a dim glaze slid across my eyes, and for the briefest moment I seemed to be standing beside him.

"What is that, Daddy?"

"A secret passage through the castle, I think."

I shrank back against his side, and he rested a hand on my head, heavy but comforting. "Don't worry, princess. We'll stay up here where it's safer." His voice turned even more uncertain. "Besides, I think I heard rats down there."

The dimness vanished, the desk lamp suddenly too bright as I rocked back in the chair, nearly tipping over. Grabbing the desk, I steadied myself.

A knock was followed by Grandma opening the door

to check in—her nightly ritual. I stood and picked up a pair of pajamas draped across the nearby hamper, an unspoken lie of getting ready for bed. She reminded me I'd promised to help her and my Aunt Mae tie baby quilts for soon-to-be Josh Junior, and I nodded. We both said goodnight, and I listened to the heavy thunk of my grandpa's feet going upstairs.

I sank down on the chair and read my father's words again, hoping that the long-ago memory might resurface. It didn't, and yet I knew it had really happened; a small, forgotten episode in the life of a four-year-old. Long ago, my father had shown me the hidden trap, and though I may have temporarily forgotten about it, that experience was the reason I knew where to find it.

My arms and hands felt tingly and I flexed my fingers, returning to the notebook. I used a small sticky note to mark that page and then moved on, reading more sentences and working hard to make out each word. I penciled in possible missing phrases and also added question marks, thinking he wouldn't have minded. On the last page of descriptions, he'd written something else that seemed important:

> There's a place where the hallways merge and then become a maze. Dust and cobwebs cover everything, and wallpaper peels away in cracked little rolls. A short flight of steps make a sharp corner before ending at a closed door. Beyond the door, a spiral staircase circles skyward into darkness.

I paused, trying to think where that might be while at the same time feeling certain Zef had never shown it to me. Several following sentences were stained and mostly unreadable, though I was able to make out some of the words: rusted hinges... broken... steps... lure... bannister... olden or wooden. And then, despite the bleeding ink, the last sentence was legible: Those circling stairs beckon to be explored.

I pulled up the blueprints on my phone and searched for the circular staircase. It was difficult to examine all the details on such a small screen, constantly zooming in and out. My father had written that the door to the spiral staircase was where hallways became a maze, yet scrolling across the vast floorplan, it seemed that could be a lot of places.

Finally I called Zef, crossing my fingers it didn't go to voicemail. When he answered I blurted, "I've found something."

"You did?"

I thought about reading aloud the passages from my father's notebook, but decided I wanted to show them to him. Checking the clock on my nightstand, and seeing it was almost ten, I lowered my voice. "Can you meet me? At the far edge of the dairy fence?"

"Sure."

In the kitchen, I opened the refrigerator to have enough light to get a flashlight from the junk drawer. Ready to leave the house, the front door squeaked, something I hadn't noticed before but which sounded too loud in the nighttime quiet. My eyes went to the stairs, expecting my grandparents' door to open. More seconds ticked by, then I slipped outside.

The air held the muggy remnants of a hot day. I hurried down the driveway where floodlights cast everything in sharp relief. Out on the road, a burst of triumph filled me for sneaking off undetected, my heart beating faster as I jogged the familiar road. Crickets and frogs along the irrigation canals took over the night, underscoring my running with a discordant soundtrack.

In spite of the darkness, a half-moon lit my way without the flashlight. I reached the far fence, but Zef wasn't there yet. A humid breeze picked up, stirring green cornstalks to make shushing whispers as cows mooed their mournful harmony.

Several minutes ticked by until I heard Zef's footsteps and he emerged from the shadows, his features etched in grayscale. A slight smile tugged at a corner of his otherwise serious mouth, and for some reason it drew me in. Being alone with him in the faint moonlight, after escaping the stuffy house, sent a pleasurable shiver through me.

Zef glanced over my head. "There are lights on in an upstairs room of your uncle's house. Let's walk further down the road."

He held out his hand and I slid mine in, fully aware of how strong his encircling fingers felt. Even though he acted casual, like he wanted to make sure I didn't stumble in the dark, I couldn't ignore the comfort of it. Maybe it was better than holding hands had ever been for me, though the weeks of lonely isolation at the dairy might have only colored it that way.

"You found something in your dad's notebook?"

I nodded, telling him about the description of the secret trap, and how I felt sure I'd been with him all those years ago.

Zef let my hand slip away. "Did you bring it?"

I got it from my art bag and handed it to him, clicking on the flashlight to illuminate the page. After Zef finished reading, I flipped forward to the final description about the spiral staircase. "But this is what I really want to show you."

He read it, then slowly closed the notebook as I added, "If there's a place like that in the Chateau, I don't remember seeing it."

Zef's face turned a little away like he suddenly found the pasture of cows interesting. Not exactly the reaction I'd expected. I clicked off the flashlight and slid it in my art bag. "What's wrong?"

"Yesterday, my dad ran into Dean's mother, and I'm

not sure what she said. But it was enough to make him have a face-to-face with me. He asked if I've been going to the Chateau."

"What did you say?"

"I lied." Zef kicked a rock with the toe of his shoe then let out a slow breath. "And it stank. But with my mom listening in, no way I could tell the truth because she'd get too upset. Which is why I've been thinking that maybe it's time to give this up."

I took the notebook from him. "But we finally have a clue. An important one!"

"Shh." He looked back at the windows of my uncle's house, lowering his voice. Then he turned in that direction and started walking. "Come on, let's get you home."

I stared at his retreating shoulders, finally going after him and grabbing his arm. "Will you stop for a minute?"

Zef turned to look at me and I added, "If we find the Hidden Room, then that money will help your mom."

He folded his arms. "Don't use that against me."

"I'm not against you."

His familiar guarded mask slid into place. I ignored it. "At least tell me one thing. Is that spiral staircase real or not?"

He shoved his hand in a pocket, the same hand that had held mine. "Yes, it's on the blueprints, though the label is missing."

"You've seen it, then?" My voice grew breathy.

He nodded.

Instinctively I knew the staircase was important, so why didn't Zef get it? "We've finally got a breakthrough. We can't stop now."

"It's not a breakthrough!"

This time, he was the one who spoke too loud, as if he'd forgotten my uncle's window.

A pulse beat in my throat and I squeezed the notebook in my fingers before shoving it in my art bag. "Whatever you say."

But Zef didn't say anything else, just stood there. A determined flush spread through me and I took off, marching away from the dairy. In the dark it would be hard to find the small path leading to the Chateau, but I ignored that fact. I didn't get far before he caught up with me.

"Where are you going?"

I increased my pace, refusing to answer, but he easily matched my stride.

"The Chateau? At night?" His tone said this was about the dumbest thing I could do. "I'm not letting you go there, Kenley."

I started running, sprinting away until his hand grabbed mine, jerking me to a halt. The fingers that felt so comforting not long ago now held on with an iron grip.

"Let go."

He didn't.

Heat rose up in me, my words reflecting it. "You think you can stop me?"

"Don't be mad."

I tried to jerk free.

"Please," he added, finally unwrapping his fingers and releasing mine.

Now it was my turn to fold my arms, keeping a barrier between us. "So what if I want to look for that spiral staircase? What's the big deal?"

A sour laugh escaped him. "That's the thing, Kenley. There's no big deal. Not at all. Do you remember Arietta's letter? She didn't describe anything like your staircase, did she?"

I hadn't thought of that. He lowered his chin, and at that angle moonlight beveled the edges of his features and gave him midnight eyes. "If Arietta's father had taken her up those spiral stairs, she would have described them in her letter, right? And she would've explained how they led to the attic."

"The attic?"

"Yeah. So even though your dad wrote about it in his notebook, it doesn't mean anything. At least not to me, because that's not where we'll find the Hidden Room."

We stood facing each other, him with his mouth set in a grim line and me trying to hold back all the upset words tumbling inside my head, until I blurted out the stupidest ones of all. "Sorry to waste your time."

I stalked off, back towards the dairy, humiliation in my steps. I wished I had never called him to meet me. From behind came the crunch of his boots on the road as he followed.

"What, you think I need an escort?" I threw over my shoulder.

I sprinted away, racing past fences as my feet pounded out a regretful rhythm. I didn't look back until reaching the *Strickland Ranch* arch. When I did, Zef was gone.

KATE KAE MYERS

25
Batter Up

The third time that I stuck myself with the needle, it left a drop of blood on the baby quilt. Grandma jumped into action, blotting up the stain with a tissue. The silent expression in her and Aunt Mae's eyes said that when it came to hand quilting I was hopeless, but since the Strickland women hardly ever said what they were thinking, she asked me to empty the dishwasher.

After lunch, I slipped out the front door before either of my grandparents could find more chores for me to do. Reaching the road, I let out a sigh that felt like freedom, just happy to be alone with my thoughts. Since last night, I hadn't been able to stop thinking about my dad's notes, or my argument with Zef. I wasn't able to forget the feel of his hand holding mine, either. But he hadn't called or texted, so maybe he was serious about not continuing our search of the Chateau.

I headed past his house and forced myself to avoid looking at the windows. A bunch of unhappy emotions propelled me forward until I took off at an easy lope, jogging down the road and eventually passing the narrow path that I usually took to reach the Chateau. I cut between the green cornfields and crossed the canal, then followed the trail that led into the wooded hill. I raced up it until my heart pounded in a way that felt good. Wandering beneath the trees still heavy with summer leaves, a calmness settled on me. I breathed in the forest scent and listened to birds.

Last night in my room, when I couldn't sleep, I spent a lot of time going over the blueprint pictures and looking for the staircase to the attic. Finally, after midnight, I gave up. Although there had to be a fourth blueprint page that showed the layout of the attic, either Zef didn't own it or hadn't brought it with him that day at the pond. It made me wonder what else he might be keeping from me, and that's when I came to a decision. The only option left was to search the Chateau by myself.

I picked up the pace again, jumping over the stream and moving quickly along the path, out of breath by the time I reached the ledge that overlooked the Chateau. Another ten minutes and I'd made it down to the bottom of the hill, just passing the gardener's shed when Jules called. I stopped to answer. Hearing her voice didn't cause as much loss and longing as usual, and the sad thought came to me that maybe I was already getting used to Uncle Josh's old room.

Next to the shed was a warped wooden bench and I sat down, relaxing as Jules asked what was new. I told her about stabbing my fingers with the needle and bleeding on the baby quilt. Sewing machines, I explained, were one thing; trying to weave a needle through fabric, another.

A smile entered her voice and we talked for a while. Jules shared stories about the play practices, costumes, and members of the cast, while I made vague comments. The whole time my eyes focused on the row of small, jutting attic windows in the Chateau's blue roof. For a minute I battled an impulse to ignore how she might get mad at me for coming here, and just tell about my childhood memory of my dad showing me the hidden theater trap that led to a secret passageway. With Zef being so difficult, I was now alone in this. I looked down at my hand, fisted on my thigh.

"Kenley?"

Jules saying my name brought me back. I realized neither of us had been talking. She seemed to sense something was wrong, but I told her my battery might be giving it up and asked if we could chat later. We disconnected and I stared at my phone, wondering when lying had gotten so easy.

Winding my way carefully among the thorny rose bushes, my steps picked up an accusing rhythm: *secrets and lies... secrets and lies...*

The French doors to the ballroom opened and I stepped inside. Zef usually kept them locked. Maybe he didn't care now, knowing it would be only another two weeks before the Chateau was brought down.

I went into the hallway, passing the library, the sitting room, and then the gallery with its ghostly outlines of lost paintings. Crossing the grand foyer, I headed up the wide staircase. I took a little time to study the beautiful filigree of the wrought-iron bannister, the marble steps and carved molding that whispered of a long-ago era. Soon it would all be crushed beneath the falling rubble of imploded walls, and I imagined sorrow emanating from the Chateau as if it somehow knew there was very little time left.

Upstairs, I spent nearly an hour searching, turning corners and going down hallways as I tried to match them to my dad's description of a door that opened to a spiral staircase. Despite checking the blueprint pics multiple times, and making mental notes of where I'd been, nothing came of my exploration. I even went as far as the dark hallway with the gaping hole in the floor, careful not to get too close. I paused to listen, fearful of hearing the sobbing like last time. The seconds ticked by but my ears picked up only silence.

I went to the room with the pile of wood where Zef had found my father's notebook. The heavy drapes were still drawn, keeping the area dim. At the fireplace, I stared into the mirror for several minutes, hardly blinking as I waited to see if the beautifully furnished room might appear again. It didn't.

I put my hands on the mantle and leaned in a little. With a discouraged sigh I closed my eyes, letting my thoughts wander until sensing a presence behind me. Not frightening, but instead calming. One of his hands covered mine.

"Why did you forget me?" my father asked.

I opened my eyes, expecting him to disappear. Instead, I saw the ghostly outline of his hand on mine and his reflection behind me—the man from the ballroom. This time, he didn't wear a mask, allowing me to see the sadness that etched his features.

"Why did you die?" I whispered, an ache swelling in my throat until it was hard to breathe.

My eyes opened, this time for real. I was alone.

Back at the main staircase, I sat down on the third step from the top. For the first time I gave serious thought to Jules warning about my coming here.

I checked my phone for texts, just in case I hadn't heard one come in. Finally I admitted that being here without Zef was not fun. Somehow, through all the sparing and teasing, I'd gotten to know a boy who was much different than I'd first thought.

Resting my elbows on the top step behind me, I leaned back and stretched. Maybe Zef was right that our search had met a dead end. If that was true, then why did it matter to him if I wanted to see the attic?

He'd once told me nothing was up there but some junk. I thought about the disappointing blueprints that didn't show enough, a new question surfacing. If a bunch of stuff was still stored there, who had carted it up in the first place? Probably not the family. Instead, servants would be the ones to climb those stairs.

I sat up, realizing I might have been looking for the staircase in the wrong place by staying on the second floor. Maybe I needed to start at the ground level service area where the staff worked. I stood, hurrying down the steps and through the formal dining room, taking the hallway that led to the kitchen. Blinking at the light coming in through greasy transom windows, I turned away and pulled up the blueprints to make sense of the service hallways.

Excited by this new idea, it took a couple of seconds to register the slight scuff of a shoe. I spun around, startled by a movement in the shadows as a guy stepped out.

"Hey, Coppertop." Riker wore a lopsided smile as he toasted me with a brown bottle.

I put on a fake smile and glanced at the worktable that stood between us with its cracked tile top. "What's up?"

He shrugged. "Just having a look around. Where's Zef?"

"Upstairs." I knew that telling him I was here alone wasn't a smart move.

"Is he," Riker said. Not a question, instead a statement saying he knew I was lying. Maybe I hadn't gotten that good at twisting the truth after all.

"So how serious are you and my little bro?"

"We're friends."

He laughed a little, like this was a lame answer. "Hope he knows that."

I glanced at the door leading out of the kitchen as he said, "I used to come here all the time when I was his age. Probably know this place just as well as he does."

This caught my attention, and I wondered if he was searching for the lost room too. I said, "Looks to me like you still come here a lot."

Riker shrugged. "Not as much as I used to. When I was still in high school, we had contests to see who could handle the fumes the longest. I hold the record."

"Really? How long?"

"Seven hours, forty minutes. Spent the night in the ballroom."

"Impressive." I meant it.

He smiled in a thoughtful way, and for the first time I noticed a slight resemblance between him and Zef. But when his eyes bored a little deeper into me, something changed. He took another drink then offered me the bottle. "You thirsty?"

I shook my head, my mouth dry but not because of what he offered. Instinct said I needed to leave, my eyes again flicking to the door leading outside but catching a glimpse of movement through the small panes. It jerked opened and a big guy stepped through. Dean's black T-shirt was tucked into jeans in a way that emphasized the roll of flab above his waist. The skull on his shirt was like a hundred others, never scary until now. He shut the door with a firm thud.

My heart started beating fast, as if it knew something I didn't. When Dean came closer, I bolted around Riker and sprinted for the door. My outstretched fingers brushed the knob just as Dean grabbed my arm, dragging me back. He towered over me, but I stomped on his foot. All he did was reach for my other arm and give me a shake that jolted my neck.

"You been helping Zef look for the lost money. What've you found?"

"Nothing!" I tried to ignore the unpleasant body odor and the way his dirty fingernails dug into my skin. "Let go."

"He will," Riker said, thoughtfully tapping the bottom of the bottle on the tile table. "Just tell us what Zef's been up to."

There was movement at the hallway entrance and Zef strode forward. "Why don't you ask him yourself?"

He held a metal baseball bat, and in one swift move swung it overhead and slammed it down on the worktable. A loud crack rang through the kitchen, pieces of tile flying in all directions. Both guys stepped back, and Dean's grip loosened enough for me to pull free. I moved to a safer distance.

"Hey," Riker said. "That's my bat."

"Want it?" Zef raised it to his shoulder and took the stance of a hitter. "Come get it. I'll keep my eye on the ball, just like you taught me. Except this time, your head's the target."

Riker leaned away, eyebrows jutting up. "What the hell's gotten into you?"

Nobody said anything until Riker suddenly laughed, like the whole thing was funny. "Take it easy, bro. We're only here to talk."

Zef didn't relax his hold on the bat but he did let it rest on his shoulder. "Okay. About what, exactly?"

"Grandpa."

The brothers stared each other down until Riker added, "Never told you I went to visit him at the care center, or how he gave me all the details of his searching this place. And about his telling you where to find the Chateau blueprints."

Zef's eyes grew uncertain. "When was that?"

"Couple of weeks before he died. He got real concerned and kept telling me not to give up. Said there really is a secret treasure room hidden here somewhere. Course that was always the story, right? It even got handed down to Dean's family."

Dean nodded, and Zef's fingers resumed their tense grip on the bat as he gazed at his brother. "You never spent time with Grandpa, so why'd he tell you anything?"

Riker shrugged. "Probably thought I was you."

He rolled the beer bottle back and forth between his hands. "He was basically out of it by then. Fact is, at first I thought he was just rambling on about that stupid old legend nobody believed. But the way you keep sneaking off to this place all the time, and even dropped out of football, got me and Dean thinking. Maybe his story is true. And now you're bringing your new little girlfriend here to help. So we came to make you an offer."

Zef blew out a disgusted snort. "Let me guess. We do the work, but you want a share."

Riker glanced at Dean. "See? Told you he'd get it."

"And what do you bring to the table?" Zef asked.

Dean grinned, folding his thick arms. "We let you keep looking."

Zef slowly shook his head. "I've got a better idea. How about I press charges against you two for what you did to my truck? Let you stay in jail until they blow up this place."

It was like a storm cloud crossed Riker's face. He threw the beer, and Zef slammed the bottle with the bat. It flew at Riker who ducked, and it crashed into a cupboard behind his head. Pieces of glass clattered to the floor and foam hit the counters. Riker swore and stood up from his half-crouch.

"You've changed, Zef." Riker pointed a finger at me. "And I blame the new girlfriend. Both times you've lost it, she's been with you."

Zef laughed, a scornful sound as he lowered the bat and started to move. "Yeah, Riker. Always gotta blame someone else. It could never be you, right?"

He kept his eyes on his scowling brother but walked in my direction. "Kenley, open the door."

Dean blocked me. "She's not going anywhere. Neither are you. You're damn well gonna…"

Zef rammed the end of the bat in Dean's stomach, who let out a woof that sounded almost comical. He folded in half, mouth opening and closing as he fought for air. Zef gave my shoulder a shove, speaking between gritted teeth. "Open the door."

I raced to it, pulling on the knob. It stuck and I yanked harder until it gave way. Not looking back, I hurried through, ready to head for the side gate. Zef followed, raising his voice. "Go to the front. It's open."

We took off running but hadn't made it far when Dean stumbled outside. "I'm digging your grave, Zef!" he shouted, his furious voice following us around the side of the house. "Digging your grave!"

26
Mad at the World

Zef drove too fast, his tires spitting gravel as we left the lane for the main road. His fingers gripped the steering wheel, jaw clenched.

Rubbing my arms that hurt from Dean's grasp, I looked back through the pickup's rear window at Riker's red car. "Think they'll follow us?"

Zef turned on me, nostrils flaring. "What were you doing inside the Chateau by yourself? You have a death wish or something?"

One hand let go of the steering wheel long enough for him to jab a finger at me. "That was stupid, Kenley."

Leaning away from him, I could feel a flush creep up my cheeks.

"I thought we had a deal," he continued, his tone lower but still heated. "We were searching the Chateau together, remember?"

It took a moment to find my voice. "What I remember is that last night you were giving up."

"That's not enough of an excuse."

"Know what? I've had it with you and your brother."

His eyes narrowed. "Don't lump us together."

I leaned against the seat, silently admitting that hadn't been fair but still annoyed enough I couldn't take it back. We rounded a bend where a huge combine harvester chugged along, forcing him to slow.

I brushed the hair off my face. "Did you ever think that maybe I'm sick of doing everything on your terms? You asked for my help, but when I find something that seems important, you're not willing to even check it out."

Zef took his usual line of defense: not answering. But I

didn't need his words to tell what he thought of me as he glowered at the slow moving tractor like he wanted to blow it up.

"Pull over," I said.

He didn't stop so I opened the door, which made him slam on the brakes. "Are you nuts?"

I climbed out and he leaned sideways, gaping at me. "What are you doing?"

"Dissolving our partnership."

I slammed the door and took off running. My legs felt shaky, arms starting to throb as they again reminded me of how helpless I'd been in Dean's grasp. Why had Zef blamed *me* for what happened? I couldn't help it if he was related to a couple of gorillas, or that I'd ended up in their path. Simmering emotions spilled over, my vision blurring. I blinked hard. He didn't deserve my tears. None of them did!

The sun beat down on my head, lungs burning by the time I slowed. Finally able to rein in my feelings, I thought of the way Zef used Riker's bat to help me escape. Of course none of that mattered now. Whatever Zef and I once had—a partnership or friendship—I'd just ended it.

The walk back to the dairy took a lot longer than I thought it would, my legs tired by the time I finally passed under the arch. Entering the house I was met with cold air conditioning, enjoying it for about three seconds until I heard upset voices coming from the kitchen. My grandparents were arguing, which didn't bother me until my name came up.

"That girl is just like her mother," my grandpa said, his voice gruff.

I silently mouthed, *"Thank you."* It was a million times better to be like Jules than him! Grandma, however, didn't deny it.

I braced myself as he started to unload. "Kenley's irresponsible. Taking off at all hours without telling you.

Where's she going, anyway?"

"She likes to walk," Grandma said. "You can't expect a girl like that to stay in the house all day."

"Have you thought about how she might be going *there*?"

My grandmother sighed, answering so softly I could hardly hear her. "Of course I have, but what is it you think we should do? If Kenley is like Julie the way you keep saying, then warning her off will only make her go looking."

I barely had time to wonder if they were talking about the Chateau when Grandma added, "Besides, she's spending most of her time with Zef now."

He let out a snort. "That won't last. She'll dump him, just the way Julie dumped every decent boy who ever fell for her."

I shoved my fists against my sides. How could he say that? Jutting my chin out, I squashed the recent memory of slamming the door of Zef's truck.

"And another thing," my grandpa said. "She's lazy. I've watched her. Kenley doesn't do one thing around here without being asked. You can't get her to pull a weed for nothin'."

"She's young, Joe. You don't understand how hard it is for her. She's never had a stable life. Didn't even get a chance to know her father."

As angry as I felt at my hypercritical, downright mean grandpa, I experienced some major softening towards Grandma.

"Would that've made a difference?" He sounded even more exasperated. "Her father never held down a real job. Spent all his time writing in those notebooks of his, even when he was staying here. And look at the trouble that got him into."

I took a couple of steps forward, ready to shout all the hateful stuff building inside, but Grandma's angry voice intervened. "Joe Strickland, you listen to me. You are being unfair! And unkind. I don't want you driving Kenley away like what happened with Julie."

This shut him up. It grew quiet, the hum of the air conditioner filling the silence. I swallowed, uncurling my clenched fingers that had started to hurt. Right then, I hated him so much.

Chair legs scraped across the kitchen floor. "Nobody drove her away, June. Our daughter left all on her own." His voice turned husky. "That girl broke your heart, running away in the middle of the night. Leaving a blasted note but not even bothering to say goodbye."

"Don't, Joe..."

"Neither of us hearing a word from her for over three months, not knowing if she was safe or even alive, until she sent a postcard from New York. Like what we'd been through was nothing! And you crying all the time but trying to hide it, thinking I didn't see."

More silence. I shivered a little, cooled off too much now by the icy air conditioning, even though my face was still warm.

"You want to live through that kind of thing again?" he said. "Because I sure as hell don't."

Without warning, my grandpa limped into the living room, stopping when he saw me. I spun around, going into the bedroom and shutting the door.

For a full minute I stared out the window, not seeing what lay beyond the paisley curtains. Finally I went to my bed and flopped down, facing the wall. There was tapping on the door but I didn't answer. Maybe if I'd shouted "go away" my grandma wouldn't have come in, but I didn't have that in me. In fact, I felt a little sick inside, an ache welling from something I'd learned but didn't want to know.

Grandma came in and sat down, the mattress dipping under her weight. She didn't say anything, just patted my arm in that funny way of hers.

"Grandpa hates me," I finally said. My voice sounded teary, which really annoyed me because I wasn't crying.

"You're being dramatic."

Runs in my family. "Fine," I said, when nothing was fine at all. "He doesn't *like* me."

"He doesn't know you."

"Whose fault is that?" I shot back.

His. Definitely. And maybe Jules. But certainly not mine. So why was I the one getting the fallout from their messed up disaster?

A big sigh escaped her, like she carried a heavy weight she couldn't put down. "He's not mad at you, Kenley. Your Grandpa Joe has some hurts he can't let go of, that's all."

I really did not want to hear her excuses for him. "Grandma, can we please not talk about this right now?" *Or ever.*

As if respecting my wishes, she gave me one more pat on the shoulder. I felt her weight ease off the mattress and listened as the door clicked shut.

27
Apology

I didn't go to the kitchen for dinner. In fact, I seriously considered staying in my uncle's old room—*not my room!*—and only sneaking out at night to search for food.

Beyond the window, the setting sun put on a gaudy display as if it didn't know the colors were wasted on unappreciative cows. My phone rang and I thought of Jules, dreading talking to her right now. But then I realized the ringtone was one I'd assigned Zef. I picked up my phone with no intention of answering until it just happened.

His opening line caught me off guard. "I'm a jerk."

I took a breath and let it slowly out. "Only some of the time."

Both of us stayed quiet, and for once I didn't try to fill the silence, deciding he needed to be the next one to talk.

"I almost didn't go inside the Chateau," he finally said. "When I got there, I saw Riker's car and how he'd cut the chain on the gate to pieces so it couldn't be used again. I thought it wasn't worth butting heads with him and put my truck in reverse, but at the last minute noticed his bat propped up in the back seat. I decided to take it, planning to just see what they were doing."

He stopped talking, letting me come up with the rest. "You didn't know I was there until you got to the kitchen."

"No." It sounded like he moved his phone to the other side. "And then I saw Dean holding on to you and wondered if I had any chance of getting you out. He might look like a stupid ox, but he's fast and dangerous. In high school, he got kicked off the wrestling team for putting another kid in the hospital. And Riker... well, no need to explain how he can get. Sometimes he seems okay, but I know how his switch can flip. And it's always worse when those two are together. It becomes a cock fight. Act weak and they'll go for the kill. I knew I had to come in swinging."

For the first time I understood Zef's reaction in the truck. He hadn't liked getting scared, and that translated to anger. I recalled my own dread at being unable to escape Dean's cruel grasp and the relief that flooded me when Zef showed up. "Thanks for what you did. Though it's made worse enemies out of them for you."

"If that's possible." He paused, like he was thinking how to put his next words. "Will you just promise me you won't go to the Chateau alone?"

I lay back on the bed, studying the way the light in the room started to soften. "I probably won't go back at all."

"You mean that?"

"Maybe. Look Zef, the idea of finding the lost paintings is starting to lose its appeal. This will probably make me sound like a chicken, but it scared me being trapped in the kitchen with those guys. And you heard how Dean was screaming at you when we left. It just adds one more danger to the Chateau's list."

"So do you think we should give up?" He kept his voice neutral, clearly not willing to let on what he was thinking.

I looked around the blue walls, my scattered possessions trying to claim the territory of a boy's room but failing. My grandpa's unkind words echoed back to me, a settling sadness in sync with the fading light.

"Yes and no. It's hard to give up the idea of my share of the profits. Without it, I'll be stuck here."

It took him so long to reply, I wondered if we'd been cut off until he said, "Would that be so bad?"

I closed my eyes, ignoring the sting behind my lids as a different mental image came to mind: me sitting on the bank of the pond with Zef. "I don't know."

"Then I have a suggestion."

"Okay."

He cleared his throat. "There's only about a week left before the detonation team gets here and starts wiring the Chateau. I'd like to go there with you one more time, just to see if we can find something."

I slowly sat up, my gaze going to the art history book sitting on the desk. "I'm confused. When we fought over my dad's notes about the attic, you were ready to give up. Now you've changed your mind?"

"Yeah. Probably a mistake."

"You are a hard guy to understand."

"In other words, you think I'm mysterious." A teasing note entered his voice. "Interesting…"

I couldn't not smile at the way he said it, surprised at an emerging buoyancy considering today had been the worst. "*Interesting* is one way to put it."

He let out a slow breath, as if wanting to say something else. "Everything I've learned about the Chateau since you got here keeps going through my head. And though I didn't like lying to my parents, I doubt they'll ask about it again. Tell you what, Kenley. I'm going to be there tomorrow morning around eight. I'll text you when I get there, and you can let me know if you're coming."

"What about Dean and Riker? I do not want to run into them again."

"I seriously doubt they'll be there, since neither of them are early risers. Just in case, I'll bring the bat."

He waited for my answer.

"I'll think about it," I finally said. "In the meantime, can we talk about something besides the Chateau for a while?"

Zef agreed and began telling me about the high school where I'd be going in the fall, the names of friends he'd had since grade school, who the best teachers were, and also how the ancient principal, Mrs. Hunchley, kept refusing to retire.

We discussed our favorite music, movies we liked, and books. He confessed he read more during school, always having a paperback with him because he hated being bored after his work was done. A mental picture came to mind of him sitting in the back row, one of those quiet, good-looking guys who read. It made me smile. And I realized that if I did end up going to school here, at least I'd have one friend.

My grandma brought me a plate of food, leaving it on the desk when I didn't make eye contact. Somehow, this led my conversation with Zef around to what had happened when I came home. I shared a little bit of my grandpa's words and how they made me feel. Zef was a good listener, and at one point I smiled to myself at how easy he was to talk to now compared to when we first met. I also decided I liked him better when his thoughts—and mine—weren't focused on the Chateau.

His mom called him to dinner, the end of our phone call returning to awkward since his unspoken question about whether or not I'd meet him in the morning hung between us.

I ate some of the dinner, now cold. I didn't care. It was better than sitting at the table with grumpy Grandpa. Maybe this could become a permanent arrangement. I wanted to hate him, but part of me kept thinking about what he'd said, how Jules had taken off in the middle of the night, leaving only a note.

Many times she had told the story of coming to New York when she was just eighteen. Right after graduation, she and her friend Lucy packed their suitcases and took a Greyhound Bus to the big city. They'd stayed with Lucy's brother and auditioned for plays, though after six months Lucy had no luck and went back home. By then, Jules had her first part in the chorus of a play and had also fallen in love with my dad.

Told from my mother's perspective, it was a wild and fun adventure. However, hearing my grandpa's version tarnished it, especially when he talked about how Grandma had cried.

Later that night, long after my grandparents had gone to bed, I thought about Zef's offer to meet him in the morning. I had to admit that after each experience at the Chateau, the place steadily lost its charm. He didn't, though. In fact, just the opposite, especially after our time on the phone. The more I came to know Zef, the more I wanted to be around him. But having an excuse to hang out with him at the Chateau meant we might chance another run-in with Riker and Dean. I turned on my side and closed my eyes, postponing the decision until morning.

My father was at the bottom of a deep well, calling up to me. I peered over the side where everything was dark, listening to his voice.

"You can't see me, Kenley, though I can see you."

"Can't you get out?" I looked around, hoping to find a rope or something else in all the shadowy clutter that surrounded me.

"Jump, and I'll catch you," he called, drawing my attention back to the well. "Trust me."

I stared down into the blackness, wishing I could see him and how far down the well went. I wanted to go to him, but fear held me back.

He called to me again, his voice more desperate. This time, when I answered, it came out a whisper. "I can't. You've been gone too long."

Trembling, I took a step back. Across the mouth of the well, half hidden in shadows, stood an old wooden rocking horse with a faded mane that had once been crimson. Thinking that somehow it might help, I carefully walked around the well to reach it, eyes cast down and studying my little girl tennis shoes. The rocking horse was just the right size for me to ride, and I stroked the smooth carving of the mane. Climbing on, I held the stiff leather reins. It started rocking back and forth, lifting up and away until I was far above everything, riding through a nighttime sky full of fragile glass stars.

My phone hummed, letting me know I had a text, and I opened one eye. *Morning so soon?* I was on my stomach, face squished in the pillow, memories from yesterday beginning to buzz around my head like annoying gnats. Finding my phone, I read a text from Zef saying he was leaving for the Chateau. No invitation to come, just a statement of what he was doing so I could decide for myself.

I got dressed, finding out I was alone in the house. Grandma had left to do her big grocery shopping that happened every two weeks, and my grandpa had gone back to his cows. I ate a bowl of cereal and thought about the conversation with Zef.

He was right about one thing. Time was running out for the Chateau. There wasn't much of a chance left to find the Hidden Room, but soon there would be no chance at all.

28
On Fire

The humid morning air forecast another hot day, and by the time I arrived at the Chateau I was too warm. Zef's white pickup was parked in front, the gate still ajar and I hesitated, resting my fingers on the iron crossbar. Hopefully Riker and Dean wouldn't come here again, at least not until after we'd left, but did I want to risk it? And if my grandparents had been talking about the Chateau during their argument, then they didn't want me to come here—the same as Jules.

I checked the time on my phone, deciding to give Zef one hour of searching and then I'd be done. Slipping between the gates, I hurried down the wide walkway, past the broken fountain and around the house to the veranda. He'd left the French doors wide open, possibly hoping to show how much he wanted me here. It made me smile when I compared it to the time I'd found him in the library and he tried to make me leave. A lot had happened since then.

The cooler air inside the ballroom felt welcoming and I called Zef's name, half expecting to hear his voice or see him come strolling down the hallway. I checked each room I passed, including the library and sitting room, finally getting out my phone and sending a text. By the time I got to the grand foyer, I didn't know whether to be anxious or annoyed. Sometimes, when Zef got focused on something, he ignored his phone. I'd noticed that the last time his mother called.

Reaching the stairs, I shouted his name again, my voice carrying in the stillness. I sent another text and decided I didn't want to go upstairs. Instead, I headed down the hallway that led to the kitchen. The only thing there was the broken worktable, pieces of scattered tile on the floor from when Zef struck it with the bat. The sun peeked over the transom windowsills, thin blades of light cutting across the darker shadows.

Still no answer to my texts, so I called his phone, turning when I heard the faint sound of a ringtone. Waiting for him to answer, knowing he had to be around here somewhere, I didn't know what to think when it went to voicemail.

"Zef?" I call. "This isn't funny!"

It definitely wasn't, and a chill passed through me. Zef was not the kind of guy to play jokes, especially after everything that happened yesterday. I redialed, listening. The sound of the ringtone soon led me through the side hallway to the stairs going to the larder—the same stairs he'd guided me down that first night. I called his name again. No answer.

My stomach tensed at the thought of heading down there by myself. For a couple of seconds I considered leaving the Chateau. But what then? Call his parents? Or call the sheriff and get fined for trespassing? My grandparents would love that. I took a deep breath like I was going for a dive and went down the stairs.

Even with the missing bannister, it was easier making my way to the larder than it had been that first time in total darkness. But at least then, I hadn't been alone. Wishing my facemask wasn't still at home in the art bag, my ears strained for any sounds. I heard nothing and assumed Zef had accidentally left his phone down there and was upstairs somewhere.

I reached the lower landing and stepped through the door into the windowless larder. Using my phone, I shone a light around to dispel shadows, sucking in a startled breath when I saw Zef in a crumpled heap.

I ran over and knelt next to him. His face was pressed

against the rough concrete floor, eyes closed, and the breathing mask around his neck. Touching his shoulder I said his name, relieved when he moaned and stirred. He slowly opened his eyes, squinting up at me as if struggling to focus. "Kenley?"

"What happened, Zef? Did you trip?"

I helped him sit up. He carefully touched the back of his head then frowned. "Someone clobbered me."

I held up the light on my phone but saw no one. He looked around too. "They're gone."

"Let me see where they hit you."

Zef leaned forward and I gently touched a bulge on the back of his head. "You've got a goose egg, all right. But it's not bleeding."

"I'll be okay. Let's get out of here."

He made it to his feet but swayed, and I grabbed him. "Can you climb the stairs?"

"Yeah, think so."

I pulled his arm across my shoulders to help steady him. "Zef, who hit you?"

"Didn't see. I set my backpack down somewhere and went looking for it. I was almost to the kitchen when I heard a scraping sound from the larder, like when that door slides open to the delivery entrance." He pointed over his shoulder to the hidden exit. "At first, I thought it might be you."

I didn't tell him that coming down to the larder on my own wouldn't have happened, and I'd only done it now because I was trying to find him.

We reached the stairs and his steps slowed. "I decided to check it out but didn't see anything unusual. Was heading to the wine cellar when I heard a sound behind me."

His eyebrows drew in as we started up the stairs, like he was struggling to put the pieces together. "I was just about to turn around when something hit the back of my head and I fell forward. After that, I don't remember anything until you found me."

I had to let go of him, since we needed to move up the stairs single file. Backs against the wall, I went first and held his hand. "It must've been Dean."

Zef started to shake his head then frowned like it hurt. "I doubt it. Dean's so mad at me right now that he wouldn't stop with a blow to the head. He'd beat me to a bloody mess."

I sensed he was right and suppressed a shiver. "Riker, then?"

"Maybe. I had his bat with me when I went down to the larder, and now it's gone."

I expected him to be mad, or at least upset enough to say something else, but he just kept climbing the stairs. I was really starting to hate his brother.

Zef froze, his head tipped as if listening. "Do you hear footsteps?"

I waited, but the only sounds came from our shifting feet. "No. You're probably hallucinating because of the gas. How long were you down there, anyway?"

"Not sure. What time is it?"

I checked my phone. "After ten."

"Oh... too long, I guess." He tugged off the breathing mask hanging around his neck and stuck it in a pocket. "This must've come loose."

We finally made it to the top of the stairs. He swayed in a way that worried me, so I pulled his arm across my shoulder again. We walked through the hallway, my nerves taut as I listened for footsteps other than ours. What if he wasn't hallucinating and I just hadn't heard? I dreaded running into Riker or Dean again, especially with Zef in such bad shape. A little bit further and we reached the kitchen, both of us looking through the doorway for intruders, as if Zef shared my thoughts. However, the room was still empty, though sunnier now since thick beams of light slid in through the high windows.

"Almost there," I said, helping him pass the table and blinking as we walked through a blinding stream of light.

"Hang on!" Zef stopped, staring at me.

"What is it?"

He smiled in an amazed way like he'd just found gold. "Kenley, you should see this!"

Reaching up, he touched my hair, lifting a strand to twirl in the light. "It's like fire."

"Okay… that's the hallucinations talking. Come on."

I tugged him forward but when we moved out of the sunbeam he pulled me back. For someone weak from getting whacked on the head, his grip felt surprisingly strong.

"I'm not joking! You should really see this."

"I can't, Zef. It's on top of my head."

"But it's beautiful." He lowered his gaze to mine and leaned in to study me with that intense stare of his. "So are you."

For a couple of seconds I felt almost weightless at what he'd said, and how he said it.

"How much gas did you inhale?"

He kept gazing at me until I decided to pull away. He didn't let go, following me into the dim surroundings. At least we were out of the light so he could get it together.

"Zef, you need to focus. We have to get out of here."

He stepped even closer, like he hadn't heard. His hands slid to either side of my face, drawing me near. The tingling warmth of his fingers on my skin, and the slight brush of his breath against my lips, caused a crazy flutter in my stomach. He bent his head to mine, kissing the corner of my mouth. Sliding down to my jaw. Tracing a tickling warmth along my throat that made me gasp. He smelled of soap and sun-heated earth and a little bit of guy aroma that set my head spinning.

My eyes slid closed as his mouth returned, pressing

full against mine. The sweet pressure and intimacy of his kiss sent a shiver up my spine. Whatever thoughts were in my head turned to mush and I couldn't process, or protest about how unsafe it was to stay here. Instead, my lips answered his.

29
Under Fire

I was driving Zef's truck, which only came about because I'd insisted, refusing to get in if he didn't give me the keys. Then we'd stopped at the main road, arguing which way to go. I wanted to take him home, he wanted to go the other direction, to the pond. That argument, I lost.

The windows were rolled down, my hair blowing in crazy swirls. "What if you have a concussion?"

He took some painkiller from the glove box and downed it. "For the fifth time, Kenley, I'm fine. I just need my head cleared from all the gas I inhaled, and that's going to take a while."

I hoped he was right. Neither of us said anything for the rest of the drive, my own mind still swimming in circles from the way he'd kissed me. Even thinking about it made my heart beat faster.

At the pond, I grabbed the blanket he kept in the back seat and spread it beneath the willow. He stretched out in the shade, his head cushioned on his arms. "This place is magical."

After a minute I lay back too, staring up at the thousands of tiny, wavy leaves hanging in an arch over our heads. Bits of faded summer sky peeked through, lazy clouds drifting by.

I decided to be direct with Zef. "The thing is, when I agreed to help you search the Chateau, I didn't know everything was going to end up so weird."

He chuckled, then rubbed his temple like it ached. "You mean your first visit there didn't clue you in?"

"Not enough." I peered up at a small wren hopping about in the branches like we didn't exist. "If I'd known, I would've asked for fifty percent."

"Hmm... not sure about that, since it is my family fortune."

I turned my head and saw his smiling eyes focused on me. In this light they took on the color of rich mahogany. Why had I not recognized, from the very first, how gorgeous they were?

"Family fortune?" I managed. "Sounds like bragging rights."

A knowing expression rested on his mouth. He turned onto his side, propping himself up on his arm to better look at me. Time felt like it was slowing down, but I couldn't let it. "How's your head feeling?"

He didn't answer. *Typical.*

I broke eye contact, dropping my gaze to his chin. Had there always been that tiny dent, and I just hadn't noticed until now? "Think the fumes are out of your system?"

His hand moved across my torso to my side, resting warmly on the indent between ribs and hip.

I swallowed. "I've been thinking..."

"Kenley," he said, his voice so serious that it drew my gaze back to his. "Stop talking."

My lips parted in protest but he leaned in, his mouth claiming mine. This time, his kiss was stronger, fearless, like he knew what he wanted. And before I could even decide what I thought about that, my mouth responded in a crazy, intense way that shocked me. One of my arms slid around him, feeling the taut muscles of his back. The other lifted up, fingers seeking the nape of his neck.

The kiss died, another instantly reborn in its place, then another and another. It made my pulse beat faster than if I was running a race. When he finally pulled back—slowly enough so that our lips still clung to each other in a reluctant goodbye—I opened my eyes to look at him. He was so near I could hardly focus, my breathing fast.

Zef released me, lying back with both arms under his

head, and for an insane couple of seconds I got the feeling it was to keep himself from taking hold of me again. He stared up at the arched willow limbs, a slow smile playing on his mouth. "So that's what it takes to make you quiet."

The friendliness in his tone kept me from being offended, as if he was letting me know how much he liked me, just laying it all out and not caring how vulnerable this made him.

"Very funny," I answered, though it sounded more along the lines of: *You kiss better than any guy I've ever been with.*

Zef and I stayed by the pond for a long time, until he felt better. I didn't talk as much, secretly admitting that being quiet with him brought about its own pleasure.

After that, we spent the rest of the day together: Walking along the trail that led around the pond, him holding my hand the entire time.

Lunch at a little Chinese buffet in town I'd never even known about. Cruising past the high school, newly rebuilt six years ago, and my confessing it was smaller than any school I'd gone to except back in elementary. Him giving me advice on teachers. Most of the art classes, he said, were taught by a math teacher who wanted kids to draw like Escher.

We went to a book store that sold new and used, where I spent half the money Jules had sent me. He showed me around the auto parts store where he worked, then we stopped at an old two story brick building housing an insurance company and the local Chamber of Commerce. They sold homemade fudge at the counter, and Zef bought us some.

"Everyone likes you," I said as we walked past a sorry-looking strip mall probably built in the eighties.

His eyebrows drew in a little, like he was trying to decide if this was true. "Maybe they're just relieved I'm not a repeat of Riker."

I finished my piece of the world's best fudge. "You're nothing like him."

"I used to try and prove how different we were, always wanting to make up for him. Then one day, I decided it wasn't worth caring what other people thought of me."

We passed the drugstore where Zef's old girlfriend worked and then a couple of businesses, heading in the direction of the park. Someone called out to us and we turned, seeing Meena coming in our direction. She wore a short flowered skirt and sleeveless white top, her dark hair hanging down her back.

"Hey," she said, smiling at us. She indicated a slim folder in her hand. "I was just heading out to drop this off for my boss when I saw you."

I asked where she worked and we chatted for a minute. It kind of surprised me how friendly she was, asking what grade I'd be in when school started and what my favorite subject was. And then she said, "After I get off work, Riker and I are driving to Fort Wayne for dinner and a movie. Would you two like to come?"

Zef and I glanced at each other. "Probably not the best idea," he finally said.

Her smile dimmed. "Why not?"

At first he shrugged but then seemed to go for honesty. "Last time I saw Riker, we kind of butted heads."

Her gaze turned penetrating. "But he's your brother."

Trying to soften the growing unease, I asked, "Do you have brothers or sisters?"

She shook her head. "I'm an only child. My dad raised me."

"Guess we've got that in common," I said, explaining how I was an only child too, raised by a single parent. Then I asked how she met Riker.

Meena motioned at the park. "I was jogging and stopped to catch my breath. He happened to be sitting on a nearby bench and we started talking. I wasn't sure about dating him, but the first time we went out, he impressed me."

She lifted her long hair off her neck. "We were playing pool when a couple of guys started clowning around. One of them threw a drink at his friend and a little of it splattered on my leg. Riker grabbed him by the collar and made him apologize."

"Sounds like my brother," Zef said.

Something in his tone made her eyes narrow. "Riker is kind to me. He's a better guy than most people know. And I think it's really sad how everyone in town keeps judging him for what he did when he was younger. No one's willing to even give him a chance. Including his own family."

Zef didn't say anything and she added, "Once he's off probation, we're getting out of here."

With that, she brushed past us, chin in the air. We started walking in the direction of Zef's truck. "Think she's right?" he asked when we were nearly there. "That my family isn't being fair to Riker?"

"I don't know. She said he's kind to her, and that's a good thing. But I didn't like the way he and Dean treated me at the Chateau. And not to mention the first time you and I met, he was shouting your name and shooting off a gun. Nothing good about that."

My phone buzzed, and I checked but didn't answer. "It's my grandma. She calls but never leaves a message."

"What do you think she wants?"

I slid the phone in my pocket. "The same thing she always does. For me to come home. Help with dinner. Sit and eat with them. Listen to my grandpa talk about how soon to harvest the alfalfa and the rising cost of feed." I exhaled, aware of what a complainer I'd become. "Sorry. I shouldn't be like that."

He reached out, taking my hand and sliding his fingers between mine. "How about you eat dinner with my family tonight? You'll probably have to put up with Kes telling more about her friends than anyone wants to know, and my dad trying to rope us into a board game afterwards."

"Sounds good."

Actually, it sounded better than anything at the ranch, so I called my grandma and got permission.

Dinner at the Webb's ended up the way Zef predicted, but I enjoyed it all: a slice of Americana pie that was a little off-kilter. His mother looked more worn down than last time, the shadows under her eyes darker, though she smiled and asked me questions that weren't too prying.

His dad did a good balancing act of being a friendly but concerned parent teacher combo. Plus dinner was pizza, something I hadn't eaten since coming to the dairy.

We all helped clean up, then afterwards when his dad tried to corner us into a game of *Risk*, Zef insisted he needed to walk me home.

Outside his front door he gave an apologetic shrug. "Warned you."

"Your family is great. You're lucky."

I didn't add what we were probably both thinking, how when Riker was around, lucky got thrown out the window.

The sun was still an hour above the horizon and my steps slowed as we reached the road. Maybe Zef knew how reluctant I felt about going back to the dairy because he gave my fingers a light squeeze. "Mind walking with me to the Chateau? I left my backpack there. Upstairs, I think."

"Sure."

It took us a while to make our way along the overgrown trail, passing through tall weeds grown brittle with the aging summer.

When we finally reached the Chateau, both of us stopped to look at it. The way the sunlight slanted sideways across the front brought out details in the muted beige and gold of the stone walls. The blue roof was brighter, the windows darker and even more obscure. I had the strange feeling that the Chateau was hiding something from me, as if it held a secret too frightening to share.

"Can't believe they're bringing it down," Zef said.

The sense of foreboding clung to me, but I didn't want him to know. "Me either."

He ran a hand across the back of his neck. "I'm going to hate seeing nothing here but a pile of stones. Mainly because I'll never know if my grandpa was right about those hidden paintings and other valuables. All of my searching and it's for nothing."

The gate was still ajar and we went through, taking our familiar route around to the veranda. We stepped inside the French doors but had only gone a few steps when Zef slowed. "What's that smell?"

I caught a whiff of it too. "Paint."

The odor grew stronger as we left the ballroom, moving down the empty hallway and into the gallery. Both of us stopped, staring at what lay before us. Scrawled everywhere, in dripping red paint, was the repeating message: *DIE!*

It had been spray painted dozens of times. Red letters covered the floor, windows, and walls, as high as the person who'd done it could reach. Half a dozen discarded spray paint cans littered the ground.

"Who did this, Zef?"

He shook his head, looking as confused as I felt.

I turned in a slow circle, surprised anyone would put this much effort into such amateur graffiti. "Dean, maybe?"

Zef wore that disapproving frown I'd come to know really well when we first met.

"I don't know. I wouldn't put it past him, though it doesn't really seem like his style."

He started walking and I followed. More scribbles demanding *DIE!* ran along the hallway, fading out and then reappearing in the main foyer, though these were now black. Huge letters also covered the marble floor, marring what had once been beautiful, though now the paint also stuck to pieces of debris and made the words lumpy. More graffiti trailed up the wall of the staircase but then ended as the last of the paint was used. An empty can recapped with a black lid sat casually on a step, like the spray paint artist was coming back for it.

"Let's find my backpack and get out of here," Zef said, heading up the stairs.

I followed him to the second floor, where he started checking all the rooms. "I'm sure I left it around here somewhere."

Our searching led us in the direction of the dark hallway, which was not where I wanted to go. I stepped into another room, one that was now familiar, with the spindly wood in the corner where my dad had left his notebook. Heavy drapes, coated in dust, blocked out the light from the window, making the room gloomy. I walked over and jerked them open, dust raining down. I shielded my head and stepped back, blinking.

"What are you doing?" Zef asked.

"You can hardly see, it's so dark."

"I didn't leave my backpack here. Let's go."

I stood near the window which looked down on the dead rose bushes, the gazebo to their far right. Beyond them, long shadows stretched out from the wooded hill, deep in the rich light of sunset. I thought about my father bringing me to the Chateau all those years ago, guiding me down the twisting path and then through the garden.

There had been something of promise in my dream of being with him all those years ago. Now, it had faded to nothing.

Zef came up behind me, his hands moving to my waist. I liked the warmth of his touch as it seeped through the thin fabric of my shirt. He leaned closer, his chin next to my temple. "What is it, Kenley?"

I shook my head, throat tightening a little, not trusting

myself to speak. He turned me in his arms. "Whatever it is, it's going to be okay."

His voice was strong, reassuring. I leaned into him.

A shot rang out, shattering the glass of a windowpane near my head.

Zef dropped down, dragging me with him. We hit the floor as more shots were fired, bullets blowing the window to pieces and slamming into the wall opposite us. Too startled to make a sound, I ducked even lower, instinctively covering my head before realizing that was no protection.

"This way," Zef shouted over the noise, tugging my arm. "Get away from the window!"

On hands and knees, we scurried along the wall to the corner, trying to find a safer place as I wondered if bullets could cut through the outside stone and reach us. Blood roared in my ears, adrenalin coursing through my body in a way that made breathing a struggle. Zef looked equally shocked, both of us hunkering down into the smallest possible targets. My eyes flew to the hallway door and I thought about running for it until the shooting started up again, more bullets coming through the window and knocking out chunks of the wooden door frame. I hunched even lower.

The shooting stopped for several seconds but then began once more, only this time not hitting the window. Instead, we heard glass shatter in the next room. Zef crawled over to a door on the wall near to us and opened it.

"In here," he said, and I hurried to join him.

We scooted ourselves into a dark, narrow room that looked like a big closet and had a second door opposite the one we'd come through. With no exterior windows, it at least felt safer, the sound of gunfire more remote.

"Who the hell is shooting at us?" My voice came out a frightened croak.

"I don't know."

He looked grim as he slid an arm around me, pulling

me near. I leaned in, feeling even more shaky as I realized how close we'd come to being killed.

Another pause in the shooting, but then more gunfire. "They keep stopping," I said. "Must be to reload."

Zef nodded. "Which means they've got only one gun."

One was enough, but I didn't say that.

He stirred a little, leaning towards the door we'd come through. "Listen. It's not so loud now. The firing has moved away. I think whoever it is, they're shooting out the windows, not firing at us."

"Why? To scare us?" I thought about Dean's threat of digging Zef's grave, and also how mad Riker had gotten when Zef used the bat. If their goal was to shake us up, it was working.

The gunfire abruptly ended as we sat in the small room, hiding in the dark and listening for it to start again. A minute ticked by, then two.

"I think it's over," Zef finally said, relaxing his grip on me.

"You can't be sure."

"They had to run out of ammo sometime."

"How are we going to get out of here?"

He turned to me, his features half hidden in shadow. "First, I'm going down the hall to peek in the other rooms."

I started to protest but he rested a finger on my lips. "I'll be careful. Just want to see what's happening, okay? Then I'll come back and we can decide our best route for getting out."

I folded my arms. "I'm not staying here alone."

He leaned in, his mouth capturing mine. At first I couldn't believe he was taking time to kiss me, but the next thing I knew, I was kissing back and it felt comforting. When it ended, both of us were a little breathless.

"Just one minute, Kenley. That's all I'm asking." And then he scurried through the door and across the shot-up room, where tiny beams of light filtered through bullet holes in the heavy draperies. He moved into the hall.

I sat there still terrified the shooting would start again, but everything remained silent. With all my being I hoped Zef didn't get hurt, and that he'd come back to me in the next ten seconds. Thinking that when he did, we might need another exit, I scooted over to the door on the opposite side of the closet and opened it. Inside was a dark sitting room with similar heavy drapes. In the center sat a broken settee covered in crumpled maroon velvet that looked ready to fall apart.

It took a little bit to realize I'd never seen that settee before, which meant for some reason I hadn't been in this part of the house. I stood, moving into the room that was gloomier than the others, making sure I stayed away from the covered window.

Another door into the hallway hung off its hinges and I went there, stepping through. It was so dim I couldn't see, and I turned on my phone for more light, looking around. With a startled gasp I took a step back from the dangerous hole in the floor.

I happened to be standing in the dark hall, on the far side of the hole that now separated me from the rest of the house. A shiver passed through me as I peered along the hallway, pale light seeping in from open doorways on either side. It occurred to me that this must be where Dean had hid with his creepy mask when he tried to scare me. Until now, I'd never known that suite of rooms was joined together and that they bypassed the hole in the floor.

Wanting a closer look at what had always seemed like a dead end, I moved away from the hole, for the first time noticing the hall actually made a sharp turn. I went around the corner and kept going until arriving at two steps that climbed up to a closed door.

A fluttering sensation inside my stomach left me shaky as I reached for the brass knob. At first it didn't budge, but I twisted with both hands until the lock clicked free. The hinges creaked as the door opened away from me, and I forced myself to step through onto a landing. There were steps leading down to the servant's quarters, but going up was the spiral staircase winding skyward into darkness.

This was the entrance to the attic.

30
The Attic

You cannot trust your eyes or ears
For in the end, you too shall die.
T'will happen sooner than you think,
In the place where whispers lie.

The Ghost Child
Act II, Scene II

I kept my arms tight around my daddy's neck. The curved wooden handrail was held up by thin spindles, all of it rising in a dizzying circle above our heads. In some places, the railing was broken away, and he stayed close to the wall. One time I peeked down, seeing the floor far below, and it made me shiver. Cobwebs hung from the steps above like little ghosts that swayed in the air current as we went by.

I climbed the rickety staircase, moving carefully. It looked the same as before, in spite of a dozen years having passed, and I carried the memory with me. Being here created an indistinct puzzle I couldn't ignore. Why had my father brought me to the attic, and why had I remembered nothing about it until now?

Pausing to listen, I thought the Chateau had never been so quiet. It seemed to swallow the sound of my footsteps and even my breathing. At a place where the bannister was missing, I moved nearer to the wall and slipped past. A thin strand of cobweb touched my neck and I brushed it away. Every so often, one of the steps felt soft, the wood rotted. I started testing them with my toe, in the back of my mind admitting that climbing up here was probably the most dangerous thing I had ever done. A couple of times I even considered turning back, but then the memory of my dad carrying me would replay itself, driving me forward.

Despite trying not to overreact, by the time I neared the top of the staircase my heart beat fast, more from emotion than exertion. I glanced down, experiencing a dropping sensation inside my stomach at the prospect of falling. Turning away, I pressed forward, expecting another door but surprised that the last steps led up through plank flooring and directly into the attic.

The wide space was filled with many items, and the stuffy air felt much hotter than in the rest of the Chateau. Wooden crates were stacked haphazardly beside broken pieces of furniture. A half-finished ball gown of what had once been emerald velvet was still pinned to a dress form, thick dust coating the folds of fabric. An empty birdcage sat on top of a writing table with missing drawers.

Overhead, the ceiling was an intricate cross-work of beams half hidden in shadow, and through slats of wood that formed an unfinished wall, I glimpsed the brickwork of a chimney rising from one of the second story fireplaces. Small windows ran along the front side of the Chateau's roof, jutting out to form the decorative edge that looked so pretty from a distance. Here, though, they were nothing more than rectangles of weathered glass through which the murkiest of light was able to seep.

Further away was a large hole in the slanted ceiling. A mangled piece of blue roof hung down inside, leaving an opening which gave a glimpse of early evening sky. Years of exposure to rain had warped and darkened the shattered wood, and from here I could more clearly see how the rotted roof beams had created a jagged gap in the floor. One massive beam still slanted down through it, precariously balanced. The weight of the rest of the collapsing roof must have continued down to the floors below, making the hole in the dark hallway directly beneath.

A shiver passed through me, followed by a warning to leave. And yet I couldn't. My breathing turned shallow and fast, increasing to a rapid pant. I took several steps forward, startled by the flapping of wings. A pair of doves abandoned their perch and escaped through the opening in the roof. Even though my heart had started its rapid pace again, I kept going, looking past the hole in the floor to what I sensed was on the far side. A drop of sweat trickled down to my jaw and I brushed it away, ignoring the tingling at the base of my neck. It took all my nerve to force myself to go forward even a little. And then I saw it.

In front of a torn fireplace screen stood a wooden rocking horse. The paint on its mane and tail had faded to a scuffed maroon, the weathered varnish on its body splotchy. A small leather saddle and reins were held in place with brass rivets, the head of the stallion carved in a smooth downward arch. The mouth opened in a horsey grimace, and a round glass eye stared at me, just the same way it had all those years ago.

"Stay right here," my father said, sitting me on top of a flat-topped trunk near one of the windows. He handed me a pen and small notebook. "Draw Daddy a picture."

I watched him bend over a crate, pulling out papers and books as he muttered to himself. "Where'd I see those?"

There wasn't much light in the attic, and beyond the panes, wind moaned and swirled leaves that made me think of brown feathers. I scooted to the edge of the trunk and peered through the warped glass. Far below stood autumn trees, an empty fountain, and gates that from way up here looked like stiff black lace.

When I glanced up, I saw something that made me

slip off the trunk and take a few steps. It was a wooden horse. His open mouth showed teeth that looked a little scary, but his shiny black eye stared straight at me like he wanted to say something. He wore a brown saddle on top of his spotted body, and his feet were set into a pair of rockers with chipped gold paint. The more I looked at him, the more it seemed we both knew I was just the right size to get on his back. I started walking over to him, my pink and purple shoes leaving a crisscross pattern in the dust.

"Kenley?" Daddy called, his voice anxious. I didn't look back, still fascinated by the horse that drew me forward.

The sound of his running feet was followed by a cry of, "No!"

He grabbed my arm, jerking me away. I fell back onto the floor as the boards beneath his feet broke with a loud crack. He disappeared into the dark hole, his choked cry cut off by loud crashing. My mouth opened to scream but no sound came out.

My body shook, terrible shudders passing through me until I couldn't stand. I sank to my knees, staring at the splintered boards on the edge of the hole—the last place I had seen my father. I couldn't breathe, certain all the oxygen had been sucked out of the attic to form a vacuum. And then, at last, I took in a breath that hurt. That's when I heard the crying. The grief-stricken child's voice sobbing, just like the first time when I had neared the hole in the floor of the dark hallway.

It took several seconds to realize the sound was coming from me.

31
Falling

My feet stumbled down the stairs, shoulder brushing the plaster wall in a way that made it flake. A buzzing noise filled my ears and seemed to come from inside my head, but I wasn't sure, since right now a great nothingness consumed me.

The heel of one shoe broke through a step, followed by the faint sound of wood pieces clattering to the floor far below. I jerked my foot free and kept going, the hum in my ears increasing. Finally reaching the lower landing, I paused, my breath coming in hard little lumps that tried to choke me.

A detached part of my mind made the decision of where to go, quickly abandoning the idea of walking through the joined rooms to bypass the dark hallway. That would mean going downstairs to the grand foyer and seeing the word *DIE!* spray painted a hundred times, an accusing message screamed at me by the Chateau. Instead, I continued down the second flight of stairs, these sturdier steps allowing me to go faster. It was gloomier inside the servant's stairwell, but I could still see well enough to make my way, fingers gliding over the chipped banister.

The last step ended at a service area that opened into one of the hallways. If I'd been here before I didn't remember, but still I somehow managed to make my way to the kitchen. I passed the battered worktable and reached the door leading outside, pulling hard on the handle. It stayed stuck even more than the time Riker and Dean had cornered me, and the hike in my fear made the buzzing in my ears worse. Just beneath the droning noise I could hear an accusing voice: *It was because of you, Kenley.*

A hoarse sob broke through my lips and I yanked harder, the door finally popping open as the knob broke free in my hand. I threw it down and stepped out of the kitchen, clamping my hands over my ears to make the condemning noises stop. They only got louder.

A desperate need to outrun them forced me to take off. I fled, a couple of times tripping over weeds but always continued on, weaving my way across the grounds in a directionless panic. Soon I found myself among dead rose bushes, racing between them as if chased by a ghost. Thorns ripped at my shirt and scratched my arms and legs. I didn't stop, pushing my way through until slowed by a memory sharper than broken glass: my little pink and purple tennis shoes staggering along this same route, tears icy on my face in the cold autumn wind.

My hair snagged on a large bramble, jerking me to a stop. Breathing in jagged gasps of air that sounded like grief, I yanked free, leaving strands of hair behind. This sent me into a thorny branch, a sharp sting on my face. I touched my cheek, fingers coming away tinged with blood. Filled with the dark sensation that these were the gnarled hands of the Chateau reaching out to grab me, I forced myself to push forward the same way as when I was a little girl.

It came to me then, with sudden clarity, that twelve years ago I'd made it out of the rose garden and up to the path on the hill. For hours I followed winding trails, lost and sometimes crying, until finally stumbling out onto the road where a car nearly hit me.

Now, my feet finally found the stone path leading out of the dead bushes. I headed in the direction of the gardener's shed and lifted my eyes to the wooded hill, for the first time noticing how dim the light had grown in the hazy forerunner of dusk.

A hand grabbed my arm, spinning me around, and I stared at Zef. His annoyed frown changed when he saw me.

The small, remote part of my mind that seemed to be in charge noted his anxious expression as I thought how my face had never been a very good place for hiding things.

His lips moved and he leaned in, talking to me, but most of his words couldn't make it through the buzzing hum. He pointed up at the hill, his mouth forming the word "shooter". Then I remembered how bullets had shattered the window, and I glanced back at the Chateau, seeing how several had been shot out.

He took my hand, guiding me over to the gardener's shed and pulling me down on the bench in front. This seemed like a good idea as it blocked us from being targets.

My fingers felt icy in Zef's hand. He brushed away the trickle of blood on my cheek and we both looked down at my scratched arms and legs. None of it hurt, not even the deep one above my knee that had a thorn imbedded in it. I plucked it out as the buzzing finally started to fade.

Zef spoke to me. It sounded like a glass wall stood between us, but at least I could understand him. His eyes were full of concern. "You went in the attic."

A statement, not a question. And that's when it hit me harder than a sledge hammer against my chest. Zef knew what happened to my father. In fact, he'd always known.

Half a dozen memories stormed down on me. The time Zef explained the dangers of the Chateau and I asked, *"Anyone ever died in this place?"*

"Yes. You don't know?"

For the first time I realized that he had stopped himself from saying more that day. How he'd always stopped himself, or turned his face away so his eyes didn't betray what he knew. It was the real reason he hadn't wanted me to go looking for the attic.

A bitter taste filled my mouth. The secret of my father's death had been hidden inside me for years, and all the times Zef and I had been together, he'd held the key. I pulled my hand away and stood. Zef did too, saying words

I couldn't hear because the buzzing was back.

In the distance I saw the gazebo, outlined with orange from the remnant of fiery clouds. Better to go that direction than up to the hill, where the shooter might have returned with more ammo. Zef hurried along beside me, not saying anything and not reaching for my hand, either. As we got closer to the Chateau my heart started racing, eyes drawn to it as if powerless.

A man stepped around the corner, a small radio in his hand. "Hold it…"

He had a badge and holstered gun. "Zefram…what…" his words faded in and out.

"Sheriff Danner," Zef answered. "Someone… shots fired… hill…"

Their muted words stayed behind the wall of glass that I couldn't seem to push through. I gazed up at the west side of the Chateau—the one place I'd never really let myself look until now. From here the damage of the collapsed roof didn't seem so severe, just a dip in the top ridge not far from one of the chimneys. And yet it was so high up… and such a very long ways down.

My vision started to narrow, like looking through a rolled piece of paper continually scrolling tighter, until all I could see was that single broken place above the attic. It shrank to a small pinprick of light as I thought of my father falling, and then I began to fall, too.

Zef leapt forward, catching me.

32
The Lies I Told

The sheriff took me home in his tan SUV and walked me to the door. I was still shaky, but at least made it on my own. He handed Grandma my ticket for trespassing and started talking about where he'd found Zef and me. I didn't look at her face but saw the way her fingers gripped the dishtowel. I swayed a little and she put her hand on my arm. Turning away, I walked inside. Neither of them called me back.

I went into my room and shut the door, then turned on the fake Tiffany lamp which gave off a little stained glass light. Lying down on the bed, I looked at the blue wall. *Blue*, the color of the Chateau's roof—a reminder, even if this wasn't close to the same shade. Shutting my eyes didn't stop me from seeing. Or remembering the questions I'd been forced to answer so many times.

In first grade I had stood with two friends at the tetherball line. We waited for a turn that wouldn't come because the boys hitting the ball back and forth were too good. Kylie put her hands on her hips. "But how did your daddy die?"

Thinking back on it now, no matter how my mind strained, I couldn't recall what we'd been talking about before. Or the name of the other little girl. Or even if the school was in New York or California. It was just one segment snipped out of time and handed to me as an unhappy little piece. What I did remember was the familiar, heavy feeling inside my chest, a stone pressing down my heart.

"Yes," the other girl said, her black bangs touching her eyelashes and moving a little as she blinked. "How did he die?"

I pulled up the word Mama always used. It came out stiff, like my lips were cold. "An accident."

"Oh…" Kylie said in the way of savvy six year olds. "He died in a car accident."

I nodded, pigtails jiggling. "Yes. A car accident." *Not because of me…*

With every move to a new school, when friends grew close enough to ask, it was always the same lie. Soon I believed it myself, the truth shoved down into a tiny black knot.

Two years ago Dana had also wanted to know. "A car accident," I'd said, ignoring the growing tightness around my heart. "He died in a car accident." *Not because of me…*

A tear slid across the bridge of my nose, dropping onto the pillow.

I'd lied to everyone, including myself. And that cowardice had built a wall of mirror around my heart, each new lie adding another layer reflecting my made-up story. A slight shudder passed through me as I admitted my greatest fear: telling Jules what had really happened.

Of course, she already knew my father had died at the Chateau. And that I'd been with him. It's why she'd warned me not go there. But did she also know the truth of how I'd walked too close to the hole in the attic floor when he'd told me not to move? And how he pushed me away to save me but then fell to his death?

In spite of the sticky summer air coming in through the half-open window, I started to shiver.

The doorbell rang and I opened my eyes, not sure how much time had passed. I sat up, mildly relieved the buzzing inside my head had finally stopped. The window framed a piece of indigo sky so dark it seemed to have swallowed the stars. I stared at it until the sound of upset voices drew my attention. Going to the door, I opened it a crack.

"We trusted you," my grandpa said with a low rumble,

and I could imagine him folding his arms across his oversized belly.

"He's here to apologize, Joe," a man's familiar voice said. A pause and then, "Tell him, Zefram."

"I'm really sorry." It came out low, but still loud enough for me to hear.

"How could you do such a thing?" my grandmother said, sounding more upset than I'd ever heard her. "You know what happened to her father! Why on earth would you take Kenley there?"

"I'll tell you why," Grandpa said, his tone reminding me of a tuba. "It's that blasted treasure he and his family keep looking for. And now he's dragged Kenley into it, too. He didn't care that it was the worst thing he could do!"

I raised my eyebrows, wondering how a man who didn't even like me could act so outraged. Moving from my room into the hallway, I heard Zef's mother say, "We're very sorry. Zefram knows what he did was wrong."

"He'll be punished," his father added.

"I thought you were different, Zefram," my grandpa boomed. "Not like that brother of yours."

This harsh accusation silenced them all. By now I'd come close enough to see them standing clustered in the front entry. Zef stared at the floor, cowboy hat in hand, head bent forward like he deserved what he was getting. Both his parents looked upset and hurt. Grandma put a hand on my grandpa's arm, an unspoken request to hold back from saying more. But the scowl he wore said he wasn't close to being done.

Not taking time to think, I said, "Stop yelling at Zef."

Their heads all whipped in my direction so fast it would've made me laugh if I could remember how. "He's the only friend I've got here."

Despite my words, I didn't let my eyes connect with his. Grandpa folded his beefy arms. "Friend! A friend would never have taken you to that place."

"He didn't take me. I found the Chateau all on my own. Zef even tried to make me leave, but I wouldn't." Telling the truth felt good, like I was finally able to stop hiding behind my wall of lies.

Grandpa's mouth opened, then clamped shut like a fish on a fly.

"Besides," I said to him. "Why are you acting all protective, when you don't even want me living here?"

"Kenley," Grandma countered with a warning tone. "Right now, we are talking about how Zefram should never have involved you in searching the Chateau."

"Why, because I might remember how my dad died?" My voice rose to a tense pitch, but I couldn't stop. "Do you think I didn't know, just because I was a little kid when it happened?"

Grandma shook her head, worry creeping into her wrinkles. I shoved a fist against my stomach. "I may have forgotten, but inside I've always *known*!"

A sob crept up my throat. No matter how much it ached, I pushed it back down. "But here's the thing I never told anyone... not even when I was four."

I pulled in a deep breath that hurt, preparing myself. "I'm the reason he died."

Their faces showed different levels of shock. Zef lifted a hand in my direction, but I lowered my gaze to the ratty beige carpet.

"We were in the attic." My throat grew so tight that my voice came out hoarser than if I had strep. "There was a rocking horse I wanted to ride. He didn't see me try to go over to it, or how close I was to the hole in the floor. Until it was too late."

"Kenley," my grandma whispered, her tone stricken.

A tear slid down my face. "He pushed me away to save me, and that's how he fell."

A renewed ache went through me from this confession, even as that little logical spot in my brain said it was right to finally start telling the truth. My grandma stepped towards me, arms opening, but I staggered back like her hug would burn.

I turned and ran into the blue room, slamming the door.

33
An Overdue Discussion

Sometime after midnight, I finally fell asleep. No dreams. Just sinking down into a dark, numb place where thinking could finally grind to a stop.

Several times during the night I jerked awake, like I was falling. I kept hearing that choked cry my father made, and how it had been cut off by crashing sounds as he hit broken boards on his way down to the lower level of the Chateau. And although I'd never actually seen it, I could clearly envision his broken body lying in a heap of odd angles.

By the time the rooster crowed, I felt more exhausted than if I hadn't slept at all. I closed my eyes and tried to ignore the scent of frying sausage as it crept beneath my door. Queasy at the thought of eating, I pulled the sheet over my head and drifted off again.

Much later, I woke to the sound of the door opening. Had my grandma now given up knocking before she came in? That was all I needed. I stayed on my side facing the wall and kept my eyes closed, hoping she'd go away. The mattress sank beneath the weight of someone lying down next to me, an arm coming to rest across my shoulders. I caught the familiar scent of cherry blossom hand cream.

"Mom?" I turned over, gazing into my mother's tired face and hardly able to believe she'd come seven hundred miles to be with me.

Her hair was pulled up in a messy snarl and there were fine lines around her eyes that I'd never noticed. She smiled, brushing a stray piece of hair from my cheek. "Hey, girl."

Wetness welled in my eyes, and I wondered when I'd

become such a cry baby. "You're here," was all I could say.

She nodded. "Just pulled in. After your grandma called me, I drove all night."

"Oh." My voice grew thick. "She told you…"

"Everything. I'm so sorry, Kenley."

"You were right. I shouldn't have gone to the Chateau." My eyes slid closed, like I couldn't keep looking at her and get out what I wanted to say. "But once I found it, staying away felt impossible."

Jules pulled me into a hug that changed me into a little kid again. All the details of what had happened in the attic so long ago came pouring out, sobs creeping in, but she never let go. Just listened until it was done and I felt empty.

I finally pulled back and saw her face was wet, too. "Let me tell you the rest," she said in a teary voice.

I wiped my eyes with the edge of the sheet. "Okay."

"The first sign that something bad happened to your father was when Mrs. McGurdy almost hit you with her car. She lived five or six miles past the dairy."

I nodded. "I just remembered that, too. I wandered across the hill behind the Chateau, trying to get home the same way Daddy brought me."

Her eyes filled with regret. "It must've taken you a long time. You were so little and had to be scared. I don't know how you even made it off that hill by yourself."

"It's okay Jules, I hardly remember any of that part. Tell me about Mrs. McGurdy."

"She was an older lady who passed away several years ago. But on that day she nearly hit you, and it shook her. Luckily, she recognized you because she'd seen you at the store with your grandma. That's how she knew where to take you."

"Didn't I tell her my name?"

A couple of lines formed between my mother's eyebrows. "You wouldn't talk, Kenley. Not to her, or your grandparents. And I was at the theater in Indianapolis, unaware of what was going on. By the time they called, I was already on stage in *Phantom*, my phone still in the dressing room. Even calling the theater, they weren't able to convince anyone to interrupt the play."

I had a simple question that came out a little choked, my heart squeezed by an iron fist. "How did they find him?"

It took her a little to answer. "Your grandma had started worrying because you and your dad didn't come back for dinner. The sun had just gone down when Mrs. McGurdy brought you to the dairy, and they called the sheriff right away. Your Grandpa may not have been all that fond of Keith, but he knew your father would never leave you alone like that."

I made myself take a mental step away until it felt as if I stood on a distant cliff, watching the story unfold. "Did I tell them he was at the Chateau?"

She shook her head. "You still weren't talking. They soon realized you were in shock. That night, whenever anyone tried to interact with you, your eyes would slide away. No eye contact, and no words, either."

Jules brushed her fingers across my cheek, giving me another faint whiff of her favorite cherry blossom hand cream.

She sighed, like trying to let go of a heavy burden. "Finally, your grandma gave you some paper and crayons, and in your little girl scribbles they saw what might be a castle. That sent them searching the Chateau."

Jules didn't finish, and I was unable to remain that mere observer on a remote cliff. Instead, tears brimmed again. "Then they found him."

Tears shimmered in her eyes, too. "Yes."

My throat ached with tightness.

Jules wiped away the wetness on her cheeks. "You didn't talk at all for more than two weeks. I was terribly scared for you, especially as the days passed and you still wouldn't speak. Even the therapist I took you to wasn't able to break through the shell you'd built around yourself."

A few bits of memory surfaced, each one blurry at the edges: Sitting on a pillow atop the hardwood floor and watching cartoons. Gray sky and bare trees outside our apartment window. Mama rocking me on her lap, a fuzzy blanket around us as nighttime settled in. How sad our home felt without my father's laugh.

"We were both grieving," Jules said in a way that let me know she was remembering, too. "Staying alone in our little apartment, everything there reminding us your dad was gone. And I felt sick worrying about you. Nothing seemed to work. I didn't know how to help you deal with all the heartache that had stopped you from speaking."

"Until you brought home a blue balloon, and we let it go up to the sky."

"You remember that?"

"Yes. It's the thing I've always remembered most." I imagined the balloon soaring skyward. "Is that when I started talking again?"

She nodded. "Two words. You stared up at the balloon until it had nearly disappeared, and then I heard you say, 'Bye, Daddy.' So soft and sad. You didn't cry, but I did. I knelt down on the sidewalk and hugged you. When I asked what you wanted for lunch, you said, 'corndog'. It was the most beautiful thing I'd ever heard."

We lay that way for a while, and I thought how most of the time Jules seemed like an older girlfriend who was lots of fun. Right now, though, it was really nice having her be my mom.

I tried to blow the bangs out of my eyes and it made Jules smile. She reached up and brushed them off my forehead. "Your hair needs a trim."

I could feel her moving away from what we'd been talking about, the way she always did. Despite her having just told me a whole lot more than ever before, I wasn't ready for that.

"My silence during those two weeks is the main reason we never talked about how Dad died, isn't it? You were afraid I'd go off the deep end again."

She sat up, putting a pillow behind her back and resting against the aqua headboard. "Not exactly. Mostly, I just didn't want you to get hurt."

I sat up too, focusing on smoothing an edge of the sheet across my knee. "When kids sometimes asked how he died, I always lied and said it was a car accident."

She slowly nodded. "I know."

"Once I started lying, I ended up believing it myself." A small catch in the words betrayed how I felt. "I never wanted anyone to find out it was because of me."

"Oh, Kenley! It was a mistake for me not to talk to you about it. All this time you've been carrying that memory stuffed down inside, and after learning the details of how it happened, I feel terrible that you blame yourself. You were only four years old, a very little girl. Your dad was the adult. Keith never should've taken you to the Chateau. Especially not up to the attic, where it was so dangerous."

I looked down at the faded flowers on the sheet. "Don't blame him."

She sighed, "If I blame anything, it's the stupid Chateau! To me, that place was never a big deal. I'd grown up hearing how it was nothing but a money pit built by a big-headed snob. And back when I was your age, instead of a ticket for trespassing, kids got hauled down to the county jail. That happened to me and my friends once when I was thirteen, after we'd climbed the fence. Your grandpa bailed me out, so you can imagine how that went. I was grounded for a month and never went back. But then your father must've happened on it and started exploring, which I didn't realize until it was too late."

"He was writing a play about the Chateau. I read the

opening scene."

"I didn't know any of that, or I would have warned him about the dangers. And I had no idea he'd be reckless enough to take you with him." A shadow of guilt crossed her features. "I was so busy with the play, spending hours getting ready for opening night after the lead was tossed in my lap."

A knock on the door was followed by Grandma peeking in. "Thought I heard voices."

She kept her face calm but it still didn't hide she was relieved I was talking to Jules. Maybe just relieved I hadn't reverted back into the four-year-old who wouldn't speak.

"You two feel like breakfast before I clean up? Plenty left."

"That'd be great, mom," Jules said.

Grandma shut the door and I stood, thinking I might be able to eat after all. Jules caught my wrist. "I've heard about how the county is bringing down the Chateau next week, and that's the best news in a long time. That terrible place took your father from us, and it could've taken you, too. You broke your promise to me, Kenley."

I sat back down on the bed as she said, "I get why you did it. My own promise to you fell through, giving you the excuse you needed. Plus that Webb boy got you all caught up in looking for the ridiculous lost treasure his family talked about for years."

Her voice turned really tough in a way I almost never heard. "But you are never to go there again, understand?"

"Please don't be mad at me," I said, my voice hushed. "Or at Zef. He tried to make me stay away, but I wouldn't."

I lifted my eyes to hers. "Don't you get it, Jules? I didn't disobey you because I was mad, or hurt, though I guess in the beginning that gave me an excuse. The real reason I went to the Chateau was because I had to face what I've always known deep inside about how my dad died."

Saying it out loud actually explained it to myself, the tightness squeezing my heart easing a little. She slid her arms around me and cleared her throat.

"Okay, then. Let's go eat breakfast. I'm starved."

34
About Our Future

I held up a green sweater that hardly looked used. "What do you think?"

"That's your color," Jules said as we searched racks at a consignment shop in Fort Wayne.

Though it felt a bit weird buying fall clothes when it was still ninety degrees, we'd learned a long time ago that off-season items were less picked over and often cheaper. As I added the sweater to the growing pile on my arm, I thought about starting school and hoped Jules would somehow find a way to let me go on tour with her. During the three days she'd been with me, it hadn't come up once. But aside from that unhappy little cloud hovering over us, we'd been having fun. It was her suggestion we drive into Fort Wayne to shop for some gently used clothes.

We went to the dressing rooms, trying on stuff and having half conversations across the partition. At one point I paused and studied the half-faded scratches on my arms and legs, remembering my race through the thorny bushes. The sadness that had been waiting to overtake me returned, but I forced it away and pulled on a pair of *American Eagle* jeans.

Jules and I modeled outfits for each other at the three-way mirror in the hall and she said, "Those jeans fit perfect. If it cools off enough, you could wear them the first day of school."

I shoved my fingers in the back pockets, our eyes meeting in the mirror. "I was hoping…"

For what, exactly? That a spot in the actor's van had magically appeared so I could now tag along? Or that Jules had been hiding an even bigger surprise and was going to tell me she'd gotten a better job in New York? Maybe already had an apartment for the two of us?

"Yes?"

I tossed it off with a half shrug.

She slid her hands down the sides of the black mini she'd just tried on, and I thought how if we were still together, I could borrow it. She looked at me then leaned against the wall and folded her arms, smiling. "When did you get so grown up?"

I turned to her. "Think I'll get these."

She exchanged her smile for a serious expression. "I'm sorry I left you at the dairy, Kenley."

Me too. But instead of saying that, I let her off the hook. "Life happens."

"All the time." She pushed away from the wall. "I've been doing a lot of thinking since getting here, and one thing's for sure. Us being apart from each other is not good."

Deep breath. "So that means I get to go on tour with you?"

Her eyes showed resignation. "It means I move back into my old room, if your grandparents will let me. Find a waitress job in town until we get enough money to rent our own place."

My mouth actually dropped opened. "What about your stage career?"

Jules shrugged in a way that was too casual. "We stay put for two years so you can graduate. Then once you head off to college, I go back to acting."

My fingers toyed with the price tag. "Can you?"

"Why not?"

Even though my pointing out the truth led us further away from what I longed for, I didn't want Jules throwing away her dreams, either. "We both know that a two year break in acting is doomsday. How many times have you told me stories about someone leaving the business for a while, but then they never came back? Or if they tried to start their career again, they couldn't find work."

I didn't add in the toughest fact both of us knew, how she'd already been struggling to get even a small job on stage. Two years from now, after living in rural Indiana, it would be ten times harder. Even impossible.

Jules sat down on the stool in the corner, shoulders slumped. "Maybe it's not in the cards for me. Maybe it never was, and I just couldn't see it."

She looked at me. "I've already sacrificed so much trying to hold onto this career. How much more do I give up?"

I didn't have an answer.

She stood, heading into the dressing room but glancing at me over her shoulder. "Try on those sweaters. Let's see how they look with your jeans."

We bought burgers. Sitting on a park bench in the shade and eating in silence, we both tried to ignore the way our dressing room conversation had dampened the fun. Jules answered her phone, stuffing her wrapper in the white sack.

I could tell right away it was Anthony. She aimlessly walked over to a nearby tree, her gaze focused on nothing as they talked. I studied how she leaned against the trunk and then lifted the hair off her neck. One minute she smiled, the next minute serious, the whole time engaged and focused in a way I rarely saw.

Crap. She was in love with him.

The mediocre burger lost the last of its flavor. I shoved everything in the sack and tossed it in a garbage receptacle. Then I waved to Jules and took a slow stroll along the sidewalk as I waited for them to finish. Good-guy Anthony, who had once shown me how to juggle oranges and now changed the oil in her car, was the only boyfriend she'd had since my dad. And not because guys weren't interested. Men were always drawn to Jules, but she hadn't dated. One time she told me it was because she'd rather do popcorn and a DVD with me, and that we'd always have more fun together than she would on a date. At eleven, I'd totally believed her. After Zef's kiss, I knew it wasn't true.

Jules let me drive home, the beat up Saab like an old friend I'd missed. "Did you tell Anthony you're thinking of quitting?"

I could see from her expression she hadn't. Did that mean she still wasn't sure?

I asked something else. "Doesn't the troupe start their first performances in two weeks, at year-round middle schools?"

She leaned her head against the backrest. "Yes. I wanted to tell him when he called, but he was really happy about his theater blog interview. And also how the portable sets are coming along."

Her eyes closed. "It didn't seem like the right time, that's all."

On the drive back I did too much thinking, watching the sunset grow dim in the rearview mirror. It was dark as we pulled into town, nearly all the stores and businesses closed for the night. Della Ray's Burger Haven was the only place still lit up, and it was slammed. Most of the kids around here didn't have any place else to go.

I stopped at a red light, no traffic coming in either direction, and turned to Jules. "I don't want to live here for two years."

She sat up a little, looking at me through the shadows as I added, "If you go on tour for six months, it might lead to another acting job. But if you quit and move here, we're stuck."

"I don't know, Kenley..."

"Well, I do. My whole life I've heard about how taking a chance on being an actress was your dream, and losing it would be losing part of who you are."

I kept my eyes on the light, wondering if the stupid

thing was ever going to turn green. "Besides, you wouldn't just be giving up acting. You'd be giving up Anthony."

The second I said it I knew it was true. Their relationship had ended once, when he went on tour and she took the job in Branson. Staying here would kill it off for sure.

"Let's face it, Jules. After I go to college, you're going to need someone to help you balance your bank statement."

She laughed, a hollow sound that tried to hide how emotional she felt. It took her some time to process, and then she sighed. "How'd you get so wise?"

The light finally changed and I drove the rest of the way back to the dairy, listening as Jules began painting a hopeful future for us with bright colors that didn't really exist.

35
The List

Jules stayed for another day, taking time to talk to my grandparents about rules for me and what my curfew should be. I stood in the hallway, watching from a safe distance. After some arguing, Jules shook her head at my grandpa.

"Kenley isn't me! She's not going to skip school or try and fake her report card. She's a good kid who actually likes school. In a lot of ways, she's more responsible than I ever was."

After Jules said that, she looked down at her hands and mumbled an apology for everything she'd put them through. It came across sincere, enough that my tough old grandpa softened a little. Of course, Jules wouldn't have done that at all if I hadn't told her about what he'd said during the argument I overheard. But if her saying she was sorry meant I could be out on weekends until eleven, it seemed a fair trade.

He stuck a thumb in his suspender. "All right, then. But she also needs to get a job. We'll cover her trespassing ticket like we said, but she's got to pay us back as soon as possible."

Jules nodded and Grandpa added, "Plus ten percent interest."

A sour taste entered my mouth. That put the total I now owed them at $462. How long would it take to earn that much cash working minimum wage?

The next morning, I drove my mother to the bus station. She left the car with me, since she would be on the road with Anthony and didn't need it.

"At least you won't have to ride the school bus," Jules

said as we stood in line.

"Misery averted." My smile felt only a little fake.

The passengers started to board and she hugged me goodbye. "I'll be back for Christmas."

With the summer heat beating down on us, Christmas felt like a million miles away. I watched her strawberry blond ponytail swish as she climbed the steps of the Greyhound, turning away before she had a chance to look back and wave like a kid going off to college—and me the one left behind. I hurried to the car that had grown stifling. From now on, I needed to leave the windows down, since no one would steal the sad old thing.

That afternoon I helped my grandma pick peas, fold towels, and make a cherry pie for dinner, none of which improved my mood. By the time the sun started going down, I hid in my room and sketched for a while. The stuff I drew didn't turn out great. Disappointed, I flipped back through the art pad to see the drawings of the Chateau and also its dancers, the best work I'd ever done.

The elusive dream had faded to near non-existence now, all of it a mental trick meant to force me into remembering something I'd kept buried. I studied the sketch of the girl in the *Phantom of the Opera* dress and the man wearing a simple black mask, finally closing the cover.

Grandma rapped on my door and opened it to say goodnight. I set the book on the desk and turned off my lamp.

In the early hours of the following morning, I was wakened by muffled voices that sounded tense. The front door opened and closed, and soon a car drove off. After that, the house stayed silent, even when five o'clock rolled around and Grandma usually came downstairs.

Finally, I got up and wandered into the kitchen, stopping when I saw my grandpa sitting at the table, eating a bowl of cereal.

He lowered his spoon. "Josh and Nora went to the hospital in the middle of the night. Your grandma's headed there to be with them."

"I thought the baby wasn't due yet."

"Not for three weeks. I'm sure everything will be fine, but June is a worrier."

He poured more Raisin Bran in his bowl. "Would you like some?"

His offer surprised me. "Uh, thanks. Maybe later."

I started to leave until he added, "Your grandma wants you to stay with us."

Turning back, I studied him. "But you don't."

His brows drew in as if searching for the right words. "I mean she'd be sad if you left. Your being here is good for her."

"Oh."

"Which means I'm good with you living here." He reached for the milk. "Think you could help out more though, without being asked?"

"Okay."

He poured the milk and I went back to my room, thinking this was as close a truce as we could come to.

I picked up the art history book, re-reading the pages on the Impressionists, especially the info on Mary Cassatt and Edgar Degas. Their studios had been close to each other and he had befriended her, both of them growing ever-committed to the new form of art which would someday become famous. My fingers slid across glossy pictures of backstage ballerinas.

Thinking of the theater made me wonder about my dad, who knew enough of stagecraft to find a secret trap in the Chateau's upper level. For the first time I willed myself to focus on him without getting too emotional. What had been so important that he risked taking me with him into the attic?

I mentally went over what I knew about him, saddened

when I realized it wasn't much. However, one of the positive things that happened by my staying here was finding his box, reading some of his plays, and looking through his notebooks.

Something about this snagged my thoughts until I slowly stood, remembering the argument between my grandparents I'd overheard. When the topic had turned to my father, there had been something about how he was always writing in his notebooks. Just then, the memory of my grandpa's upset voice came back to me. *"And look at the trouble that got him into."*

What did he mean by that? Had something my dad written led him to the attic, and therefore to his death?

I heard the back door slam, Grandpa heading out to his cows, and I hurried upstairs. In the sewing room, I slid my dad's box from under the bed and carried it down to the blue room. I sat and started pulling everything out, setting his plays in a pile on the desk then focusing on the notebooks.

Unlike the small, portable one Zef had found hidden at the Chateau, these were full sized. Before, I'd only flipped through them. Now I searched the pages, finding one held notes for a comedy and another for some sort of relationship story. The third had an outline for *The Ghost Child*.

Biting my lower lip, I turned pages, seeing a heading labeled: *Chateau de Beauchene History*. This held his research on the architect, Phillipe Moncharde. I scanned my father's precise printing—rows of facts, including the theaters Moncharde had built as well as the *Chateau de Lévesque* in France. There were other pages of notes on the Broderick family, though he didn't have as much info as what Zef had already told me.

Most revealing of all was on a dog-eared page titled *Research*. It held a list of things that my father wanted to check into:

- County records dept. for blueprints?
- Library, local history section
- Broderick descendants in area?
- Attic, onion skins
- Order Pevsner's books
- Character chart
- Timeline

The fourth item jumped out at me, simply because of the word *attic*. I wondered if this was why my father had taken me up there that fateful day. But what would onions have to do with it? I leaned back against the headboard, closing my eyes and forcing my mind into the attic once more. Even though this was the last place I wanted to think about, I made myself remember.

The image of my father looking through crates came to me right away, almost as clearly as last week when the truth had overwhelmed me with shock and pain. Now, as if those freed memories were just waiting, they replayed themselves with sharp precision.

I recalled how he lifted aside a box, murmuring that he'd *seen them somewhere...* but what? Onions? That made the least sense of all, since he'd been sorting through papers and books. Of course on that day, I'd only noticed a little of what he was doing, my attention drawn first to the window and then the rocking horse.

Unable to think about the rest that followed, I used my phone for an Internet search of onion skins. After wading past health recipes and articles on how to make natural dyes, I finally came across a key bit of info.

Onionskin was the name of a light-weight, translucent paper. Not actually made from onions, it was named for the thin, papery skins it resembled and could be used as tracing paper. Though still around, it wasn't as common as decades ago.

I did another search for the next item on the list, finding a man named Nikolaus Pevsner, an author who wrote about European architecture. I'd never seen any of those books in my dad's things, which probably meant he hadn't gotten a chance to order them.

Sitting on my bed, knees pulled up to my chin, a dozen thoughts circled through my head until my eyes went to the digital clock on the nightstand. With a jolt I realized I'd lost track of the date. It was the first of August, the day the Chateau was scheduled for destruction.

36
Convincing Zef

I put my tennis shoes on, slid the notebook into my art bag next to the flashlight, and left through the front door. This activated a warning voice inside my head about how upset my grandparents would be if they learned I was sneaking out before sunup, but I squashed it. Grandma was at the hospital, and my plan was to be back long before either of them noticed I was gone.

Zef's house was dark when I got there. I looked down at my cell phone, debating, until finally calling him. I almost hung up but then he answered, his voice groggy.

"Kenley?"

"Hey."

"How are you?" he managed.

"I think you mean, *where are you?*" I paused, suddenly uncertain, then added, "I'm in front of your house."

Curtains at the window closest to the road stirred and he said, "Okay." Then he hung up.

I stood there thinking Zef really needed to work on his communication skills, until the front door opened and he walked out, tugging down the hem of a shirt he was pulling on. He didn't smile, though he did study me in a way that felt almost too intense.

"This is early for you."

I nodded, wondering how I'd become the one who was hesitant to talk.

"I wanted to call," he said. "Came close like fifty times."

I adjusted the strap of the bag on my shoulder. "Why didn't you?"

He made a half shrug. "Didn't know what to say.

Maybe: *sorry I put you in danger*. Or, *sorry I made your life worse*."

"What about, *sorry I kept the truth from you*?"

"Yeah, that too." He blew out an exaggerated puff of air.

"Wow, your parents must've really loaded on the guilt."

He smiled at the way I said that. "Kind of, though it was deserved."

His hands moved to my shoulders then slid down my arms, fingers warm against my skin. "I never meant for you to get hurt like that."

"Zef, I'm not mad. What happened in the attic didn't really have anything to do with you."

I managed to keep the emotion out of my voice, though it wasn't easy. "I've been thinking a lot, and it feels like I needed to go up there and finally remember. That way, I could stop lying to myself and pushing down the facts about how he really died."

"Then I'm glad you finally got to the truth." His fingers gave my arms a slight squeeze before letting go.

I missed the feel of his touch. "How much trouble are you in?"

"Grounded."

"For how long?"

He shifted his weight. "Indefinitely. Can only go to work, and my schedule is on the fridge, which my mom marks off. Plus yardwork every day until football practice starts. And a lot of household chores."

"Wow."

"It's not so bad now, since she and Kes are visiting Mom's sister in Pittsburgh. Also, my dad let slip that once the Chateau comes down, she'll probably lighten up."

"That's happening soon, right?"

Zef nodded, his expression defeated. "At ten. The demolition crew's been working all week."

He reached out and took my hand, tugging, and we headed to his truck. "There's something I want to show you."

I asked, "By the way, did the sheriff find out who was shooting up the Chateau?" I didn't add that I'd been curious but hadn't felt able to broach the topic with Jules or my grandparents.

"No. All he found were a bunch of empty casings on the hill. He's assuming it was just bored kids doing target practice on the windows, since the place is going to be destroyed anyway."

"You think that's all it was?"

"Probably. After the shooting stopped, when I went to look, I couldn't see anybody."

He opened the pickup door and dug around in the back seat, retrieving a black binder. He glanced up at the dark windows before quietly shutting the truck door which didn't latch all the way. "Come on."

We went through the fence to his back yard and sat on the swing. Handing me the binder, he turned on his phone but I pulled the flashlight from my art bag. "I've got this."

Before I could open the binder, he laid a hand on the cover. "More than once, I thought about showing this to you. Even left it in the back seat, hoping you'd find it."

"Why, what is it?"

"My grandpa's collection of newspaper clippings about the Chateau."

"Oh." I suddenly got it. "There's something in here about my dad."

He nodded, opening the cover. Inside a plastic sleeve was an article about the lawsuit against the county by the parents of Mandie Parkston, the girl who had fallen to her death at the Chateau.

Zef said, "The most current stuff is in the front, and it goes backwards."

I squinted at the glare of the flashlight on plastic and

flipped through a couple more pages. There was a collection of small articles about the ongoing lawsuit, until the next large clipping blared: *Girl Dies at Chateau*. It included a picture of Mandie who had straight blonde hair and a pretty smile. Another photo showed emergency vehicles near the front gate.

"This is sad." I skimmed the details, including dates. "It happened three years ago this month. Says she was visiting cousins in the area, and they took her to the Chateau."

"Met some friends there, though none of them were named."

"One thing I don't understand. How'd she get on the roof?"

Zef touched the picture of the Chateau. "There's a place above the solarium where the eave nearly reaches an outside decorative wall. It's an easy way up."

"I never noticed it."

He turned his head to look at me, shadows enhancing the contours of his face. "I wasn't about to show you."

"You think I'm that reckless?" I flipped through more pages with small articles about county hearings.

"Yeah, kinda do," he finally answered.

The way he said it made me want to laugh. But then I turned another page and saw a large article with a photo of my father, the same one from the back covers of his plays. The headline read: *Man Falls to Death*.

There were two additional pictures, one of the local sheriff and the other of the Chateau. I leaned over the article, tilting the flashlight to better see. I read until the words began to swim. It made my father's death seem more real, proof of what happened bringing back the sharp bite of pain from last week.

I closed the cover, handing Zef the binder. "It didn't say anything about me being with him."

"No. Your grandparents wanted to keep you out of it."

"As if pretending I wasn't there would make a difference?" I could hear the irritation in my voice and let out a slow breath. "Not that it matters. You knew, though, didn't you?"

He nodded. "My mom is friendly with your grandma. She heard how you went into shock and they were worried."

He looked down at the binder, his posture humbled. "She said my taking you in the Chateau was the most irresponsible thing I could've done, and that your grandpa was right when he said I wasn't any better than Riker."

I let out a disgusted snort. "Trust me, I've seen Riker in action. You're nothing like him. Zef, you wear the good guy hat better than anyone I've ever known, so do me a favor will you? Drop the guilty verdict and get it together, because acting like this means you're not any help to me."

His eyebrows raised halfway to his hairline. "What're you talking about?"

I dug my dad's notebook out of the art bag. "I'm going back to the Chateau."

He stared at me with a stunned expression until a small laugh escaped me. "Before you freak out and tell me I can't, just take a look at this."

"No."

"You don't even know what it is."

He folded his arms. "There is no way you're going back there. I won't let you."

"How are you going to stop me?"

It took him a moment to find an answer. "Call your grandpa."

I stood up from the swing and glared at him through the shadows. "Do that, and so help me I will never talk to you again, Zefram Webb."

In typical Zef fashion, he didn't answer. I stomped off but hadn't gotten far when he caught up and grabbed my arm, spinning me around. Even in the moonlight, I could see his annoyance.

"You are the most difficult girl I've ever met," he said, his voice a growl.

I started to pull away but he took hold of my other arm, too. His fingers, gentle the last time, now had a firm grip.

I glared at him. "Let go."

"You are impossible, know that?"

My lips clamped together in a silent warning, but he continued. "There's no reasoning with you, ever. You couldn't just stay in that upstairs room while I looked for the shooter, could you? Instead, you had to take off on your own and end up in the attic without me."

"Fine! Since you can't stand me, let go and I'll get out of your life."

I tried to jerk free, but he pulled me near. The next thing I knew, his mouth was on mine, kissing me in a way that sent a surprising zing along my nerves. I struggled until his hands let go, arms sliding around me like strong bands that held me even closer. A tingling warmth spread from our lips through the rest of my body, and though I tried to hold onto my anger, my mouth surrendered to his.

Zef kissed me for a long time and when he pulled back just enough for our lips to separate, we were both breathless. I slowly opened my eyes. "That's cheating."

"Whatever it takes."

We stood facing each other for a while, neither of us saying anything. Finally he rubbed the back of his neck. "You're still determined to go."

I glanced to the side, unwilling to meet his eyes.

"All right. Tell me what's in the notebook."

I dug it out, handing it to him along with the flashlight. Then I walked through the gate to the front drive and rested my hip against his pickup. Zef came and leaned beside me, putting the notebook on the fender and flipping through it under the beam of light.

"Okay, so your father took notes on the Chateau and

Phillipe Moncharde. Not a surprise."

I pointed at the list and he read through it, his finger stopping at the notation about the attic. "Onion skins?"

I pulled up the info on my phone, showing him. He read, his eyes growing thoughtful. "It's paper."

"An old kind of tracing paper. My dad must've seen them before, in the attic. Because the day he took me with him, he was really focused on searching the crates." *Not watching me, until it was too late...*

"So?"

"I'm guessing the first time he saw the onionskins, they didn't mean anything to him. But later, maybe after he found the secret trap on the second floor, he realized they were important. Think about it, Zef. What if those papers hold a clue that leads to the Hidden Room? And all this time, they've been sitting in the attic with a bunch of unwanted junk."

Zef closed the notebook and clicked off the flashlight. "My grandpa searched up there. He would've seen them."

"True, but maybe he didn't recognize what they were. Maybe nobody did, until my dad, who unraveled it because of what he already knew about theaters."

"It's a really long shot. Even if we find those papers, there's no guarantee we'll know what to do with them. Besides, if it was just about us going into the Chateau, that'd be one thing. But not the attic, Kenley."

I slid my fingertips in the back pockets of my shorts, studying his darkly attractive features. "They were friends, did you know?"

He looked confused until I said, "Edgar Degas and Mary Cassatt. They used to visit each other's studios. And he helped her succeed as an artist, since it was a lot harder for women back then."

During a moment of quiet I heard the distant chitter of crickets along the irrigation ditches, a white noise I'd learned to ignore.

"I keep thinking about Arietta's letter tell of the Degas dancer in a purple sash, and Cassatt's mother and infant. And then there's Monet's garden. I can hardly breathe when I try to imagine what his painting is like. All of them masterpieces the world is never going to see, since in a few hours they'll turn to dust."

He looked past me but I moved closer, drawing his gaze. "Do you want to save those paintings or not? Because no one else is going to do it. And if we don't try, they'll be gone."

He glanced back at the house. "Kenley..."

"Don't give me excuses. Either come or don't." I blew out a couple of short breaths to get control of what I wanted to say. "The Chateau stole my dad from me. And because of that, I need to solve what he started."

Turning, I walked away. This time he didn't stop me, or even try to tell me how stubborn and difficult I was. What he did do was catch up with me as I passed the mailbox, taking my hand in his.

37
Return to the Attic

Neither of us said a word as we walked along the weedy path leading to the Chateau. After we squeezed past the wire-bound post and rounded the bend, it finally came into view. A demolition services equipment truck and a huge tractor with a long excavation arm were parked in front of the gate. There was also a security vehicle with an inside light on, revealing the outline of a man. He didn't move, or seem to notice us, but that didn't help my nerves.

"What now?" I asked in a quiet voice. "And don't say we should go home."

Zef lowered his tone to match mine. "Maybe he's reading."

I squinted, still unable to see more than the shape of a head and shoulders. "With the light on, he might not be able to see us at all. Let's just get past him and go through the side gate."

"We'll have to. They have a new padlock on the front."

Zef was right, and this chain was so fat even a pair of big bolt cutters wouldn't get through it. In the low slung moonlight, the blue roof of the Chateau gleamed an odd shade of muted silver, the stone walls a deep slate gray. The windows looked like charcoal smudges, and the cement fountain gleamed a pearly hue that reminded me of frozen water.

He tugged my hand. We moved quietly, trying to stay in the shadows of the half-dead oaks, our eyes on the security car. When we reached the corner, the light clicked off. We scurried around the side, our backs against a stone pillar as we listened. The vehicle's door opened and closed.

My heart started tap dancing as I strained to hear footsteps. I thought about running off along the fence, but the noise might give us away. However, if he came around the corner and saw us standing here, we'd be in trouble. What if he called the sheriff? I dreaded the idea of another ticket.

Zef peeked around the corner but pulled back fast and whispered, "He's at the front gate. Go, but be quiet in case he's doing a perimeter check."

We followed the fence, watching where we stepped, the pale moon our only light. At times, the tall oaks cast long shadows across our path and it was impossible to see. I stumbled once, catching myself on the fence and grimacing at the rustling noise, hoping we were far enough away that the security guard hadn't heard.

Zef whispered my name and I turned back, realizing I'd passed the side gate. It surprised me how he found it so easily, when I had to search. Shoving aside the vines, he opened the latch and guided me through. I was ready to say something when he dropped down, yanking on my arm to join him. About two seconds later, a flashlight beam slid over the bars of the fence from the other side.

We scrunched down tight, our backs against the stone base and heavy vines around us. My pulse pounded and I clamped my lips together to silence my breathing, thinking this was a terrible hiding spot. Even though the vines were thick, there were still lots of holes. If the security guard shone his light just right, he'd see the tops of our heads.

I heard him stomping through the brush. He hadn't made if far when his footsteps faltered and the beam of light zoomed skyward before disappearing. He said some swear words, as if he'd tripped or stepped in a hole. Zef and I didn't move, a cramp forming in my calf at the way I crouched. We listened as the guard searched for the dropped flashlight. I wanted to take off for the shadows by the gazebo, but when I started to move, Zef tightened his grip—a good thing because the beam of light came on again. It seemed my heart was beating loud enough for the guard to hear.

Finally, he began moving away from us, back the direction he came. "That was close," Zef said so softly I hardly caught it.

We raised up enough to look through the fence, just in time to see the man round the corner. Once on our feet, we hurried past the gazebo to the Chateau. I didn't let myself look up at the west end of the roof, remembering how hard that hit me the last time I was here. Instead, I kept my eyes on the shadowy kitchen alcove until we reached it.

Missing its knob that had come off in my hand, Zef pushed it open and we stepped through. He left it ajar so it wasn't completely lightless inside. "We can't use a flashlight or he might see."

I held out my hand. "That first night we met, you guided me through the dark, even though we couldn't see a thing. I asked how you knew where you were going, and you said you had the place memorized."

His fingers slid around mine. "I remember. At the time I kept thinking, this girl is gonna be trouble." A teasing note entered his voice. "Man, was I ever right about that."

I slapped his arm with my free hand. He chuckled and I smiled. "Want to know what I thought of you?"

"Nope. Pretty sure I've already got a clear idea." He tugged my hand. "This way, Miss Trouble."

As on that first night, he blindly led me through the dark. Unlike that time, though, it wasn't awkward or scary. Instead, I felt relieved he'd come with me. In fact, I was happy about being with Zef again.

We moved slowly, feeling our way along one of the servant's hallways, until he stumbled over something. Covering his phone with his palm, he let out the barest light to look down. "My backpack. What's it doing here?"

"This isn't where you left it?"

He shook his head, sliding the pack out of the way with his foot. "I'll pick it up later."

Turning off the phone, we kept going, each of us quiet until his hand squeezed mine. "I'm sorry I didn't talk to you about your father, and what happened to him here. I kept thinking I should bring it up. But since you didn't seem to know, I was worried it might make things worse."

I sensed it was easier for him to say this in the dark, where our eyes couldn't meet. "That's okay."

He hesitated a little. "It really isn't. And I don't get why you're not mad at me."

That was a good question, but I didn't have an answer. Finally I let out a sigh that sounded sad, even to my own ears. "I don't know. Mainly because there's so much to sort out when it comes to my dad and this place, it's going to take a long time. Maybe most of my life. Or at least that's the way it feels right now."

I blinked several times, trying to decipher images in the total blackness within the narrow hallway. I began to understand why it really did feel easier to talk as mere voices in the dark.

He didn't comment, so I added, "When I told my grandpa you were the only friend I have here, that's the truth. Who else would come back inside the Chateau with me after everything that's happened?"

"Don't make me answer that," Zef said in a dry tone.

We reached a doorway and he guided me through, then turned on his phone. "No windows here."

He sounded relieved, which is how I felt since the small light from his screen seemed an encouraging beacon. Lifting it to focus on what lay ahead, he said, "We'll be okay until we get to the attic, but with all the windows there, we'll need to be careful."

It didn't take us long to reach the storage room, the door on the far side opening to the second set of stairs I'd come down the last time I was here. I got out my flashlight and pointed the beam upward to the first landing, this spiral staircase much sturdier than the one above it that led into the attic.

"Look," he said, pointing to a gray rectangle attached with heavy silver tape to a section of the threshold. On top was a red sticker, and thin wires ran down from the plastic explosive, disappearing into a drilled hole in the plaster.

"That's meant to take out one of the weight-bearing walls. From what I read, the blasts are usually set in a series of three to get the best implosion and collapse. Red goes off first, followed by green. Then the blue, which should be upstairs."

My mouth went a little dry, and for the first time I got the full picture of how dangerous it was to be here. We started up the spiral staircase with its heavy plank steps made for servants' work and soon came to the first landing. Zef gazed up at the second staircase spiraling up into the dark, the delicate bannister rotted and missing in places. "Wish they'd made that stronger and less for show," he murmured.

It looked different at night, the shadows so deep my flashlight didn't penetrate them. A nervous chill ran through me as I went up the first steps. Zef's hand moved to my waist. "Maybe we shouldn't."

"We have to."

"No, we really don't."

I started climbing anyway, hoping he didn't chicken out because I was fairly sure I wouldn't have the nerve to go on without him.

Our climbing the second staircase took longer. We tested the steps that seemed soft in places and stayed close to the wall, especially wherever the bannister was missing. I kept the flashlight focused ahead, but every time I glanced down into the darkness below, it gave the illusion of a bottomless well that caused a clenching sensation in my stomach. Finally, I forced myself to keep eyes forward.

Something touched my arm, startling me, and I brushed away thin strands of cobweb. "Yuck!"

"Let's hope they're aren't black widows up here." His voice sounded mostly serious but a little playful.

I kept going. "If you're trying to make me turn back, it's not working."

"I must be outta my mind…"

There was a breaking sound, and Zef cried out as his foot dropped through a rotted step and threw him off balance. One hand hit the bannister, which crumbled away. I grabbed him, pulling back with all my strength. As his hands flailed, I knew he was going to fall. But then he threw himself sideways and hit the wall, plaster crackling. Both of us panted like we'd been running, and I hung onto his arm, his muscles taut beneath my fingers. Finally, he was able to pull his foot free.

Neither of us said anything for a long moment, my throat tight and fingers of the other hand squeezing the flashlight so hard they ached. Finally I flexed them, turning it in his direction. Whether from the white beam or the panic he'd felt, his face looked washed-out.

My voice came out a scared croak. "You all right?"

"Yeah. But let's not do that again," he joked, though it didn't come across funny.

My chin dropped in shame. "What if you'd fallen?"

His hand reached out and took mine. "I didn't."

A tremor passed through me, reaching my voice. "You could've died. Like my father."

"Kenley. Look at me."

I didn't. His fingers touched my jaw, gently turning me in his direction. I blinked away a blur of wetness. "Then that would be my fault too."

"I'm okay," he said firmly, forcing me to meet his eyes.

I let out a slow, quivery breath. "Turn around, Zef. Let's get out of here before we both die."

He shook his head. "It's only a few more steps 'til we're there. No way am I going back now, especially after surviving that."

I started to say something but his finger moved to my lips. "For once, will you please not argue?"

He took the flashlight from my hand and then carefully inched his way around me. We were so close it would've felt intimate if I hadn't been afraid of him falling, my hands grabbing his sides.

"Not far. Come on." Now he was the one going ahead, checking each step with the light and a little bit of pressure from the toe of his shoe.

I kept my eyes on him, copying where he stepped. Taller than me, his head brushed against cobwebs that clung to his dark hair. "I really don't get you, Zef. You're the one who wanted to turn back."

He chuckled. "Then we're even, since half the time I don't get you, either."

My eyes traced the nape of his neck, the muscles of his shoulders and back. *You may not get me, but you still kiss me. And hold my hand. And put your finger against my lips...*

He moved up to the attic landing. I emerged through the opening, my legs wobbly and a palm pressed over my thudding heart.

His hand cupped the front end of the flashlight so that his fingers glowed red but stopped it from letting off much light. In the dark, the attic seemed a very different place. It felt closer and, at the same time, vast. Through the hole in the roof, the sky appeared gray and pearly compared to the abysmal black here. Beneath it, the wooden beam slanted down through the break in the floor. This made me shiver, even though the attic still held onto its stuffy warmth.

Just then I felt grateful I couldn't see much, though I remembered well enough the hated little rocking horse that had tempted me—now thankfully hidden in shadow—and the splintered boards that collapsed beneath my father. I swallowed, turning away.

Zef clicked off the flashlight, plunging us into blackness that made me bite back a nervous gasp until the screen of his phone lit up.

"I don't think the security guard will see this. Where do we start?"

"Over here." I led him to the wooden boxes near the corner. "This is where I remember my father searching."

The top crate was half empty, books and papers randomly stacked on the floor where my dad had set them twelve years ago. We bent over the crate, pulling out items. There were several old ledgers of household accounts and a folder with bills of receipts for delivery, the papers inside now brittle with age. We worked our way through a pile of antique almanacs, seed catalogues, and gardening manuals. Zef lifted off that box and we started on the one beneath.

It held a container of dried out fountain pens and children's primers that fell apart, their binding separating in our hands as we picked through them. Some were in Latin, others in French, and I guessed they'd belonged to Arietta's brother who was still a little boy when he died. It struck me then how much grief the Chateau had caused. At first I'd only thought of it as an amazing castle-like building. Now I understood all the lives it ruined. Jules was right; it was time this place got destroyed.

"Nothing," Zef said, sitting back on his heels. "I'm not seeing anything that looks like onionskins."

My frustration matched his, releasing in a theatrical sigh. "I guess coming up here was a mistake. I mean, my dad didn't even remember where he'd seen them, so what if they're not in these boxes? No way to search this whole place."

"Let's not give up yet." Zef moved to another crate.

I opened a small trunk with a curved lid, the leather hinges creaking and then the lid falling back with a bang.

We both stopped, afraid the sound might have carried. Zef inched over to the nearest window, peering out. He was a dark silhouette against the softening dawn. He stayed there a while until I asked, "See anything?"

"No. There's no light in the security car now, and I don't see the guard out there, either."

"Maybe he's sleeping."

He turned back to another box. "I say we give it twenty minutes. If we don't find anything, we get out of here and don't come back."

"Agreed."

The trunk was full of folded clothes. I pulled out a black riding skirt and jacket, a shawl, old-fashioned slips and pantaloons. "Think these belonged to Arietta?"

Zef looked up from a box that held a wooden rabbit on wheels and rusty tin soldiers. "Five more minutes and we're out of here."

I hurried through the rest of the things in the trunk, then looked into a crate that had wooden spindles wrapped with discolored wool. My knees ached and I stood. "It seemed simple, just find those papers."

Zef stood too, kind enough not to point out that he'd tried to warn me. We heard a distant thump somewhere below. He moved past me to the opening in the floor, going down two steps to better listen. He took his phone with him, leaving the attic even dimmer.

Now that it was quiet, I tried to rationalize the sound as merely something falling, probably another piece of the bannister. Or the wind moving an unlatched shutter. It could be anything... or nothing. Hopefully, it wasn't the security guard.

I glanced around the attic, heavily draped in night. Defeated, knowing this had been a waste of time and worse than that—a risk to both Zef and myself—I headed to the steps leading down.

"Kenley."

I spun around, grabbing my phone out of my pocket and clicking it on. Dispelling the shadows only a little, I squinted through them, heart hammering. I didn't see anyone, but I did recognize my father's voice. He wasn't there... not even his ghost. Just a memory of how he'd once said my name, how real it had been and how the sound of his love for me now squeezed my heart in a painful grip.

Staring at the broken boards across the attic that had taken his life, I whispered, "I'm so sorry."

I closed my eyes to shut out the attic, swaying a little as if all courage had left me.

"Don't give up," he said.

A shiver passed through me, despite the stuffy air. Maybe I'd been downstairs too long, exposed to the hallucinogenic fumes that were finally catching up with me. It wasn't him, even though I wanted it to be. Slowly, I opened my eyes, hoping for one last glimpse of my dad. All I saw were stacks of junk.

I glanced down at my feet, for the first time noticing I'd taken several steps, once again standing next to the first crate Zef and I had searched. I knelt down, looking inside. All the same items, none of them the onionskins. My gaze drifted to the floor beside it, books and papers left there long ago by my dad. That's when I knew.

I scooted over, staring at the scattered stuff on the floor, my hands shoving aside books Zef and I had taken out. Underneath was a small, square folder not more than eight inches across. I set my phone on the corner of the crate and picked up the folder, brushing away thick dust. I unwound the string wrapped around a flat brad, and opened the flap. Zef came back and called to me in an edgy whisper as I slid out the stack of papers. Thinner than vellum, the edges were brittle with time. It felt like a bolt of energy hit my nerves, a tingling sensation tracing my spine.

Zef came up behind me, saying we needed to leave. I

finally found my voice, holding onto the folder with both hands. "You'll never guess what I found."

38
Star-Crossed

We sat on the floor of the master bedroom, early morning light filtering in through the window as we studied the papers.

Zef shook his head. "I just don't get it. Why did your dad think these were important?"

His words echoed my thoughts but I didn't want to admit it, so I reached up and brushed the last of the cobwebs from his hair. He sat there patiently, which made me smile, until my attention returned to the onionskins.

They were all the same size, about seven or eight inch squares, thin and lightweight. The color was an odd shade of ivory, now heavily yellowed at the edges. Each had straight lines drawn in all directions, except diagonal. Some lines ran parallel to each other or formed right angles, and a few papers had tiny half or quarter circles. Two others also had small dots on them. Like tracing paper, the onionskins were sheer enough to see the markings on several of the sheets beneath, all of them forming a confusing mess.

"What if this isn't even what your father was looking for? They might just be papers stuck in with the school workbooks. Did kids learn geometry back then?"

"I count sixteen papers. These must be the onionskins," I said with more confidence than I felt.

"How can you be sure?"

I looked up at him, my focus drawn to his deep eyes beneath straight eyebrows, the serious yet full mouth that was exceptionally skilled at kissing.

"Kenley?"

"Don't give up yet, okay?"

I started spreading them out. "Let's see what they have

in common."

"Same size, same shape, same kind of paper," he listed off.

I touched the one closest to me. "Looks like all of them have eight or more lines. Four have arcs, two have dots."

"And each one has a small angle drawn in a corner."

"I noticed that too. Either obtuse or acute, but not facing the same direction. Though they do seem to be the same size." I put my fingers on a couple of them.

He picked up two other papers with acute triangles in the corners and lay one sheet on top of the other. "You're right. They match."

I started to get excited, turning papers and even flipping some over to make pairs of angles. But when I looked at the markings, the lines in the middle overlapped in an even more jumbled way. Zef, I suddenly noticed, happened to be study-ing me, a slight smile on his usually somber mouth.

"What?" I asked.

"I didn't say anything."

Still, his eyes stayed on mine in a disconcerting way. Self-conscious, I pointed to the papers. "You going to help me with this or not?"

"How, Kenley? I don't have any idea what that even is. And I think for all the time my grandpa spent searching here, he must've run across them. He was the Chateau expert, but didn't bother with them. What does that tell you?"

He rubbed his chin. "I know it's not what you want to hear."

"You're probably right. It's just that after all we went through to get them, it's disappointing."

Even worse, had my dad lost his life trying to find something that ended up having no value?

The sound of engines distracted us, and Zef made his way over to the window and peeked out. "Trucks from the demolition crew."

I checked my phone. "It's eight-thirty."

"We've got to get out of here."

"Okay." I grabbed random sheets, stuffing them into a pile, but paused when matching lines on two of them drew my attention. Lifting the top papers, I stared at the pattern they formed. The markings fit, almost like a strange sort of linear puzzle.

"Zef, I think I've got something. Look at this."

He sank down beside me. "I think that's a match."

His finger touched the tiny angles in the far corner of the overlapping papers. "And what about those? They're both obtuse, though turned in different directions."

I lined the outside edges of the papers exactly together, and the ends of the angles met, forming what looked like half a star.

A surge of electricity passed through me, and I shuffled the other papers, searching for more obtuse angles and turning them in hopes of a match. A third one lined up, but two more angles didn't. Then I found a fourth that fit. Now we could barely see the lines of the bottom page through the top three layers of the thin onionskins, but it was still visible.

"Zef, it's a four-pointed star!"

He let out a disbelieving breath. "And now all the lines and angles on the main part of these papers match up."

We studied the rectangles they formed and two arcs that created a small half-circle. Outside, I heard a truck door slam. "Quick, let's match the rest!"

We gathered the four remaining obtuse angles which easily came together, as did all the markings on their pages, and I let out an amazed laugh. "We've got half of them sorted!"

Zef shuffled through the unmatched papers. "The rest of these only have acute angles."

"Bet they make stars, too."

We put them together in several combinations, trying to find which four went together by matching up the lines and markings within the body of the papers.

Zef glanced up at the window, brighter with sunlight. "We've got to get out of here."

"Look, it's done!" Now there were four groups of onionskins. I turned them so the stars were all at the outside corners, but none of the main lines on the pages came together.

We studied them a little longer, then Zef turned all four stars inside, to the center.

Everything within the four quadrants lined up exactly right. We'd solved it!

Heart beating fast, I stared at the large square formed by the four stacks of papers. The lines now created a precise drawing of hallways and rooms, the small arcs even showing where doors opened. Most important of all, a square surrounded the four stars—a square that indicated the walls of a small room with steps leading down into it.

"The Hidden Room," Zef said with a hoarse exhale.

"But where in the Chateau is this?"

He indicated the stars. "That's the key. There's one of those in the architect's logo on the blueprints!"

I suddenly remembered the small four-point star drawn between Phillipe Moncharde's first and last name. We looked at each other, eyes wide.

"The blueprints!" we said at the same time.

"They're in my backpack. It's still downstairs."

Each of us grabbed two stacks of onionskins and headed through the door. We ran down the stairs and along the winding hallways until finally turning into the servants' hall behind the kitchen. Zef snatched up his backpack.

"Where now?" I asked, trying to catch my breath.

His head jerked up, as if listening, a finger moving to his lips. Then I heard it too, distant voices inside the house. We were too far away to hear what was said, but the sound grew in volume.

I mouthed, "They're coming this way."

We moved cautiously, checking as we left each area.

Peeking around a corner, we saw a man and woman with their backs to us. They wore fluorescent orange safety vests and hard hats, and were busy checking the wires of an explosive pack.

Retreating, we made our way to the kitchen and headed out the door. "That was close," Zef murmured.

I followed him along the back of the house, skirting bushes and dead flowerbeds to reach the veranda on the far side. Once there, we sat in a corner least visible from the inside windows, and Zef unfolded the blueprints, spreading them out.

The two of us began pouring over the Chateau plans, starting on the second level and seeing if we could match up the onionskins. When they didn't, Zef grabbed the top sheet and slid it off so we could study the ground floor. Sensing we were on the brink of discovery, my heart pounded. "I don't know how he figured it out, but he did," I whispered.

"Your dad?" Zef asked, his low tone matching mine.

"It's why searching for a copy of the blueprints was the top thing on the list in the large notebook. Now all we have to do is find out where the room is."

More minutes passed, a tightness growing inside me. "It's not working. Why can't we see it?"

"Because of this," Zef whispered, rotating the four sets of papers. "We were looking at these upside down."

He slid the onionskins forward, hallways lining up and walls of the surrounding rooms coming together. I gaped at it. "The Hidden Room is underneath the sitting room that's next to the library." I pointed in that direction. It was mere yards away. "The entrance has to run between the walls!"

"Of course! Moncharde put it together that way, so the extra two feet were masked by the bookshelves on the library wall. We did it, Kenley!"

Zef hugged me and I grinned at him. His face sobered. "We've got to get back inside."

Staring at each other, knowing how insanely dangerous this was getting, I shrugged. He glanced at his phone. "It's almost nine."

"Maybe we can explain to the demolition guys." I held up the papers. "Show them these."

"They'll just think we're a couple of kids who don't know what we're talking about. We ask for permission and don't get in, then it's over." He shoved fingers through his hair.

"Come on, then," I said, moving to the French doors before we had more time to think about it.

We paused to listen, the only sounds coming from noisy equipment engines parked in front. Inside the ballroom, I glanced around a last time, thinking of how this place had once haunted my dreams. Now, a line of holes were drilled in the lower sections of the walls, red cords leading from explosives planted deep inside.

Zef checked the hallway, motioning me to follow. Further down, towards the gallery, I caught a glimpse of the red spray-painted letters declaring: *DIE!* It sent a tenseness up my spine as I again wondered who had done it.

We hurried past the library and into the sitting room next to it. I left the door ajar, since all the way shut might be suspicious. Looking at the wide east wall adjacent to the library, we started searching.

"You see anything?" Zef whispered.

I didn't. The room was in better shape than many of the others, large squares of elegant wainscoting inset with brown and tan fleur-de-lis wallpaper. I ran my fingers down a piece of decorative molding, freezing when voices drew near.

Zef and I stepped behind the door, not daring to move.

"Did you check the wires on charges fourteen through twenty-six?" a man's voice said.

"Yes. Everything's in place," a woman answered.

"And they're all labeled?"

"Just the way I always do." This time she sounded miffed, as if she didn't like being micro-managed.

They continued walking down the hallway to the ballroom we'd just left, their voices fading, and I let out the breath I'd been holding. Kneeling, I pulled the onionskins from my art bag and lay them on the floor. Zef joined me, both of us silently studying the outline of the Hidden Room beneath us.

He put his finger on the lines indicating the narrow walkway between the walls. "But where is the door?" he mouthed.

We stared at the schematics, neither of seeing anything that indicated the opening which Arietta had written about in her letter.

I leaned closer, finally pointing to a small dot on the second page of the stack outlining that wall. "What's this?"

Zef shrugged but continued studying the papers, finally turning back to the wall. He went to the area indicated by the dot, and I joined him. We ran our hands across the wallpaper and along the edges of wainscoting. I thought about the secret trap in the upstairs service area and knelt, pushing on the corners inside the molding. Zef did the same. We made no progress, and I sat back on my heels just as a corner of the wall inside the molding gave way beneath his hands. A small section seemed to release a pressure latch, falling open in much the same way as the secret trap upstairs.

I started to squeal but slapped a hand across my mouth, eyes wide. Zef and I looked at each other with incredulous expressions. He swallowed, his Adam's apple bobbing in a way that said he couldn't believe it.

A lever was inside the opening, also like the one upstairs. Grabbing it with both hands, he turned, a rusty squeak escaping the metal parts. Before we had time to check the hall and see if anyone from the demolition team had heard, there was the whirring of gears and an entire three-foot section of wall slid outward to reveal an opening. A narrow walkway ran between wooden beams within the walls of the Chateau. Not far ahead, it ended in steps that led down into darkness.

Zef and I gaped at each other, both of us wanting to scream and jump, but forced to be quiet. He grinned, silently laughing, and I could feel the heat rise in my face. My cheeks were probably flamingo pink, but I didn't care. I fumbled around in my art bag until finding the flashlight, a little shaky as I clicked it on.

He reached for it, indicating he wanted to go first. I put my hands on my hips in a wordless, *"What, you think you need to be the big protector?"*

His intense gaze beneath raised eyebrows answered, *"My family's house. I take the risk."*

"Fine," I mouthed, still too excited to be annoyed as I handed him the flashlight.

Zef stepped inside the opening and I went after, our shoulders brushing the wooden beams as we headed down the stairs.

39
Inside

We stood at the bottom of the tight stairwell, a small door in front of us. The first thing we saw was a deadbolt lock that needed a key. "Oh no," I whispered. "How will we get through that?"

Zef gave it a try, both of us surprised when it unlatched. "It's not locked. Henry Broderick must've left it like this the last time he was here."

Instead of a knob, the door had a large handle formed of an iron bar. Zef pushed down on it but nothing happened. I glanced back up the steps to the opening far above, a small rectangle of gray light showing how far down we'd come.

"It's stuck," he said, handing me the flashlight.

I kept the beam focused on the door as he used both hands and all his body weight. Finally, it moved downward in a slow arc. There was a click of the latch sliding back, and the door swung inward.

"This is it," Zef said, his voice tense and jubilant at the same time.

I held the light up so he could see, following him down two steps into a very small room. Shelves lined one wall, some of them empty but others holding neatly arranged items. In the corner opposite was a large, freestanding iron safe with the door halfway open. I shone the light around. The Hidden Room was just the way Arietta had described in her letter. And unlike nearly every other place in the Chateau, there was no dust.

Zef went over to a kerosene lamp with a brass body and glass chimney. Beside it lay an open box of safety matches about eight inches long.

"Let's see if this still works," he said, striking a match.

The wick caught the flame, which he turned up, filling the room with flickering yellow light. I glanced at some of the items on the shelves. A coin collection sat next to a jewelry box. I opened it, seeing cameos, a jet necklace, and pearl jewelry. A gorgeous art nouveau mantle clock of a forest nymph changing into a tree was beside half a dozen pocket watches in mahogany stands. A satin-lined box held a single silver pistol, the indented spot next to it empty.

"The missing gun must be what old Henry used to end his life," Zef said, standing at my shoulder.

A shiver passed through me as my eyes scanned more items. Realizing the shelves weren't large enough to hold paintings, I turned and looked around the room. Zef reached the unlatched door of the standing safe, pulling it all the way open. He started to say something but the words caught in his throat. I went over and we stared at stacks of U.S. bonds in hundred dollar increments, their printing and design antique. Beside them were more piles of U.S. Treasury notes.

I shone the flashlight across them. "I'm guessing those are worth a whole lot more than the printed amount."

"Oh yeah. Those bonds have been earning interest for more than a century."

Bending down, we looked at a lower shelf, both of us audibly gasping. It had layered rows of small gold ingots, each perfectly molded and about two by three inches in size.

"You are so rich," I managed.

We stood, gazing at the safe and then each other, and I wondered if I looked as shocked as he did. "You too," he said. "Twenty-five percent!"

I giggled. He laughed. We hugged and he lifted me off my feet. The warmth of his arms around me felt like sheer happiness.

"I can't believe it," Zef said, sounding hoarse. "All the

months and years of looking, and no one really believing my grandpa or me. But now we've finally found it."

I pulled back, scanning the four walls. "What about the paintings, though? Where are they, Zef?"

He let me slide from his embrace and we both turned in a slow circle, eyes searching every corner for anything large enough to be a painting. There was nothing.

"They aren't here." Just saying it felt crushing. "How can they not be here?"

Zef slowly shook his head. "I guess Arietta got it wrong about her father sneaking off with the paintings. Maybe they were stolen, like the estate manager thought."

He checked the time on his phone. "We have to get out of here. Put the bonds and notes in your art bag."

On the bottom of the safe was a large velveteen pouch with draw strings. He knelt down, shoving gold ingots into it while I grabbed handfuls of the bonds. I said, "If we call the sheriff and show him how we found this room, I bet he'll stop the demolition. That'll give us time to get everything out."

"If we do that, he'll confiscate all of this for the county, which technically owns the Chateau because of back taxes."

"Oh."

After that, we worked quickly, my mind still spinning at the wealth inside the safe, especially the gold. This money was going to change our lives.

A noise behind us caught my attention and I glanced back, startled to see two people step in the room. I squeezed Zef's shoulder and he turned, standing, his hands clutching the pouch filled with heavy gold.

Riker sauntered forward, Meena in his wake. He clapped his hands slowly in a mocking sort of praise. "Can't believe you did it, bro."

Zef's posture stiffened, eyes angry, like this was the culmination of a lifetime's worth of crap from his brother.

"How'd you find us?"

"Meena and I were on the hill, getting a good spot to watch this place get blown up. Saw you out on the veranda with the blueprints and decided to see what you're doing."

"Typical." Zef didn't hide his disgust. "You don't deserve a share of this. You didn't do one thing!"

Riker scowled, ready to say something when Meena stepped around him. Her thick black hair was in a pile atop her head, the makeup on her dramatic features perfect. "Not true. We did one thing. We brought a gun."

We stared at the handgun she raised. "Get those sacks, Riker."

With a laugh, he stepped forward and jerked the art bag from my grasp. When he tried to take the pouch, Zef wouldn't let go. "You're a lot of things, Riker, most of them bad. But you're not a killer. You won't shoot me."

"No," Meena said. "But I will."

Riker glanced her way. "Don't make her mad. She's got a temper."

I stepped back and put my hand on Zef's arm, giving a squeeze that said all the wealth in the room wasn't worth risking his life. He finally surrendered the pouch.

Riker dropped it at Meena's feet then pulled my dad's notebook from the art bag, tossing it on the floor along with the onionskins to make more room inside. He went to the safe and began grabbing money and bonds, shoving them inside until the bag was stuffed.

"Get their phones," Meena said. "We can't have them calling the sheriff."

Riker nodded, holding out his hand as we surrendered our phones. He dumped them in my bag and hoisted it on his shoulder, looking nervous. "How much longer until they bomb this place?"

Meena stared at him. "Give me your phone, Riker."

"Huh? Why, what's wrong with yours?"

"Do it."

She pointed the gun at him and his mouth opened in surprise. "What the hell..."

Meena lowered the muzzle and shot him in the leg.

I jumped, the sound echoing around the room and making my ears ring. Riker staggered backwards with a howl, dropping my art bag. He hit the floor and grabbed his lower thigh where blood began to seep through his long shorts.

She smiled. "That felt so damn good."

Now she aimed the gun at his chest. "Your phone."

Riker got it out of his pocket, trembling fingers damp with blood but still able to toss it to her. With eyes and gun on us, she slid it in her back pocket.

"I can't even tell you how many times I wanted to shoot you, Riker. More than once, it took all my control not to blow your head off."

The color drained from his face. He squeezed his leg, grimacing in pain, and looked crushed. "I thought you loved me!"

Meena's features distorted. "Only someone with your gigantic ego wouldn't get how my dating you was pure slumming."

She leaned forward a little, studying him like he was a nasty bug. "Today, up on the hill, I had it all planned. After we watched this place get blown to pieces, I was going to kill you. But then these two showed up, acting like they'd found something."

Riker gaped at her. "Kill me! Why?"

"For what you did to Mandie."

The room got very quiet. "Mandie Parkston?" I asked. "The girl who died here three years ago?"

She nodded. "We were best friends since seventh grade, both of us only kids. Mandie and Meena, like sisters. Closer than sisters." For the first time, her tone got emotional.

"And then the summer before her senior year, those

pea-brained cousins brought Mandie here to meet their friends. To meet you, Riker." Her tone was accusing, eyes hot with hatred.

"Even though I didn't see it happen, I still have nightmares about Mandie falling to her death. It got bad enough I had to drop out of college, so I came here and found work. Made friends with one of her idiot cousins, and eventually wormed out the facts. She confessed everything. You're the one who took Mandie up on the roof."

Zef turned to look at his brother. "Riker?"

He didn't deny it as Meena kept going. "You knew about how bad the hallucinations could get but didn't warn her. And you gave her beer."

"Dean brought the beer, not me!"

"Yes, good old Dean." Her mouth looked as if she'd just tasted something nasty. "I plan on taking care of him next."

Riker licked dry lips. "Mandie kept asking me to go on the roof with her. She said she was a gymnast and rock climber, that it'd be easy. Said we could sit and count the stars. When she started walking along the top peak, I tried to warn her. Called her name, but she wouldn't come back."

He stared at his bloody leg. "She lost her footing and fell. It was an accident."

The muscles in Meena's face grew taut. "At first, I blamed myself. Mandie asked me to come to Indiana with her, but I didn't want to waste my time with her backwoods cousins. Maybe if I had…"

I took a small step forward. "My dad died here, too."

She shook her head in a way that said she didn't believe me. "Trying to trick me won't work."

"It's the truth!"

"Then why would you keep coming here, when you know what this place is like?"

She turned to Riker. "Remember the first time you brought me here, to see how long I could handle the fumes? You made fun of me for getting upset and wanting to leave. But what you didn't know is that I heard Mandie's voice calling to me."

Her tone turned hoarse. "She kept crying out for me to help her. And then she started blaming me."

I thought of the article about Mandie's death and remembered the date. "Three years ago last week was when she died."

The same day someone fired a gun at the Chateau, sending me into the rooms on the far side of the dark hallway that led to the attic. "You were the one shooting out the windows."

"The anniversary of Mandie's death," Meena said. "I also did the graffiti, hardly able to wait until this damn place dies."

Zef said, "You've been searching the Chateau, and you're the one who knocked me out in the larder."

"Why worry about that now? Because very soon the Chateau is going to take your lives, the same way it took Mandie's."

She picked up the art bag, putting it on her shoulder while keeping her eyes and the gun on us the whole time. Next, she hefted the pouch of gold. "Mandie's death broke her parents. And so did the cost of their lawsuit. They settled for almost nothing, just to guarantee the Chateau gets destroyed. This money will help."

Riker licked his lips again. "My kid brother doesn't deserve to die in here, Meena. I made the mistakes. I admit it. But he's innocent."

Her gaze only hardened. "So was Mandie."

She backed up the steps and across the threshold. Zef bolted forward as she slammed the door shut, the outside lock clicking into place.

40
Trapped

I hammered on the door, shouting until my throat hurt and my fists ached. Finally, I slumped against it. "Someone had to hear that gunshot. Why aren't they investigating?"

Zef knelt by Riker. He used a strip cut from his brother's shirt with his pocket knife and tightly bandaged the wound. "Maybe they can't hear it over the noise from their equipment. Besides, if she closed the opening in the wall, they'll never find us."

He stood. "Is there something in here we can use as a lever? Let's try to get that door open."

We both searched but found nothing promising. Fear closed in as I looked around the tiny room dimly lit by the wavering kerosene flame. At first, finding this place had seemed like the world's greatest adventure. Now, it felt like a tomb; would be one, in fact, when tons of the Chateau crashed down on us.

"What are we going to do?" My voice sounded scared, but I didn't care.

Riker, still sitting on the floor, had his head buried in his arms atop one knee, his wounded leg out in front. "Die," he said in a muffled voice. "Just like Meena spray painted upstairs."

He raised his head, eyes damp and nose red. "Can't believe I trusted her!"

Zef had managed to unscrew a metal leg from the bottom shelf, which now slanted downward, items sliding off and hitting the floor. He tested it on the edge of the door, trying every angle to pry it open. Minutes ticked by as he worked. I could see it was hopeless but kept quiet. Finally, he slammed the metal bar against the door. It ricocheted off and landed on the floor with a loud clank. The drooping of his shoulders told everything. There was no way out.

I bent my head, staring at the floor and determined not to be a crybaby like Riker. But the thought of what my death would do to Jules, and my grandparents, caused a clenching inside my chest. My mother had warned me about the danger of this place, but I'd been stubborn and stupid. It had taken my dad's life, now it was going to take mine. And would Jules even know it? What if she just thought I disappeared, ran off without saying goodbye?

I shoved away these thoughts. My breathing grew shallow, the air stuffy. Maybe the oxygen was getting used up, too. Did it matter?

"How much longer until they detonate, do you think?" I asked.

Riker looked at his watch. "Seventeen minutes."

Zef came over, stricken. His arms slid around me, our foreheads coming together. "I'm so sorry, Kenley."

"It's not your fault," I whispered. "I'm the one who showed up at your house this morning."

We stood that way for a moment, then he took my hand and led me over to the open safe. He bent down, bringing out four small gold ingots. "Not all of them made it in the bag." He handed me one, trying to smile but failing. "Twenty-five percent."

The gold felt cool in my palm, and I slid it in my pocket. He did the same with the other three. After that, I walked over to my father's notebook and the onionskins that Riker had dropped in a messy pile when he'd dumped out my art bag. I picked them up and straightened the pages.

"Zef," Riker said in a choked voice. "I've been a terrible brother."

Zef walked over to him. "Yeah, you have. And a lousy son. I was going to use the money so Mom could get better medical help. All you cared about was getting rich and impressing your girlfriend."

"Meena tricked me!"

"For once, own it, will you?"

"Uh, Zef?" I said, waving a hand in his direction and staring at the stack of onionskins. "Come look at this."

He joined me and studied the papers. I pointed to a dot. "This marked the upstairs entrance to this room, right?"

"Yes."

"I'm sure I saw another dot on one of these papers. It might not mean anything…"

We shuffled through them, trying to find it. Finally, I knelt and put them together on the floor, all four stars in the center. "Right here," he said. "Third paper down. One of the walls for this room, I think."

"What if it marks an exit?"

We looked at each other and then started figuring out where it might be. "There," Zef said, motioning to the wall with all the shelves. "Look for a secret trap!"

Shoving items off the lower shelf, we pushed our hands against sections of wall. Nothing happened. We went over it again.

"It's not here!"

"Hey guys," Riker said, panic making his voice squeak. "Eleven minutes."

"Move up," Zef said, shoving aside the art nouveau clock and pushing on the wall.

"This is taking too long!" I stepped on the bottom shelf and climbed up, which let me see the top of the wall near the ceiling. I used the flashlight to get a better look, noticing a vertical line.

"It might be here, but I can't reach it!"

Zef hopped up, seeing where I focused the flashlight beam. He punched it with his fist and a secret trap popped partway out. I squealed, still more panicked than relieved. Yanking it all the way open, he grabbed the lever inside and turned, the muscles of his arm straining. The shelves moved and I almost fell, jumping down. He did too.

We ran to the far end. "That's it," I said with a half sob.

Grabbing the side of the shelf, we both pulled until it opened wide enough to reveal an archway. A tunnel lay beyond.

"Riker get up," Zef shouted, running to grab his brother. "Go, Kenley!"

I hurried into the tunnel, shining the flashlight beam ahead. Much tighter and less well-built than the other tunnel we'd found, these walls were formed of crumbling brick, the floor packed dirt. Despite gnarled roots that had broken through the ceiling, and the earthy smell that reminded me of worms, it felt like hope.

I tried to run, though it was tough in the tight space, the floor rising in a steady incline. Glancing back, I saw Riker leaning heavily on Zef with an arm across his shoulder.

"Move it!" Zef shouted. "We're not safe yet."

He was right. When the Chateau came down, if it landed on the tunnel this crumbling passageway couldn't support the weight. The thought of it collapsing on top of us made my heart pound even faster. I reached a sharp turn, racing around it, my hair snagging on a tangle of roots. Zef and Riker caught up, ducking under them.

Ahead lay a pile of moldy bricks fallen from the sides. I clambered over and turned another corner. The tunnel soon became a series of zigzags, and I wondered where it could possibly lead. My flashlight beam bounced off the walls in rhythm with my wild chase, so disorienting I pointed it down and hurried on. Stumbling, I rebounded off a wall, and the sound of my ragged breathing echoed back to me until I was startled by the distant sound of a siren.

"What's that?" Riker called from behind, hobbling as Zef practically carried him.

I looked back as we all braced for the explosion. When it didn't come, Zef said, "Check your watch."

Riker did. "Nine fifty-five."

"That was a five minute warning. Go!"

He didn't need to tell me. I scurried around debris and turned corners. The sound of menacing voices ahead startled me, and I slowed. The flashlight hardly cut through the darkness, and I couldn't see what lay beyond. The voices began telling me I was going to die.

"Not real!" I hissed, ignoring the fear creeping up my spine.

We'd definitely been underground long enough for the fumes to start causing hallucinations, so I pushed forward, telling myself that no matter what lay ahead it wouldn't be as dangerous as what was behind. The tunnel straightened out, and in the distance I saw something, squinting as I hurried closer.

"A ladder!" I shouted.

The flashlight beam dimmed and went out. I gave it a frantic shake and it flickered on again. "Over here!"

Zef let go of Riker, stumbling forward. I climbed the ladder, touching wood. "I think it's a trapdoor. An opening to get out!"

The flashlight beam revealed planking and a rusted latch, which my fingers yanked. It wouldn't budge. "It's stuck!"

"Let me try."

Zef and I switched places, but he didn't seem to do any better. I looked around. "The tunnel keeps going. Maybe we should, too."

"Give me a second," he said between clenched teeth.

We might not have a second. "Better to keep going," I called.

The flashlight dimmed again, winking and fading. Then the beam vanished, plunging us into blackness, and no matter how much I slammed it against my palm, it didn't come back on.

Riker swore and I stood there, mouth so dry I couldn't swallow, pulse hammering at my temples. My hand felt for the wall. Why hadn't I grabbed the kerosene lamp?

I heard a grunt from Zef, a wince like he'd hurt himself, and then the raspy sound of sliding metal. A thin blade of bright light suddenly pierced the darkness and I squinted as the trapdoor banged open. Sunshine poured into the tunnel; beautiful, glorious light that made me want to shout.

Zef jumped down. "Get up there, Kenley!"

I scampered up the ladder, stepping into what looked like a rusty wire cage. It took a second to realize I was standing inside the gazebo. Riker pulled himself through the opening, Zef shoving from behind. Another siren blared, this time much louder. Zef climbed out just as a series of blasts filled the air, dust billowing out from the base of the Chateau. More explosions and then more again, too loud despite covering our ears. And then the building began to collapse, dropping straight down as huge clouds of dust roiled upwards and out, heading straight for us.

We turned away, covering our heads. I squeezed my eyes shut, hands over my mouth and nose. Bits of sand-like debris pummeled our backs. The floor tilted and I lost my footing, but Zef grabbed my hand and we jumped out of the gazebo. We hit the ground, lying flat where we could breathe better. Slowly, the dust began to thin.

I finally opened my eyes and sat up, bending forward to blink the layer of dust off my lashes. Zef coughed and wiped grime from his face. In the distance we could hear excited shouting, a crowd cheering and horns honking in celebration.

Riker sat up, so covered with dust that he could pass for a ghost. Along the ground, all the way from the back of the Chateau, was a crooked depression, the reason the gazebo had nearly fallen over. I studied it, realizing the collapsed zigzag in the earth was the tunnel. If we'd still been inside it, we would've been crushed.

Zef and I stared at each other, heads and arms coated with gray dust. He grinned, a joyful look that let me know exactly what he was thinking. It was good to be alive.

41
Discovery

When I got home, my grandma was still at the hospital. Good thing, since I was a mess. I spent a long time in the shower. Toweling off, I noticed a thin scratch along my jaw, not even aware how I'd gotten it. After getting dressed, I dropped onto the bed, my head so tired I couldn't even guess how many hours I'd been up.

I slept for a long time, so that waking felt like swimming upwards through a murky pond. Lying on my back, I held the little rectangle of gold. I ran my fingers over the shiny surface and turned it to catch light from the window. It might be worth a thousand dollars or more, so at least I could pay off the money I owed my grandparents for the ticket. But I couldn't get over knowing how much Meena had stolen from Zef, or the fact that we'd come so close to dying.

In the kitchen, I scouted out some chocolate cake and poured a glass of milk, one food item we never ran out of. I sat in the nook, listening to the tick of the old farmer's wall clock that had been hanging in the same spot since Jules was a girl.

Afterwards, I put my plate in the sink that was half full of dirty dishes, not the way the kitchen was normally kept. I rinsed them off, loaded and ran the dishwasher. The back door opened and Grandma came in, carrying her handbag. She set it on the counter, smiling at me.

"You have a new little cousin. Four pounds and nine ounces."

"Is the baby okay? And Nora?"

"Yes, they're both fine. Little Josh Junior will have to stay in the hospital a few more days, is all. Nora and Josh are already calling him J.J."

"That fits," I said, thinking how I was the only non-J grandkid in the family, which suited me fine.

My grandma moved closer. "Are you all right? There's a scratch on your jaw."

"Yeah... not sure how I got that."

She kept staring at me, worried. I smiled, stepping in to give her a hug. "Know what? Little J.J. is lucky to have such a good grandma."

She gave me one of those odd pats. "Well... thank you, Kenley."

Grandma pulled away, her eyes damp, though I couldn't see how a hug from me would make her teary. Maybe she'd just had an emotional day, spending so many hours at the hospital and worrying about the new baby.

She went to put her purse away and the doorbell rang. She answered before I got there. It was Zef. He wore a clean shirt and jeans, no sign of the dust that had covered him last time we were together. "Hello, Mrs. Strickland."

"Zefram."

He took off his cowboy hat. "I was wondering if Kenley could go for a walk with me."

I could see her debating what trouble we might get into. "Well, I suppose that now the Chateau's been torn down, it shouldn't be a problem."

She looked at me. "Be back for dinner."

Zef and I headed under the archway. Despite the afternoon heat, a lazy breeze helped it feel less stifling. "How's Riker?" I asked.

"Still at the hospital. So is Meena. Just hope they're in opposite wings so they don't kill each other... Or maybe that's what they deserve."

I stopped, gaping at him. "What happened?"

Zef smiled, pushing back the brim of his cowboy hat. "Sheriff Danner went to Dean's place about some past-due speeding tickets. He found Meena there, her gun on Dean. I don't know the details, but according to my dad, she fired at the sheriff and he shot her. Self-defense. Her condition is serious, but she'll recover. Enough to get arrested."

"What about the money and gold she stole?"

"Sheriff Danner has it. For now, it's part of the evidence. After that, the county will try and claim it."

"That's not fair!"

"My dad's on it. He's already talked to his college friend, an attorney in Indianapolis. According to county law, if we pay the back taxes and interest, the Chateau and all of its property is still ours. It'll just take time to work out everything."

He reached in his pocket, pulling out my cell phone and handing it to me. "At lease the Sheriff gave my dad our phones."

I eagerly took it from him. "By the way, what did your father say when you told him about us going to the Chateau?"

Zef reached out, taking my hand as we walked down the road. "He was not happy, but it's kind of after-the-fact. Especially since we're okay. Except for Riker getting shot, which would have happened anyway but been worse because Meena planned on killing him. Besides, right now he's excited my mom can finally get the medical help she needs."

I looked down at his hand holding mine. "Zef, your knuckles are skinned."

"From when I opened that trapdoor leading out of the tunnel." He slowly shook his head. "We sure cut it close on that one."

Without hardly realizing it, we'd turned onto the trail leading to the Chateau. Passing the barbed wire post and finally coming around the bend, both of us stopped, staring at the huge pile of dusty rubble behind the tall fence. The demolition crew was gone, their equipment waiting for their return.

"It looks so wrong," I murmured, remembering the blue roof and how the stately windows had reflected the afternoon sun.

He didn't say anything, just squeezed my fingers. I moved closer to the gate, peering through the bars. "Jules was right when she said this place ruined our lives. Guess I should be happy it's gone."

He tugged my hand, guiding me around the west side of the fence to the secret entrance. He lifted the vines and unlatched the gate. This time, he left it open since nothing remained to safeguard. The mounds of crushed debris, formed from bits of blue roof and crumbled stone, looked even sadder. We neared the gazebo, still tilted from when the tunnel had collapsed beneath it.

"I spent so much time looking for the Hidden Room," he said. "But finding it almost got us killed."

"It was worth it, though, don't you think? The money for your family?"

He shrugged, seeming to struggle with what he wanted to say. Finally, he sighed. "Not if I lose you."

I studied the handsome, serious face I'd come to know well.

"Kenley, I get that you don't like it here. You once called this the middle of nowhere. Everything you've done to help me find the lost money was to buy yourself a way out. So when you get your share, you'll go, won't you?"

I tried to put my thoughts together, to make a plan for my future. To even figure out what I wanted. My gaze dropped to his more deeply tanned fingers encircling mine.

How could such a simple touch make me feel safe, and happy, and like it didn't matter if I went to school in a tiny Indiana town with kids I didn't know? Because most of all, I didn't want to lose Zef the way I'd lost just about everyone else in my life.

I swallowed. "Maybe I won't go. Not if you ask me to stay."

He touched my chin, thumb gently stroking my jaw. "Will you stay?"

"Yes."

Zef smiled, and then he kissed me in a way that made a crazy little bubble of happiness well up inside. After that we stood near the gazebo, his arms around me as we watched the sun sink lower on the horizon.

The rays pierced through tree limbs, too bright in my eyes. I looked down and studied the sunken line of the underground tunnel, how it made a zigzag path to the gazebo. Then I noticed how it kept going a little ways past. I pulled away from Zef's arms to turn and look at it.

"Remember when you were trying to open the trapdoor under the gazebo? I told you the tunnel kept going."

"To where?" he asked.

Both of us followed the line with our eyes, slowly pivoting to look across the back property.

"The gardener's shed," we said at the same time.

We hurried away from the gazebo, catching the path to the shed.

"Why would it lead here?" I wondered aloud.

"No idea."

The shed's wood had aged to a grayish brown, the swollen door stuck. He kicked it until it broke free. We stepped inside, and I used the light from my phone to look around. Shovels and spades with splintered handles were piled against one wall. Dusty shelves held cracked and stained pots, and an aged wooden wheel barrow sat atop a filthy canvas in the middle of the tiny shed. It was filled with soil that had dried into a rocky mound.

Zef walked over to the wheel barrow, moving it to the corner as I pulled aside the canvas. I knelt down, running my fingers along a horizontal line crossing the slats in the floor. "I think this is a trapdoor. Just like the one under the gazebo."

"But how do we get it open?"

I stood. "Look for a secret trap, of course."

We started searching the shed, moving aside tools and testing portions of wall. One section, behind clay pots, shifted beneath my fingers. The pressure latch clicked and a small square fell open, sending a pot crashing to the floor.

"Here!" I called, grabbing the lever inside and turning.

There was the pop of a lock releasing, and both of us stared at the floor, the trapdoor now sticking up about an inch. Zef got his fingers underneath and pulled it open, the hinges groaning. A ladder led down into a dark chamber.

We looked at each other, eyes wide, and then clambered down inside. I shone the light from my cell phone around. The tiny cement room had bare shelves on one wall and a large storage crate sitting in the middle of the floor. Zef picked up a lever and mallet left in a corner, using them to pry the lid up. I helped him lift it off. Inside, a yellowed sheet of paper sat atop slots holding canvas covered frames. I lifted the paper, focusing my light on it, and we read together:

> Arietta,
> You were right to leave the Chateau.

I handed it to Zef. "Do you think her father wrote that?"

"Yes." He slid it in his pocket, reaching for one of the covered frames.

My heart beat fast at the possibility of what we'd found. I helped him lift it out, hardly able to breathe as he peeled back the canvas tarp.

It was a painting of a red sailboat on choppy green water, the sky holding the promise of a sunset. "This is beautiful," I managed. "Definitely impressionistic."

Carefully setting it aside, we took out another and I removed its tarp. Inside the gilded frame was the painting of a dark-haired woman in a fringed turquoise shawl, a tiny baby on her shoulder. I blinked several times, mouth open, unable to speak. Pointing to the signature at the bottom, I finally managed, "Mary Cassatt!"

It came out a squeak that would've been embarrassing except Zef made a half-choked sound. I started squealing, jumping around. He grabbed me in a hug, and I hugged back.

"We did it!" he cried, and I'd never heard him so elated.

We laughed, blurting out stuff like, "Can't believe it!" and "This is crazy!"

"More!" I said, turning back to the crate.

Working very carefully, we lifted out the biggest painting in a thick, ornate frame and removed the covering. A path meandered through a garden blooming with yellow and fuchsia, a small white cottage in the distance.

"Monet," I whispered, my tone reverent.

"We are going to be so rich," Zef said in a stunned voice. "And famous. Guess no one will call my grandpa a crackpot now."

"No they won't."

I reached inside the crate, gently lifting out the last item wrapped in a faded child's quilt. Before I opened it, I already knew. It had to be Louisa's painting, taken from her wall the day of her funeral. The Degas.

A young dancer posed in second position, body slightly angled, and soft white tutu fading into the hazy background. Wavy brown hair pulled back with bows, she wore a black ribbon around her neck. And at her waist, a purple sash of gathered satin. She seemed to gaze at me with questioning eyes beneath dark eyebrows. It was the most beautiful thing I'd ever seen.

Zef relinquished his hold on me, and we stepped outside the shed. He called his father to come meet us.

The setting sun was at that blazing point right before the sky would start to fade. I propped the Degas on the bench and stepped back. Impressionist works were always meant to be seen from a distance, where the blur of colors could meld together and tell a story. And yet, as it was also meant to do, it eventually beckoned me closer.

I picked it up again, sitting down on the bench and looking at the place where the Chateau once stood. The thorny rosebushes were still there, storybook guards with nothing left to protect. Closing my eyes, I let the long-ago memory resurface of my father holding my hand as we walked towards what I'd once believed was a castle.

He was the reason why, after I found the Chateau, I had to keep coming back—to learn the truth that brought heartache but would also, in time, finally bring healing. It gave me a sense of release that I was able to finish what he started. And because of him, Zef and I had been able to discover the Hidden Room, the tunnel, and eventually the lost paintings.

"Thanks, Dad," I whispered, slowly opening my eyes to look up at a sky streaked with color, as Zef's fingers encircled mine.

Kate Kae Myers lives in Boise, Idaho. She is the author of *Inherit Midnight* and *The Vanishing Game*. Kate encourages you to visit her website:

www.katekaemyers.com

If you enjoyed *The Hidden Room*, watch for the upcoming release of *Someplace Safe*.

Someplace Safe
Preview Chapter

1

Reflection
Shadow
Frost

I saw him for the first time as a reflection in a shop window.

An outfit on the mannequin caught my attention and I paused, ready to move on when my eyes refocused on the glass. Mirrored behind me, across the street and off to one side, stood a teenage guy in a thin tan coat that hung down to the top of his hiking boots. Weird, since this was the last warm haze of September when the rest of us wore shorts and flip-flops.

He stood by a parking meter, one hand in his coat pocket as he gazed my direction. His features were vague in the reflection, but still I felt caught in his stare.

A pickup drove down the street, followed by a car, and they cut off his image in the glass. After they passed I turned to look at him but saw only his back as he disappeared around a corner. Despite my lifelong shield of paranoia that helped keep me and Dwin safe, it didn't set off any mental alarms.

*   *   *

The second time I saw him, the air had turned dusty with October. An evening storm with more wind than rain rolled across the new city we'd moved to, and as I headed down the sidewalk, a breeze exposed the pale underbellies of leaves. My thoughts far off, I hardly noticed the rapid click of wheels on the sidewalk. Glancing up too late, a girl on a skateboard nearly plowed into me. I jumped to the side but not fast enough. Her elbow hit my shoulder, leaving me staggering. At the edge of an alley, where concrete was missing from the sidewalk, I lost my footing. A hand shot out and grabbed my arm, steadying me but squeezing too tightly. It belonged to a boy about my age.

He had on a long tan coat with a collar of black suede worn thin. His overall nice-guy appearance seemed ordinary enough, except for his eyes. They were a dark brown that reflected the halo of a nearby streetlight, and something about them sent a chill through me.

In the handful of seconds we stood there, nothing happened. A regular nice-guy would smile and say, "Watch your step," or, "Be careful." And a regular girl would thank him. But I was not a regular girl, and when his hand let go of my arm and he disappeared into the alley shadows, I realized he wasn't a regular guy, either.

Hurrying back to the apartment, I told Dwin we needed to move. Two hours later, that place was a memory.

*   *   *

Five weeks went by before I saw him again. Frost covered the ground as I jogged. Thanksgiving morning in the small Vermont farming town left the air icy. Even with a hooded scarf and insulated jacket, the cold still found ways to bite. It was worth it, though. Glittering frost covered everything: trees, weeds, even an old tractor abandoned in a field. The air held its breath, the only noise coming from my shoes slapping pavement.

I passed cozy farmhouses set back from the road and imagined turkeys cooking in ovens as football games droned in the background. Dwin and I didn't celebrate holidays. "It's the way the unintelligent masses mark the passage of time," he once said. For us, celebration meant making it through another day.

I followed the narrow lane around a bend and headed to the covered bridge straddling a shallow river. That's when I noticed footprints in the frost. Someone walked this way ahead of me; not ran, since there weren't the deeper toe marks followed by long scuffs. Instead, the person had taken solid steps that left repeating waffle patterns on the white ground. I looked up.

A dark-haired guy stood waiting. I stopped and squinted against the glare of the morning light. Close to my age, he wore a long coat with a black suede collar turned up, the front hanging open. Beneath were a blue shirt and worn jeans. The thin coat wasn't warm enough to protect against the cold, and he looked out of place in the frosty light.

Just then two flashes of memory came: a window's reflection in September; a city alley back in October. The breath went out of me. I turned and ran.